AUSTIN DUFFY grew up in Ireland and studied medicine at Trinity College Dublin. He is a practising medical oncologist at the National Cancer Institute in Washington DC, where he lives with his wife and two children. In 2011, Duffy was awarded RTE's Francis MacManus award for his short story 'Orca'.

'Duffy interrogates the human fear of both emotional closeness and mortality, while demonstrating the power of human connection' *Sunday Business Post*

'Well-written and authoritative' *Sunday Herald*

'[With] precise prose [that] can often be subtly disarming . . . The story is dominated by its thought-provoking ideas and will appeal to readers who share the central character's fascination with the beauty and absurdity of life' *Phoenix Magazine*

'[Duffy] immerse[s] the reader in the world of medicine . . . It is the details that bring the narrative to life, the clinician's eye for spot-on summaries . . . convincing . . . pensive and stark' *Irish Times*

'Despite its chilly subject, the book has a certain lightness of touch' Keith Miller, *Spectator*

'Blends experience with fiction and offers more than informed opinion and insight into medicine, science, life and death . . . loss and replacement' *BMJ Blogs*

This Living and Immortal Thing

AUSTIN DUFFY

GRANTA

Granta Publications, 12 Addison Avenue, London, W11 4QR

First published in Great Britain by Granta Books, 2016
This paperback edition published by Granta Books, 2017

A CIP catalogue record for this book
is available from the British Library.

2 4 6 8 9 7 5 3 1

ISBN 978 1 78378 168 3 (paperback)
ISBN 978 1 84708 169 0 (ebook)

www.grantabooks.com

Typeset by Patty Rennie
Printed and bound by CPI Group (UK) Ltd, Croydon, CR0 4YY

For Naomi

Star, therefore, to start,
like waking on the best day of your life
to feel this living and immortal thing inside you.
You were in love, you were a saint,
you were going to walk the sunlight blessing water,
you were almost word for word forever.

Stanley Plumly, from 'Cancer' in Orphan Hours

Henrietta is not long more for this world. There was never any doubt about it, placebo or not, although in her case she is getting active drug. For some stupid reason that makes me feel better. She will have a small chance for a while at least. I started her treatment today, Day 1 of the protocol, but I fear it is too late for her. When I came into the lab this morning she was crying red tears. I had to look it up, their significance. The manual says it's because of the porphyrins in them. They dried into a rust beneath her eyes.

At eleven o'clock I left the lab to go to the procedure unit. They were doing a pleural tap on a patient who wants to take part in my study. 'Be on time,' Jorge Seabat, the radiologist, had told me in his email. OK, I replied, but I was surprised. Normally Jorge is way more laid back than that. Jorge is an interventional radiologist, as opposed to the non-interventional kind, who are simply witnesses to everything, sitting in front of monitors all day long, murmuring into small dictaphones which they hold up to their lips.

The patient was a Chinese man. According to the nurse he is some sort of entrepreneur. I'd say he is worth billions. The room was full of people. Bodyguards, advisers, two interpreters. Officials from his embassy even. The patient himself seemed like a nice man, although he didn't look like an entrepreneur. If anything there was more of a rural vibe to him. After the interpreters finished explaining what I had told him about my study he bowed his head repeatedly to me. I added that what I am doing is pure research. It wouldn't benefit him in any way. The interpreters whispered some more to him and once again he bowed his head.

'How much fluid do you want?' Jorge asked me when we were over by the sterile trolley, setting up.

'A hundred mls about, I'd say,' I replied.

Jorge was being more formal than he usually is. Generally you can joke around with him, but not today. He seemed nervous and was clumsy opening the equipment. I nodded in the direction of the lethal-looking bodyguards. They were dressed all in black and standing by the door, not knowing what to do with themselves.

'You'd better not give him a pneumothorax,' I said to Jorge.

'Shut up, will you,' he said, looking around to see if anyone heard. But then he gave me a big grin.

On my way back to the lab I sat for a while on the smoking bench in front of the hospital on First Avenue. I gave up smoking some months back and you'd imagine that it would be pure torture sitting there, surrounded by the exhalations of others. But I like it actually. I could sit for hours watching the angry traffic held back at intervals by the traffic lights. The cars vent and scream like livestock before moving along. In any case there's nowhere else to sit around here, just a small playground on 63rd Street between 1st and 2nd that has a sign saying 'No Childless Adults'.

There was a girl sitting beside me. She was beautiful but I didn't want to stare at her too much. She was sobbing away quietly to herself, using a bunched up tissue to dab at her eyes. She was also smoking a cigarette but she didn't know how to smoke it properly. As soon as she removed the cigarette from her mouth the smoke wafted out of her. It reminded me a little of my wife, who is an occasional or social smoker. She could never get the hang of it either. The memory made me smile.

The girl and I sat together on the bench for a while. She wept and smoked the entire time, lighting a second cigarette from the first. I felt under some internal pressure to say something to her, maybe try to comfort her a little. But if it was me sitting there weeping I know that I would rather be left alone. The girl was wearing purple underwear, a thong, I think. I saw that when she leaned forward. Her skin was very white.

Because of the procedure on the Chinese man all my other work got pushed back. It was evening by the time I got out of the laboratory. Instead of heading directly back to my apartment I decided to go for a walk to clear my head. I'd spent the whole afternoon under the sterile hood, fixed in more or less the same position. My neck was stiff and the small joints of my hands hurt. I must have used the pipette a thousand times.

When I stepped through the sliding doors of the institute the bubble of silence was lanced by the street noise and the wind jumped on me like a large dog happy at my return. I went across town, making my way slowly along 64th Street until I got to Lexington Avenue. My mind was blank and empty and my body was exhausted. It felt good, like I had given everything to the day, leaving nothing behind. All the avenues and cross-streets were packed, Manhattan's iconic steam rising out of the ground, also emanating from the backs of cars. I stopped at a small diner on Lexington called Eat Here Now and spent a while trying to read the menu but I found it difficult to focus on the words. There was still some daylight left. Even so, every light was on in every window in every building, the entire city looking down at me through the whites of its eyes.

In my old job, before coming here, I used to leave work in a similar state of blankness but I would arrive at it through a different process. In that job I took care of a lot of sick people, most of whom are dead now. I recall some of them very fondly but to be honest I have forgotten most of them.

2

The girl has a Russian accent. I heard her today when she asked for a light off a builder who was sitting next to us on the bench. The builder handed her his lit cigarette. But when he got it back off her again the cigarette was broken. He looked at it in a bemused fashion and discreetly threw it away. Then he put on his orange helmet and trudged off. The girl and I followed him with our eyes. Or at least, she followed him with her eyes and with mine I followed the perfect outline of her body. She was wearing the same underwear as the other day. The same colour anyway.

The builder headed in the direction of the new research institute on the corner of 1st and 67th that has been flying up out of the ground at a rate of knots. They've got a real expertise for that sort of thing over here. Just a few months ago the building was nothing but a large hole in the ground. If it had been up to these guys that Babylonian tower would have made it all the way up to the pearly gates. We'd all still be speaking the same language.

The girl wasn't crying today. I noticed also that her cigarette smoking had gotten slightly better in the few days since I last saw her. She kept glancing in my direction but we didn't speak and after a while I left to go back up to the lab. But when I got to the door of the institute she caught me looking back at her and gave me a wave. I looked away instinctively before turning around and waving back. We both laughed. I went through the door of the institute.

Henrietta was a touch better today. She has been tolerating the treatment well. It is already Day 4. This first ten days of the protocol are fairly intensive, involving six-hourly injections of the drug. It means that I have to be in the lab at midnight and then again at 6 a.m. It's just as well I live nearby. Henrietta's bloods today were fine. The protocol says to check them every seventy-two hours, to make sure there is no liver inflammation, a known side effect of the drug she is getting. I decided to check them on a daily basis instead, just to be on the safe side. If you wait too long the inflammation can become fulminant, the liver shot through completely. In any case the bloods were fine, better than baseline actually, no liver inflammation. Her overall condition is similarly stable. The red tears have dissipated. The manual doesn't comment on this, but I imagine it can only be a good thing.

3

I saw the Chinese entrepreneur today. It was late at night and I was staying up. There was no point sleeping until I had given Henrietta her midnight dosage. The man was standing at his window looking out. He seemed to be pretty bored. Every now and again something down in the street would attract his attention and he leaned into the glass trying to get a better look at it. None of his bodyguards were visible. Perhaps they aren't needed any more. I was standing at my own window, in the staff quarters on 65th Street. My apartment looks directly out on the hospital, which at night looks like an enormous cruise ship seen from the side, all of its berths lit up. You can see easily into the patients' rooms, right down to what they are watching on television. They must feel that we are continuing to observe them as part of our studies, taking notes on their activity levels, what is called their performance status. For their part they can also see into our rooms, which are mostly single-roomed quarters like the cells of a monastery, or a prison.

When I moved in here for some reason they put me on the floor for surgical residents who rotate around the various New York hospitals. Every three months somebody new will be standing in front of the elevator in their scrubs. I meet them when I come out of my room in the morning to go over to the laboratory. Sometimes it's a gorgeous girl and you get to know her a little with chit-chat. Then the three months are up and you regret not having asked for her email address. The only exception is the apartment at the end of the hallway which contains an Indian family. They've been here longer than me and have several small children. I haven't been able to work out how many exactly. If I was to guess I would say four.

Unfortunately for the Chinese man they've put him into the corner room, a worrying development for him. Those quiet corner rooms are for pure palliation. You don't come out again, or at least that has been my observation.* The previous resident had been in that same room for weeks. I watched as she became more and more bed-bound. She didn't get any visitors until the end, and then of course they came in their droves. On the final night one of them produced an enormous candle out of a sports bag. The type they carry at Corpus Christi. He mounted it on a table in front of the window and it made the entire room glow red as if it was on fire. The next morning the room was empty, the bed stripped bare. Now the Chinese man is there, down to my left as I look across.

I have been here for two years now. That was when I came over from Ireland to do a postdoctoral research fellowship at

---

* If you are ever being admitted to hospital and the nurse starts leading you in the direction of the single room in the corner, you should dig your heels in and refuse to go. You don't stand a chance otherwise.

the world famous Lincoln-Pryor Cancer Center, one of the best cancer hospitals there is. Unsurprisingly the Americans have a league table to decide these things, although what it goes on I have no idea. A crowd comes in auditing every once in a while. Presumably the number cured must count. First place is always between us and a place in Texas. When it's us they hang a banner over the front door.

The fellowship was part-funded by the Irish government and was too good an opportunity to turn down. You're encouraged to go overseas after completing basic clinical training in whatever specialty you've chosen and I'd been putting it off for years. The move came at the right time for me for other reasons too, because my wife and I decided to separate just before we were due to leave for America. 'Taking a break' was the phrase that was used in telling others about it, as if we were children playing in the sun, merely pausing out of thirst and exhaustion. As yet there is no sign that play will be resumed.

Several people had applied for the fellowship and I was very fortunate to be awarded it by the interview panel. I was the oldest applicant – I'm forty-two now – and had been on the scene in Dublin for several years, whereas the others were all younger, fresh out of their various senior house officer schemes. There were two slots and Cillian Deasy got the other one. He lives a few floors up from me with his wife, who is a dietician. They're both from Cork in the south of Ireland.

My contract is due to end soon but I may try to extend it if my supervisor – Dr Solter – allows me. It is easier than you think to get accustomed to new surroundings, especially if you have enough money and are open to things. And my family has grown used to my absence. When I call home on weekends my brother Donal, who has Down's syndrome, doesn't ask me any more when I will be home. And my parents, who sit behind him on the computer screen, their images flickering in and out on account of their poor internet connection, appear also to be resigned to it. But they are old – my father is well into his eighties.

4

I finished the bulk of Henrietta's treatment this evening. Day 10. I just have to give her a boost on Day 15. After that she'll be done. I will simply observe her then, until Day 90, when that will be it for her.

I always feel bad giving her the injections. It is a huge relief for both of us to have finished the course, or nearly finished, once the boost is given. Henrietta hates them with a vengeance. I have to stretch her backwards over my hand to get at the tiny vein near one of her hind legs. The vein has become more and more sclerosed recently. As a result each administration has been getting more difficult from a technical point of view. Sometimes it takes a few minutes just to get some blood return so that you can give her the drug. And sometimes I am not sure if I have gotten all of the drug into her. On those occasions I give her a little bit extra even though this is strictly prohibited by the protocol.

The observation period will be easier for both of us. For sure I will have to monitor her closely and take notes, but the night-time visits will not be necessary and I can go into the lab slightly later in the mornings. Henrietta is the last of her cohort. The others are already in their observation periods.

Half of them got active drug and half got saline solution, which served as the control or placebo. Control is the more accurate terminology given that there is no placebo effect in mice, or at least not as far as anyone knows.

There's been no sign of the Russian girl. I've been keeping an eye out for her, leaving the laboratory more than strictly necessary to sit out on the bench or even just to walk by it. Today for example Deep asked me if I thought it was raining. At the height we are at it is sometimes hard to tell. I told him I would check. Down I went. The girl wasn't there. I sat on the bench and watched the traffic for a while before heading back upstairs. I told Deep it was dry outside, although the sky was indeed threatening. The clouds were like a million fists pointed at the earth.

Deep is one of the other postdocs. The two of us share lab space in the Nathan Institute, which is just across 68th Street from the hospital, on the other side of it from my apartment building. The institute is part of the hospital, the brains of it you could say, where most of the research gets done. All the laboratories are here. There is a connecting passageway, all glass, which joins the two buildings umbilically at the level of the nineteenth floor. It is a good place to stand during storms. Our laboratory is up on the twenty-fifth floor. We have the entire floor pretty much to ourselves.

I don't know why Deep was so curious about the weather. He rarely leaves our small office at the back of the lab, where we spend a lot of our time staring into anachronistic computers from the 1990s. I wasn't surprised to find him there last night when I came to give Henrietta her midnight injection. And then again at six this morning when I found him sprawled out in front of his computer, fast asleep and wearing yesterday's clothes or even those from the days before that. When the sound of the door woke him it took him a second or two to remember who I was. Then he rubbed his eyes and got back to work on his computer, with its nebula screensaver, the Orion, I think. John Coltrane is on mine. In the picture he is playing his saxophone furiously. The photo was taken near the very end of things, when for the first time in his career Coltrane had to sit on a chair in order to play and he was barely even producing music any more, just sound that has a searing quality.

Both Deep and I are affiliated with the same laboratory, the Solter lab, but you would never guess it, as our research could not be more different. Deep's is in signal transduction. He incurs mutations in fruit fly larvae, then transplants them into the adult drosophila. By studying cell signalling in fruit flies you can gain insight into the human situation. We are apparently not all that different from them genetically. Sometimes Deep spends whole nights watching over his flies in their dark green glass cage that he keeps beside a fan heater even in the height of summer, staring at them for hours on end, no doubt discerning all sorts of patterns in how they arrange themselves in the air. He makes notes in a small pad with a yellow biro, then transfers all the data onto his computer. On the wall he has hung a poster of a larva ripped from a *National Geographic* and stuck up by one corner with a bit of white tape. It is a fearsome sight, with massive eyes and sharp teeth. Other than that the walls of our small office are bare.

My own research involves giving cancer to mice and then giving them drugs to see what happens. Either way they are screwed. Even if they don't die of the cancer you have to sacrifice them, as it is quaintly said. As if there was a god of science that needs mollifying, lounging on some altar. I can picture him, actually – a blood-lipped Jabba, the mice dangling by their tails above his gob.

After I had finished with Henrietta's treatment I stood for a while looking down on her and the others, watching as they scampered about the floor of the cage like children in a play-ground. I took some food granules from the dispenser and sprinkled them from my thumb and index finger. Then I planted my hand down on the sawdust base and left it there, enjoying the sensation of the animals rubbing up against my skin and running over my fingers. They must think my hand and arm a strange visiting creature. A benevolent multi-pronged thing coming out of the sky every day. For all anybody knows they might anticipate the moment when it appears in their midst, look forward to it, recall it later after it is gone. Worship it even. Alternatively it is a startling phenomenon to be endured each day as a brand-new terror. Perhaps they even associate it with the deterioration amongst their number, which I suppose would not be wrong.

5

I was on the smoking bench this morning for half an hour
or so when the Russian girl appeared and sat beside me. I
was reading a textbook, which I much prefer to do out there
in the air and noise. The girl smiled at me and was looking
very pretty. She was wearing the same yellow cardigan as the
last time I had seen her, almost a week ago, and a short denim
skirt. Her legs were bone coloured.

'You pay for sex?' she said.

I stared at her and my thoughts became nothing more
than a rubbish truck that happened to be going thundering
past us on First Avenue at that very moment, men hanging
from it precariously. When I was young that was what I
wanted to do, to simply hang off a truck like that.

'What?' I said.

'You play the sax?'

'No,' I said. 'Trumpet.'

'Sax. Trumpet. Whatever,' she said, taking out a cigarette.

'How did you know?' I asked her.

'I see you at the window. Every day, actually.'

'From where?'

'Where do you think?' she said.

We looked at each other for a moment without speaking.

She must have seen me from somewhere in the hospital. Every day I stand at the window of my apartment and practise scales on an old trumpet which I only began learning when I came to New York. I bought it at a flea market in Chelsea on one of the first Saturday mornings. Patients point me out to their relatives and whole groups sometimes stand looking over at me as if they are listening intently, which of course I'm glad they're not. I can't play the thing at all. I can barely even produce a sound – it's much harder than it looks. Once somebody across the way clapped when I removed it from my mouth.

'Are you a patient?' I asked the girl.

'Do I look like patient?' she said quickly back to me, the cigarette between her teeth. Then she lit the cigarette, with some difficulty. The wind kept blowing out the flame. She covered it with her hand and sucked hard on it until eventually she was able to blow out some smoke. She sat up straight and stretched her neck by moving her head from side to side.

'You don't have a job?' she said.

'Yes,' I said, 'I'm a postdoc.'

'Post. Doc,' she said almost musically to herself. Then she looked at the ground and repeated it a few times. 'Post. Doc . . . Post. Doc . . . What is it? Post. Doc?'

'I'm a doctor, a scientist,' I said.

'Ucch,' she said, almost in disgust.

She stared at me then for a few seconds that felt longer than that – her eyes are green, I think, she really is beautiful

– before turning away abruptly to face downtown. A rush of cars came at us.

'So are you in a band or what?' she said, turning around to me again.

'Jesus no!' I said, laughing at the idea of it. 'To be honest I've only just taken it up.'

There was more silence then, at least in terms of conversation between us. Of course New York is never silent. A half-block away from where we sat a group of hard hats, cordoned off with orange, gathered around a gash that they had opened up in the centre of the avenue. They worked in disregard of the obstruction they were causing, cars honking at them, drivers' heads out side windows yelling at them. It was as if the city under their boots was kicking and screaming as they attacked her skin, exposing New York's nerve endings, one of them with a pneumatic drill, others with picks.

'You should join a band, make some money,' the girl said.

'What about you, what do you do?'

'Me? I'm more or less a translator here. Volunteer.'

'What language?' I said.

'Russian, of course.'

'Is there much call for that?'

'What?'

'Are there many Russian patients?'

'Of course there are,' she said. 'They drink, they smoke, they get cancer. Then they need me because of course they don't speak English despite that they live here thirty years.'

She took a long drag of her cigarette. The smoke came out her nose.

'But I don't like it, actually,' she continued. 'You have to tell people crap horrible things, you know. The treatment isn't working . . . the . . . the lesions in your liver are getting bigger . . . we need to discuss your resuscitation status . . . the . . . the cancer has gone to your brain . . . Ucch. It's so shit, you know. The other day I had to tell a guy his wife wasn't going to wake up. She was on a ventilator unconscious, in a coma or something. They want to turn it off, the machine, but they need for him to sign form. He was refusing. I wanted to say, yeah, don't fucking sign it. You never know. These doctors don't know everything, y'know? Despite of it all, what they think.'

'Did you?'

'What?'

'Did you tell him not to sign it?'

'Of course not. Don't be stupid. I'd get fired.'

'I thought you said you were a volunteer.'

'You know what I mean,' she said.

Neither of us said anything for a while. Then she said 'Americans' and shook her head.

'I'm not American,' I said. 'I'm Irish.'

'I wasn't talking about you.'

A yellow cab pulled out abruptly ahead of an SUV right in front of us. The SUV came to a screeching halt and the driver leaned on the horn for a prolonged moment. Then the traffic moved on and it was as if nothing had happened.

'Is that why you were crying the other day?' I asked her.

She stared back at me and I noticed again her eyes, which I never usually notice in a person. They are striking, a sort of whitish green like those of a cat. She blew more smoke out.

'I do lie a bit, though, now and again,' the girl continued, ignoring my question, 'make it nicer a bit, you know. Change words a little. The lesions are a small bit bigger maybe. Not by much. We think the cancer has gone to your brain. Pretty sure maybe. It doesn't take much. Doctors are so stupid fuckers sometimes, you know? No offence. If it was me I'd want them to lie a little. You know – just tell me, yeah yeah, you know what, it's fine, don't worry about it. In fact, don't come back! Go to the bitch.'

'The bitch?' I said.

'Yes, the bitch . . . Sand and all, you know? What, you don't have bitches in Ireland?'

'Ha!' I said, laughing. 'Yes, we have bitches in Ireland.'

She took out another cigarette and lit it from the butt of the old one. She puffed on it intently, her eyes narrowed, until a tiny ember showed and small wisps emanated from it. Then with real effort she flung the spent butt as far as she could towards First Avenue.

Neither of us said anything. We watched the traffic. Over her shoulder I noticed the builder from the other day, walking back towards the Tower of Babel carrying his orange helmet under his arm. He was stopped by one of the protesters standing out the back of the hospital. The protester asked the builder in mime for a cigarette by putting two fingers in front of his lips. The builder took out his cigarette pack and then he took out his matches and shielded the struck flame with his other hand as the protester bowed his chin towards it. When smoke appeared they nodded at each other and the builder headed back again over to the unfinished tower. The protester upended his sign and rested his foot on it as he smoked, facing out towards the traffic.*

'What's the book?' the girl asked me then.

I lifted it up to show her the title: *The Biology of Cancer* by Robert Weinberg.

'So what sort of doctor are you anyway?' the girl asked me.

'I work mainly in the laboratory.'

She shook her head and looked away.

'You're not a real doctor? A regular one? Med school and all.'

'I started off as a regular one but then recently I stopped.'

'Why?'

'I don't know. Humans are tricky, I suppose.'

'Tricky?'

'Unpredictable ... more or less anything can happen.'

'Tell me about it,' she said.

---

* The hospital seems to attract these protesters. I've noticed this particular man a lot. He's there most mornings, an old man who wears a long overcoat even in summer. His sign says ST MICHAEL – PROTECT AND SAVE US. A big hefty thing which must make his shoulder ache. I don't know who St Michael is; perhaps he is a surgeon. There is also another woman who now and again sits on the ground outside the main entrance getting in everyone's way. She never has a sign. Security have learned to leave her be. It is unclear what their agenda is. Perhaps it is a picket against sickness in general or even death itself, in which case it's a wonder there aren't more of them. And the ones there are are always solitary. They would be better off organizing themselves into a union.

'I decided to work in the laboratory instead,' I said.

'Tricky,' she said, after a delay, as if she was making an effort to remember it.

A police van appeared and went by blaring its sirens, crossing in the direction of the West Side. Cars grudgingly tried to get out of its way. An ambulance turned the corner at 64th, following in its wake, its siren also sounding. The sun sharply bisected the avenue and an elderly tramp pushed a trolley full of junk across it head-down, oblivious to the irate cars. Both the girl and I followed his slow and miraculous progress. When he reached the kerb I got up from the bench.

'I'd better head off,' I said.

'What?'

'I'd better go.'

'Go then!' she said and laughed.

'I'll see you around,' I said to her.

'When?' she asked.

'I don't know,' I said. 'Around.'

'OK,' she said.

As I was going through the door of the institute I met Dr Solter, my supervisor, who was coming down the steps.

'Where were you?' he shouted out to me.

'Fresh air, to read,' I said, and I lifted the Weinberg up in front of me with both hands.

He looked at it suspiciously.

'Great book,' he said. Then he continued on his way.

6

This morning I gave Henrietta her boost. According to the protocol I was supposed to give it on Day 15, but I ended up giving it today, a day early. Her condition has slightly improved and I was anxious to get more drug into her in case the disease takes off again. After I injected her she started shivering, so I set her down in the corner and just observed her for a few minutes. I tore off some tissue paper and placed it over her to keep her warm but the shivering continued, fairly vigorously. After about five minutes it finally stopped and she looked up at me as if to say: 'Why did you do that?' I stroked her back and smoothed her fur, which was moist. It is possible that she has developed a mild allergy to the drug. If I had to treat her again I would slow down the rate of administration, perhaps give her some acetaminophen first, or Benadryl or even a small dose of steroid. I stood with my elbows on the rim of the enclosure peering down on both her and the rest of the mice, my face a moon in their sky. Henrietta appeared to be completely exhausted. After a minute she closed her eyes and fell asleep.

For the first few months of my fellowship over here I continued to do mainly clinical work – treating patients, just as I had done back in Ireland – but now I am entirely in the laboratory, which I much prefer. It is more controlled and predictable there, in contrast to clinical work, where you have only an illusory or – at best – superficial control over things, and the truth is that you never know what is going to happen. Just ask any number of my former patients. One lady in particular comes to mind, a woman in her sixties who I used to see a lot of when I first came here. I will call her Mrs X on account of patient confidentiality. She would come in once a week for treatment. We would chat and I would do a physical and check her bloods. Then one day she died outside the hospital just minutes after I saw her. She simply went down in the lift and collapsed in the middle of First Avenue. Her blood work was perfect, and her physical examination revealed nothing of what was to happen just a few minutes later. Even the autopsy was negative.

In the laboratory on the other hand it is rare that something totally out of the blue occurs. You set your own conditions and to a large extent the future is predetermined. Only some of the details are fluctuant. And even if something unexpected does occur you can usually work out the mechanism, uncover a logic that is always present in nature even if we don't see it a lot of the time. Whereas in the clinic it sometimes felt as if there was no logic at all and that, when you were talking to the patients about what might happen to them, trying to answer their questions and so on, you might as well read out their horoscope. 'We'll see' you would say whenever a patient asked something as basic as 'Will it work, doctor, the treatment?' or 'What will happen?', entirely reasonable questions, you might think, but completely un-answerable. 'We'll see,' you could only say, 'we'll see.'

I was sick and tired of saying this and I didn't want to do it any more. In particular I didn't want to be confronted by that particular look that patients have when they come to you on their best behaviour, sometimes even dressed up for the occasion, because they think that will make a difference. It even happened the odd time that a person – generally some-body wealthy or in business – would try to intimidate you a little, making it clear that they knew someone on the board of the hospital or that after this they were also going to Dana-Farber or MD Anderson or wherever to get a second or a third or even a fourth opinion. I would always feel bad for them at those moments, for not knowing the trouble they were in, as they looked out at me from within their fine Brooks Brothers suits, now a size or two too large. They seemed to be under the impression that my job came with additional discretionary powers, or that I could at least shade it a little in their direction one way or the other, that I had the ear of some superior being. It made me think of that old joke where the doctor gives a man six months to live. The man settles his account, paying the doctor all the money he owes him, so the doctor decides to give him another six months.

But people like that are very much in the minority. Most simply overestimate your power. My life is in your hands, doctor, they would sometimes say, which it never is in medicine, unless of course you are going out of your way to deliberately cause harm. For the most part there is nothing to do except sit across from them and be kind, to make sure your white coat is clean and that at the very least you look the part and don't mislead them too much. That last part is harder to do than it sounds, because of course we all share the same basic predicament.

Certain patients come to mind. That lady from New Jersey. I don't remember her name, but her elderly husband wouldn't let her flush the toilet after she used it, so that he could go in and record the appearance of her excretions. He set great store by this and kept a detailed record, which he would then read out to me and I would pretend to take an interest. The lady sat looking at her husband as he went through his record with an expression on her face which I would like to forget if at all possible: it was full of love, and also indulgent, as if he were a small boy. (She was less impressed by what I had to offer, but was not bitter about it in any way). I would have liked very much to have had her life in my hands. And there were others, of course. As I said, I've forgotten the vast majority of them.

In the laboratory my main research revolves around an enzyme called telomerase. I'm trying to find ways to inhibit it and neutralize its effects in cancer cells. The rationale is that if you can do it in mice then you might eventually be able to do it in humans, although that is more difficult. It is actually quite easy to cure cancer in mice, which under other circumstances would make them fortunate.

In this current experiment there are a total of eleven mice. They all have cancer, which I gave to them and which is easy to do. You take tumour cells – human cancer cells – and grow them in a cell culture flask, and then inject the cells into the fat beneath the animal's skin. You wait a few weeks before the cells take and form tumours, growing to a measurable size that you can test the drugs on and which can serve as the baseline, generally half a centimetre, against which future growth or shrinkage can be quantified. While that is happening there is nothing to do. It is like having pets. You come in and look at them for a while. Weigh them. Run your fingers over them individually, massaging their bellies and their backs trying to detect the gristly nodules of the incipient tumours taking root. The people from the Research Animal Resource Center (RARC) come by regularly to check on their food and water supplies, and to make sure you're not doing a Captain Kurtz and making a necklace of their heads.

I get the malignant cells from a variety of sources, from patients over in the hospital, from their fluid collections generally (either pleural or peritoneal effusions), but also from other laboratories who may have established a cancer cell line with particular properties. Or sometimes I get them from private companies who sell cancer on the internet. It is a good thing to test your drug or your hypothesis on a variety of different cancer types. One of the mice – whom I have nicknamed Mr Miyagi – has a bile duct cancer that was originally taken from a seventy-two-year-old Japanese man who died of that disease fifteen years ago. I ordered that particular

26

cancer on line because of its unusual growth pattern. Rather than appearing as hard, discrete masses, the cells grow in sheets. In Mr Miyagi they have spread out over his back and are pushing up in bunches through his thin felt skin, almost as if he is wearing a backpack. It doesn't seem to bother him too much, although occasionally he staggers a little under the weight as if he were dazed or drunk. In general the cells that you get online are more reliable in forming tumours. They have a proven track record, whereas the ones I get from the patients across the way in the hospital are more hit and miss. It is hard to make them grow outside the body. A lot of the time they just die out.

Before coming here I had never worked with animals. We didn't do much of it in college. We dissected cadavers, of course, but that was purely for anatomy and was never as informative or as useful as you would imagine it to be. I have vivid memories of a particular day in secondary school where we had to bring in a cow's eye to physics class when we did the eye chapter. My eye was infected. When I cut into the vitreous humour a foul-smelling, thick yellow gunge emerged. The lens was a firm pastille. After class the teacher collected the torn eyes in a black refuse sack and put them in the dumper container in the corner of the yard. But he forgot to close the lid. In the afternoon a plague of gulls descended on the sack of eyes. Thousands of them. Maybe even tens of thousands. After school I ran through the yard to get to the bus. The air was thick with gulls, their agitating wings, their pointed probing beaks, the cow's eyes they were letting fall spattering the ground, making it greasy. I ran across the yard with my arm across my face. Gulls eat anything.

7

WHERE ARE YOU?
That was the email waiting for me this morning when I went into the office and booted up my computer. It was from Dr Solter, my supervisor. He sends me these messages on a regular basis from whatever lecture or seminar he happens to be at in the hospital and which – for whatever reason – I have decided to skip. There's always something going on over there. If you went to every talk or seminar you wouldn't get a stroke of work done. I don't have a BlackBerry, so by the time I get his email there's usually another one above it in my inbox, that he sends afterwards.

WHERE WERE YOU?

When I first came here I found all of this amusing but now it is getting tiresome, particularly as I am actually older than the guy (and have more medical experience). But he has my immediate future in his hands, and given that they are so hierarchical in America, I have to keep him onside.

But he is a bit of a mystery to me, Solter. Everyone seems to be afraid of him and he is generally considered to be a rising star. I don't see it myself. He is on the short side and has a somewhat theatrical – almost clownish –quality, especially when he shouts and rails and embarks on long, ranting monologues, which he does frequently in departmental meetings, where he is completely disinhibited.

Solter has been very lucky in his career to date, because he happened to do his own postdoctoral fellowship with a famous professor somewhere in the Midwest, Michigan, I believe, who is in with a shout of winning the Nobel Prize because of the work he did on telomeric DNA. Telomeres are at the ends of DNA strands. They act as a kind of molecular clock, telling the cell when it has divided enough and needs to enter the senescent state and then die.

As it happens, I was at this morning's seminar, the one Solter was on about, demanding to know where I was. For a while anyway. I had been on my way to get a coffee when I saw a crowd of young white coats heading somewhere in a hurry, about twenty or thirty of them, squeezing to get into one of the small lecture halls by the canteen. I was curious to see what was going on so I joined the queue. They were clinical fellows and in general the clinical people are better informed than the lab people about what's happening around the hospital – what lectures or seminars are taking place – or even what is happening in the world at large. In contrast, if you asked Deep what year it was or who the president was he would have to stop and think about it for a few minutes.

The seminar was called 'The epigenetic highway – how to see clearly ahead'. The title was on a placard mounted on an artist's easel outside the door. There was no sign of Solter for the period of time I was there, which admittedly was not for long. The guy giving the seminar seemed to know a lot of the white coats by name. He was very matey with them, and had a long and carefully cultivated ponytail. In the first five minutes he managed to drop in the twin boasts that his wife was a professional dancer and that she was from Argentina. I was half expecting him to show a picture of her, which would have made the seminar more interesting. I left early. Solter must have come in late because when I got back to the lab his email was already waiting for me. He had attached the flyer for the seminar and when I opened it there was the ponytailed lecturer I had just seen grinning out at me, his arms folded. He seemed to be standing in a garden, which meant the photo hadn't been taken here at the hospital because there are no gardens around here. Just concrete. Perhaps he was standing in his own garden at home. Maybe it was his wife who took the photo.

I was sitting looking at it when the second email arrived from Solter.

WHERE WERE YOU?

I had to laugh. Then I deleted both emails without reply. In any case I assumed that both questions were rhetorical.

I also had a message from Jorge, the radiologist. He said that he would be doing another paracentesis* on Thursday. 'If

---

* Paracentesis = A procedure where body fluid within the abdominal cavity is either sampled to make a diagnosis, or removed in quantity in order to relieve symptoms of pressure resulting from fluid build-up. If it is just for sampling purposes you only need a few millilitres. But if you are relieving symptoms of discomfort you take as much as you can get, which can be several litres. The abdomen can hold more than you'd think. I once took twelve litres from someone, back in Dublin, a builder with one finger missing. He was a Tottenham Hotspurs fan, but when Abramovich bought Chelsea he began to support them instead, even wearing their jersey on his hospital visits. He never waited for the fluid to build up again. For a while he made a weekly appointment.

you're still doing that study of yours, that is,' he added at the end, and which Jorge always adds, as if one of these days I am liable to reply to him saying that 'No, actually, Jorge, we just found the cure. All studies are on hold. We're going to set the mice free. And the patients too.'

Jorge generally emails me once a week, sometimes twice or even three times. He contacts me whenever he has a procedure scheduled and knows that there's going to be a lot of fluid removed. My research protocol allows me to collect the fluid and study it. It would only be thrown out otherwise. I collect it so that I can extract the cancer cells in order to study them. There are all sorts of things you can do with them. You can establish cell lines, keeping the cells growing in a culture flask, in a special medium consisting of foetal calf serum, which nourishes them. It is easy enough to keep cancer cells going but this is not the case with normal cells. Normal cells die out pretty quickly, whereas cancer cells never do. They are immortal.*

It is a simple enough procedure to remove the fluid. It comes out easily under the internal pressure and gravity, depending on the angle. It's even more straightforward if there's a lot of it. The worse the disease is and the more free fluid there is, the easier it is. I don't know if that's ironic or not. All you have to do is inject a bit of local anaesthetic into

* There are certain characteristics that differentiate cancer cells from normal cells in culture. Normal cells, when you place them in nourishing media, exhibit what is called contact dependent growth, meaning that when they come up against one another or a surface they stop growing, whereas cancer cells grow in a contact-independent fashion, insensitive to external moderating signals and multiplying regardless.

the skin and then put the trocar needle into the area of the abdomen where the fluid is, usually down low and at the sides. What is removed is totally extraneous and will not be missed by the body. It is free fluid, in the so-called third space, meaning that there is no relationship or equilibrium between it and the fluid within the vascular space. Fluid should never be free.

I replied to Jorge's email: 'Thank you very much, I'll see you on Thursday!'

Over here they are always adding exclamation marks to the ends of their sentences and it is an Americanism which I have adopted. At this stage it almost feels rude not to.

8

Henrietta is definitely getting better. Day 20 today and her red tears have not returned. Her weight – which is probably an even more sensitive indicator of her well-being – has increased compared to both yesterday and the day before that. Granted, her visible tumours have remained unchanged in size, but this is acceptable. They are more or less stable, as is the case for the rest of the animals, meaning further growth has at least been inhibited by the treatment. Henrietta's tumours are a little bigger than those of the other mice, two moderate-sized masses on her flank. They had really taken off in the period before I started her injections, reflecting their more aggressive biology. Their consistency is also a little different compared to the other animals. They are as hard as stones. Which makes it even better that the growth has stabilized. Mr Miyagi is the only one of the subjects who has manifested a visible response to treatment, the lesions beneath his skin having shrunk right down, now being barely palpable. He seems to have more nervous energy as a result. For an old guy he never sits still. But even Henrietta appears to be a little bit more energetic than before. At baseline – before she got any treatment – she was a little on the sluggish side.

Now that the animals are in the observation period I have more free time. The protocol is relatively quiet for this phase of the study – mandating only daily weights and tumour measurements – whereas for the first two weeks during the treatment and preparatory phase, it was relentless in its demands. Centrifuge at 1,500 rpm for 15 mins . . . Discard the supernatant . . . Suspend in 50 microlitre of solution . . . Repeat steps 3–7 . . . et cetera, et cetera. Even during weekends I had to go over to the laboratory. And any time I left I would need to have a timer in my pocket which summoned me back to the lab and made sure that I kept to the letter of the protocol as if it represented the commandments of a stern and inflexible Godhead. It has to be that way, otherwise you will end up with unreliable data. In any case I find it calming, to thoughtlessly follow the minute commands of the protocol, to suspend my own volition for a change and be simply a cog in its mechanism, as if I were standing at the centre of a machine. It is as quiet as a planet there.

This is what I have so far discovered in my just under two years of laboratory work:

– if you inhibit AKT signalling with a particular kinase inhibitor you get compensatory phosphorylation immediately upstream of it;

– if you then halve the dose of the drug this can be ameliorated, the downstream phosphorylation being eliminated completely.

It is not a big truth, and for sure it is not the cure for

cancer. But it is verifiable and reproducible by others*. And as a phenomenon it is something that already existed in nature, entirely independently, like a hard stone or piece of metal lying in the earth waiting to be dug up.

The last time I was talking to my wife in person she laughed out loud when I told her that I had changed jobs and was now working in a laboratory.

'That sounds about right,' she said quickly back at me, and which had the tone and feel of one of her barbs. I let it pass. I was just off the plane and the conversation had been going well. I didn't want to jeopardize it. This was over a year ago when my brother Donal got sick and I travelled back to Dublin to see him. Yvonne happened to be working in the hospital he was admitted to. We agreed to meet in the canteen on the first morning.

'Ha!' she said again, warming to the idea. 'I can picture it. You bloody well have the personality for it. That's for sure.'

More laughter, but there was a clear edge to it. I didn't delve. Evidently the mental image she had of me in a laboratory was providing her with some sort of confirmation. What was being confirmed I didn't know exactly but I could have hazarded a couple of guesses. Yvonne was post-call; she was sitting with both feet up on the chair next to her, still dressed

---

* When you publish your experiment you include in the Methods and Materials section exactly how you went about doing it. The point is that any lab anywhere in the world, assuming they use the same methods and materials, should get the exact same result every time. If they can't reproduce your findings they will write an angry letter to the editor accusing you of fraud or incompetence.

in her surgical scrubs. Her hair was up and she wasn't wearing make-up, which I always much preferred. Yvonne is naturally very pretty although she herself never thought so. She said hello to somebody walking past. Then she leaned forward and took out a cigarette from the pack in front of her on the table. She looked tired.

'Well,' she said, 'you can tell the rats I know exactly how they feel!'

I looked around the canteen, which was largely empty. They had just stopped serving breakfast. I reached over and took out one of Yvonne's cigarettes. One of the cleaning ladies glared at me as she pushed a large cart of trays containing dirty dishes. We were not supposed to be smoking indoors, despite the fact that we were in the staff section near the back door, which was open right beside us. I looked back at Yvonne.

'They're mice, actually,' I said.

Yvonne threw her head back and laughed again, this time without any edge to it.

9

This evening as I was heading back to my apartment I saw the Russian girl again. She was in a queue to get into the Knopler building where the library is and which is right next door to where my apartment is in the staff quarters building. The line went all the way down 66th Street. There must have been a hundred people in it. I knew that they were there for an Awards Lecture that was due to take place. Solter had circulated an email about it to all the postdocs saying GO TO THIS. The girl was near the front of the line; her yellow jumper caught my eye. The doors were still locked but just then ushers opened them and the crowd began to move forward. Some people were dressed up as if for a night out. A few men were even in tuxedos.

I joined the rear of the line and followed the crowd in through the large glass doors of the building. The event was being held in the large room across from the library which they call the ballroom for some reason, although I can't for the life of me imagine any dancing ever going on in it. It is more like an enormous vault, its ceiling two or three stories high. When I came into the room I saw the girl sitting up near the front, to the right of the small stage. There was an empty seat next to her which had her bag on it. I went up and stood beside her.

'Hello there,' I said, and she looked at me over the rim of her glasses, which I hadn't seen on her before.

'Postdoc,' she said after a slight delay, and I was relieved. I smiled at her.

'Are you expecting someone?' I asked.

She turned and picked up her bag without answering and I went in and sat down beside her.

'Why are you here?' I asked her, turning around to look back at the entrance. They had closed the doors.

'Why?' she said back at me quickly. 'Do you guys have some big conspiracy or something, that you don't allow public general to see?'

'Not that anyone has told me about,' I said.

'I saw sign that say this woman is bracka expert,' the girl replied. 'Your work involves this?'

It took me a second to realize what she meant.

'You mean BRCA, the breast cancer mutation?'

'Yes, of course,' she said. 'Ovarian cancer also.'

'No,' I said, 'I don't work on it.' The girl looked at me for a long instant.

Bracka, or BRCA, has been in the news a lot recently, mainly because of Angelina Jolie, who underwent the only really preventative treatment there is for it (radical surgery, including bilateral mastectomies), and then – just as bravely really, considering the nature of her day job – revealed to the world that she had undergone it.

39

'Anyway,' she said. 'It's a Jewish thing. I'm Jewish so I want to know about it, you know. You need to know these things, what might affect you.'

'Ashkenazi?'

'Wow, postdoc, I'm impressed. You actually know some things. Yes, Ashkenazi. One guy marries his cousin ten thousand years ago and everyone is screwed as a result.'

'Not everyone,' I said.

'Right. Just the lucky ones.'

I looked around the auditorium, which was fairly packed, with still more people coming in to stand at the back. I didn't recognize anybody. There was no sign of Solter. If I had a BlackBerry I would have been tempted to email him saying 'Where are you, David?'

'Where are you from?' I asked the girl.

'Like you know it already, postdoc. Russia. St Petersburg, actually. But I haven't been back since I left five years ago.'

'Why did you come to New York?'

'My brother works here. He arrange visa, everything. He's quite successful actually. Rich, or going to be anyway, soon enough. He loves it in America. Runs two businesses, what he could never do in Russia. Completely opposite to me. I study. No money. For this I would be better off back in Russia.'

'Where do you study?'

'Postdoc, you're so full of questions today!'

'Yes, I admit I'm very nosey,' I said.

'Nosey? What is it?'

'Curious . . . about life and . . . things.'

'OK, me too then, nosey. I like it, actually. Anyway. I don't do anything at the moment. In Russia I did architecture. Basic course. Foundation. But over here you need to do all over again. You have to save lots of money for that. Grad school and all. It cost arm and leg over here,' she said. 'So basically I'm on break.'

There was some activity on the small stage and it looked like proceedings were getting under way. Beside the lectern a group of people had gathered, including an elderly lady who presented another, very attractive, woman with a glass bowl. They stood with their faces frozen for a picture. Some men in suits joined them and more photos were taken. Behind them enormous red curtains swooped down from the high ceiling. It was a very impressive auditorium, almost like a cathedral. In between the two strands of curtains were the names of benefactors chiselled into the marble. Some of them were multinational corporations. Chrysler automobiles. Ford. KPMG. Dwarfing them all though was the name Albert A. Knopfler, after whom the building was named. Old Albert must have donated billions.

'By the way, I've never properly introduced myself,' I said and turned towards her, saying my name and extending my hand.

She laughed as she shook my hand.

'Yes. I know it already,' she said, 'I see it on your identification badge. But I prefer postdoc. No offence.'

'What's your name?'

'Marya. Here, I have card,' she said, removing a card from

her purse on her lap. She handed it to me. The card said her full name, followed by her email address. I sat forward and put the card in my back pocket.

Her phone made a noise and she took it up out of her bag and looked at it. She made an indignant sound and put it down again, turning it to mute.

'What is wrong with male species?' she said. 'Always sending SMS, every ten minutes, checking, always checking . . .'

I automatically looked down at her hands. There was no ring.

'How are your mice?' the girl asked then, putting the phone away.

'They're OK.'

'OK but doomed, right? Where do you get them, anyway?'

'There's an animal facility in the basement. You order from there, whatever type you want.'

'And you get right away?'

'It depends. If it's just a regular mouse then yes. But if you need to build a mouse, that can take months.'

'Build mouse? Like from scratch? Arms, legs, everything?'

'More like change its DNA, knock out a gene in it, or in one of its parents, so that they have a particular deficiency and develop cancers more naturally, instead of just injecting the cancer into them.'

'Yeah, right, sounds very natural, postdoc.'

Her phone vibrated again and its face lit up from an incoming text.

'He must be really worried about you,' I said.

'No . . . friends,' she said after briefly checking the message. 'They always want to go out dancing, partying. Say Marya, you come, you come. But I can't, y'know.'

'Why not?' I asked.

'Ucch, that's what they say too, postdoc. Why not? Why not? Always why not? Everything must be explained to every-body, y'know? It make me so tired, to be honest.'

Nevertheless she typed in a reply and then put the phone back in her bag.

Up on the stage more photos were being taken. I felt her gaze on the side of my face. It heated up as if she was really focusing on it.

'So . . . how come you're not married?' she said. 'You're like, what, forty, right? Forty-five? Are you homosexual?'

I laughed.

'I am married,' I said then, 'but we live apart. Separated. She's back in Ireland.'

'How long were you together?'

'In total, about three years.'

'Kids?'

'No, not really.'

'What do you mean?'

I didn't get a chance to answer because at that moment the lights dimmed and the chairperson walked up to the podium. The people who had been having their pictures taken stepped down off the small stage, apart from the attractive lady, who remained standing next to the lectern, still holding the glass bowl she'd been presented with. The chairperson tapped on the microphone and introduced her. We all applauded and she replaced him at the lectern, handing him her glass bowl.

The lecture was interesting enough. It was on the role of PARP inhibition in breast cancer, with a special focus on BRCA, just as the girl said. The event was in honour of a dead scientist I had never heard of, although you would think he had discovered the cure given the way they spoke about him in the introduction. The Italian woman giving the talk was really beautiful, so beautiful that for the duration of the lecture they projected her face onto a massive monitor that hung on the wall to the left of the sweeping curtains. They don't usually do that. She told the story of BRCA, going back thousands of years to when it first occurred in the germline of the Ashkenazi Jews and which over time is now present in a significant percentage of them. It is what is called a founder mutation.*

Throughout the lecture the girl took fairly copious notes on a large pad. At the end of the talk, when the lights went on,

---

* BRCA is a tumour suppressor gene. Any gene or part of your DNA can be damaged by random mutations. These happen all the time, every second of every day. The vast majority of the time it doesn't matter a whit. The areas of the DNA which are damaged are of no consequence, like getting a scratch on your car. But certain parts of your DNA are more crucial, controlling how the cell grows or divides, which is generally very tightly regulated. Instead of a scratch on the car exterior it is more like the brakes going or the accelerator being permanently pressed down. The cell grows and divides when it is not supposed to, ignoring the signals telling it to stop (becoming totally contact-independent), resulting in a tumour. These parts – whose absence or impairment causes cancer – are called tumour suppressor genes. We are all at risk. But some people inherit a damaged or mutated tumour suppressor gene in their germline, meaning that that risk is present in all their billions of cells from birth – placing them at much higher risk – and then handed down through the generations.

she listened closely to the questions that people asked. I thought she might even get up to the microphone and ask one herself. At the end there was a standing ovation for the Italian woman and more photos were taken with her and the elderly woman, who it turns out was the dead scientist's widow. A bouquet of flowers were also handed to her, the Italian woman, that is. I don't think the widow got anything. Then we drifted with the crowd out of the auditorium towards the foyer, where everyone had gathered, and which had been transformed. There were tall tables set up around the cavernous entrance hall of the library building, each with a white tablecloth and a single candle. I had never seen the building like this. We picked an empty table and stood at it, both of us looking around. Waiters wearing bow ties circulated with champagne flutes on silver trays. There was also a food station at which people were queuing. There was even a jazz band in the far corner.

I was staring into the intermediate distance when a woman standing in the centre of the room waved at me. I didn't recognize her, but she kept waving. It took me a minute to realize that she was actually waving at the girl. The woman was dressed in a long, flowing robe and wearing a bright yellow bandana. She walked over to us and, without any introductions, started speaking to the girl in Russian, her voice raised a little. She appeared upset. At one point the girl rested her hand on the woman's arm. I could tell her tone was now warmer.

It looked like an intense or certainly a private conversation, so I stood off to one side looking over at the jazz band.

I took out my own phone to check the messages, even though I knew I would have none. I rarely give my number to anyone. The only people who have it are my parents and brother, and Donal is the only one who uses it. He texts me frequently, usually relating the scores he has just achieved in whatever video game he is currently obsessed with.

After a while the girl and the woman said goodbye to each other and I turned back to her.

'Who was that?' I asked the girl.

'More being nosey, postdoc,' she said.

'She looks like a patient,' I said.

'Yes, she is,' said the girl. 'Ha! Be careful, postdoc! Half the people here must be patients! Or certainly public general . . . They want to find out what you guys are saying behind their backs!'

We stood around the table again.

'Anyway,' she continued, 'she's up on fifth floor of hospital. All week she is here, for tests and to decide on next step, you know? She fly in from Florida. Her husband is rich. But her English is not so good. I don't know why she come to lecture. She wants me to help her talk to her doctors tomorrow. Marya, she say, they come this morning to my bed, a crowd. Big crowd. They descend on me like eagle even when I eat my breakfast and half sleeping, no make-up, and talk all type of things to me. You come tomorrow, Marya, she say, you come, please come. And what am I supposed to say? No? Get lost? So anyway she go to the library to study. Every day. Check the net, see what is out there, you know.'

'What treatment is she on?'

'Nothing. She come to decide. All I know is that she spend fortune on white shark.'

'Shark?'

'You know it. Like Jaws. Big white.'

'Yes,' I said, 'I know it.'

'She buy it online. The fin. The cartilage. The teeth. The bone. You name it.'

'What does she do with it?'

'To eat it, of course. Crush up. Make soup. Tea. And why not? It's not like you guys have cure figured out. Apparently big white shark never get sick. No cancer. Infection. Nothing.'

'They're evolutionarily conserved*,' I said.

She stared at me without saying anything, slightly shaking her head in frustration. Then her mobile phone vibrated again. She laughed once more at whatever the message said and then she started coughing.

'Anyway, postdoc. I'm tired, and maybe coming down with something. I think I'm going to skip,' she said. And she pretty much rushed off, catching me a little by surprise.

---

* The same process underlying evolution also underlies cancer. Genetic mutation, which occurs all the time within a cell's DNA. Evolution also depends on random genetic mutations. Some of the mutations may actually be of benefit, producing certain advantageous traits that are then selected for over time. No mutations would mean no cancer, but also no evolution. Cancer is basically the flip side of the evolutionary coin. A great white shark is supposedly relatively conserved by evolution, because it hasn't had to change much. It is a myth though that they don't get cancer. The truth is that they can get the same nasty ones that the rest of us get, or at the very least those which aren't induced by behavioural patterns such as smoking or drinking. In any case, shark cartilage is useless as a treatment. It does nothing in mice when compared to placebo.

I watched her as she cut quickly through the crowd like a pickpocket.

I wandered about the foyer for a bit and had some wine, which was available at one of the stations. There was also pizza, served on silver platters. I went up and got a closer look at the jazz band. I ate and drank my fill and stood listening to the jazz for a good long while. They were excellent. They played a Coltrane number, 'Equinox', and when it ended I clapped loudly. I was the only one paying any attention to them.

10

When I came into the lab this morning Deep was standing facing the door as if he had been specifically waiting for me.

'There's a p-p-p-package for you,' he said. 'I p-p-p-p-put it downstairs. In the liquid n-n-n-n-n-nitrogen.'

He turned his back on me then and walked towards the office.

'Thanks,' I shouted after him, 'I'll go down and get it in a while.' He closed the door of the office after him.

I walked over to the animal enclosure and lifted off the lid. It may have been just my imagination but Henrietta seemed even perkier. More and more I think the treatment is kicking in. Perhaps the drug is doing what it is supposed to do. Or what we think it is supposed to do, because with drugs you are never a hundred per cent sure. It also has to be the case that whichever process the drug is interrupting is a relevant one to the cancer's biology, central to the vitality and persistence of the cells, and not just a peripheral process of no importance or which the cancer cell can easily overcome.

It is still early, though. There are a lot of variables. But it is encouraging that her weight is up a little on yesterday, stable, and it is not from free fluid, which would artificially increase the weight. I examined her abdomen carefully but couldn't detect any. In addition she seems more alert, more interested in her surroundings. Not that her surroundings are very interesting. I put some clean tissue paper in her cage. She gets great enjoyment out of that, they all do, tearing it to shreds.

Henrietta is named after Henrietta Lacks, whose cancer she has growing inside her. The original Henrietta died at age thirty-one of cervical cancer back in the 1950s. Her cancer was so tenacious it was able to survive independently outside her body after killing her. Like an alien that kills its host then scuttles about looking for another one. Scientists trapped it and used it to form the first cancer cell line. They wanted to study cancer cells in captivity, to figure out their circuitry, the mechanics of how they divide and grow (and grow and grow, the fuckers). Also to test drugs against them. So they took some of the cells from Henrietta Lack's cervical cancer and put them in a culture flask. Got the nutrient balance in the medium right to get them to grow. Were able to construct a replenishing of the nourished cells, dividing and dividing. If you do that with normal cells they die out after a number of cell divisions. Their telomeres get whittled down to nothing. The DNA strands are exposed. They develop karyotypic instability, which is quite beautiful under the microscope. You see them enter the senescent state and simply stop, having no thirst for immortality.

But this did not happen with Henrietta Lacks' cervix, or – to be precise – the part of it that went bad and wanted to keep going on forever. Her cancer cells became the first cell line, a feat of bioengineering. They called it HeLa after her. The cells are now immortal, dividing endlessly, forming new populations in unlimited culture flasks and growing in laboratories all over the world. You can mix them with drugs in various sequences and doses in 96-well plates to get an inkling of what might work and what probably won't. Or you can inject them directly into animals, a better approximation of what occurs in the human. The cells are introduced like soldiers onto an enemy beach, under the animal's skin or injected directly into an organ – Special Forces style – a surreptitious parachuting directly into the liver or under the kidney capsule, also fertile ground. You sit back then and wait as the cells assemble the architecture of their invasion, co-opting the host's vasculature and lymph into an insurgency against the host, instigating rebellion, erecting a bridging network to structurally support the budding friable vessels of the in-process tumour, or attracting inflammatory cells that buzz in a flap at barriers, breaking them down. The cells switch off their apoptotic or suicide mechanisms and survive, invade, metastasize.

Henrietta Lacks has been immortalized. Not in a metaphoric or literary sense. But literally. Unrecognizably her but at some level still her all the same, her molecules present in the cells which contain, somewhere in their DNA, the original her, driving forward with a life force grasping blindly for the next moment.

I've seen photographs of her as she once was, the original Henrietta. In one she is wearing a fur coat and standing beside her husband. They look like they're on their way out for the night. In another she is standing with her hands on her hips, smartly dressed and defiant, but in a jokey sort of way, as if she is making fun of someone she knows who stands that way and takes themselves seriously. I'm guessing she had a sense of humour. It is strange to think that she is here in my lab right now, having taken on this strange form, like in a fairytale, locked into the present, existing piecemeal and in mutated form, her cells dividing fifty years later. It's as if we've managed to trap alive someone from history to study them. Someone who should not be here. One out of the trillions of the past generations who have walked the planet before us. Not just an artefact belonging to one of them like in a museum – a farming implement or a piece of jewellery – nor a photograph or video imagery; or a skeleton or corpse; not even the peat-preserved leathery actual body, broken-necked, hauled from a bog. In Henrietta's case we actually have one of them, one of the previous trillions, alive. We snared her from the part of her cervix that went bad, dividing and dividing and dividing. Away off in her future that never happened.

It is these cells that I put inside Henrietta the mouse, to see if the process could be reversed by drugs. To see if their immortal thirst could be quenched, their behaviour modified. I stroked her skin and tipped her on the nose. She briefly opened her encrusted eyes. I replaced the lid of the cage.*

It was decent of Deep to put my package in the liquid nitrogen vat. He would have had to go downstairs to Solter's lab to do it. The easy option would have been to place it in the four-degree fridge on some ice, in which case most of the cells probably would have died. I knew that in the package were cancer cells taken from a group of patients who had enrolled in one of Solter's early studies, at least five years ago but maybe even longer than that. The cells had been frozen and then put in storage at minus eighty. I have been expecting them for weeks. Solter wants me to analyse them before they go completely out of date. To start with I am to thaw them and culture them in a flask filled with complete medium – a purplish liquid containing foetal calf serum and all the amino acids and nutrients necessary to sustain the cells. It is very straightforward to do. You simply add the cells to the medium and leave the culture flask in an incubator at thirty-seven degrees, body temperature. After a few days you will find that

* Henrietta is also special because of her genetic make-up. She is a transgenic mouse – a knock-out – meaning that she has a genetic defect that was purpose-fully imposed. When she was at the blastocyst stage (very early on, just after her parents' egg and sperm had fertilized, and when she consisted of only about thirty cells) I injected a stem cell into the middle of her which then grew along with the other cells, multiplying to become part of her. The stem cell had a particular genetic defect which means that Henrietta grew up to have it too. I implanted her into the uterus of her mother, who wasn't really her mother but a surrogate. I had to perform the operation on ten different blastocysts but Henrietta was the only one in whom the stem cell took. The other nine grew into normal mice. I thought we could still make use of them, but Solter told me to just kill them.

the cells have proliferated, attaching themselves to the bottom of the flask, covering it in a monolayer that you can easily make out under low power microscopy. Under higher power you can identify the individual cells. They are surrounded by a rim of fibrous tendrils like tiny teeth, with which they adhere tenaciously to the plastic bottom of the flask, biting into it; or like fingernails that they use to dig into the surface of the container, clinging to it and to their life. Under other circumstances we would encourage them, admire their tenacity, their ability to survive in extreme circumstances – severe hypoxia, et cetera – like the strange creatures or resistant microbes that you hear about living at great depths on the ocean floor.*

When the cells overgrow the plate the fluid medium becomes acidic and changes colour from purple to yellow-orange, indicating a build-up of waste which will cause the

---

* According to Weinberg there are six hallmarks of cancer:
– Self-sufficiency in growth signals: the cells are capable of growing autonomously, irrespective of what's going on around them, in contrast to normal cells which only grow if they are allowed to by their environment.
– Insensitivity to growth-inhibitory (anti-growth) signals: the cancer cells ignore the signals of social restraint; like a belligerent neighbour cutting down your fence and building an extension onto his house, deaf to your protests.
– Evasion of programmed cell death (apoptosis): cells are supposed to die and are programmed to do so after a defined number of divisions. Cancer cells avoid this.
– Limitless replicative potential: the cancer cells divide and divide interminably like ants.
– Sustained angiogenesis: the cells which clump together and form a tumour need a blood supply in order to suckle whatever nutrients they need. The tumour creates its own network of blood vessels to supply itself, although this is often chaotic and unstable, like a scaffold erected by chancers.
– Tissue invasion and metastasis: The cells do not respect the integrity of anatomical borders and traverse them at will, as opposed to benign growths which often have a capsule around them.

cells to die unless you split them. Then it is necessary to remove the majority of the cells and to add fresh medium to the ones that are left, diluting them; and you need to do this every other day, keeping a close and watchful eye on the cells, the way you would with a pet or a plant, because in actual fact it is easy enough to kill cancer cells when they are outside the body and completely dependent on your efforts to sustain them, adding the right nutrients and clearing out their waste, as opposed to when they are inside your body – adhering to you with their tiny teeth or digging into you with their finger-nails – when you keep them alive without making any effort at all.

When I went back into the office to get my lab coat Deep quickly closed down whatever screen he had up on his computer. I got a glimpse of a woman in Indian dress, a sari, it looked like. Certainly she was fully clothed, although to judge by Deep's flustered reaction it was as if I had caught him looking at pornography. He became very embarrassed, and even went a little red in the face. I was going to say something, crack a joke perhaps, but instead I pretended not to notice anything and, after quickly grabbing my lab coat off the chair, backed out of the office, leaving him to it.

The liquid nitrogen vat is in Solter's main laboratory on the twenty-first floor, just one floor down. When I got there I saw that there was nobody about, at least not in the main part of the laboratory. They were all gathered in the small conference room out the back. I could see their silhouettes through the

Venetian blinds. It looked like they were having some sort of party. Solter was giving a little speech and everyone laughed intermittently and cheered.

I made for the liquid nitrogen vat, which is near the front of the lab. A smouldering mist emanated from under its lid as if it was on fire. I put on the thermos gloves and climbed the small ladder. When I lifted the lid off the vat the freezing mist totally engulfed my head, nipping at my ears and neck like insects. I could barely see what I was doing. Meanwhile in the conference room they started to sing 'Happy Birthday'. I could even make out Solter's voice leading the way and without any inhibition, miles off key.

They were singing to someone called Cindy, who I knew actually. In the early days – because I had never worked in a laboratory before and had to be taught pretty much everything from scratch – Solter would send one of his other postdocs upstairs to show me how to do certain things, such as performing a particular ELISA assay or titrating an antibody. Procedures which seem basic to me now. Cindy appeared one morning wearing a white long-sleeved shirt through which you could clearly see her nipples, despite the fact that she was wearing a bra. It was as if they were made of iron.

'I never realized there was, like, a whole lab up here,' she said when I let her in the door.

She wandered around then looking at all our equipment. At that stage it was mostly stuff that belonged to Deep and the majority of it was out of date. I think he had even brought some things over from India with him.

'Wow,' Cindy said, picking up one of his glass pipettes, 'this stuff is awesome, like from a museum or something.'

Deep said nothing and remained seated by his computer for the duration of her visit, following her with his suspicious eyes. At that stage he was still getting over the shock of my own appearance into his lab space. I wasn't even clear how good his English was.

Cindy showed me a lot, like how to separate the buffy coat from a blood sample using Ficoll-Paque density gradient. We used my blood, which I took from my own arm – neither she nor Deep could do it – biting the tourniquet between my teeth and accessing the cephalic vein like a heroin addict. She came up on a few other occasions but it didn't take me long to become fairly independent, just a couple of months, and in fact I was surprised to discover that I was quite good at laboratory work. I had a knack for it, which I would never have guessed before. I liked the strict and exact adherence to the protocol which is completely necessary if your results aren't to end up as just another source of noise in the world.

The other thing that surprised me about lab work was how much manual labour was involved – the centrifuging, pipetting, separating, measuring, twisting, the minus eighty hand burning, not to mention all the walking, bending, lifting and the sheer repetition of all of these things times two hundred on any given day. I found that I liked this purely physical aspect to it. It was very satisfying in the way manual labour can be – not that I've done much of that – making yourself part-machine and following on thoughtlessly, the burden of discretion having been removed. Whereas with clinical work it is ninety-nine per cent discretionary. In the evening time I was taken aback by how exhausted and physically drained I was, and how well I slept after all that rooting around and digging downwards, like a construction worker in an area known for artefacts, hoping to hear his shovel sound brightly as it came up against some hard thing. That sound is very rare. Mostly the earth merely gives way, not easily but soundlessly, and the best you can hope for throughout the span of your entire laboratory career is the odd glancing blow of steel on steel.

Solter used to come up himself every now and again, which he rarely does any more. He never taught me anything directly, which was a shame, because back then I was badly in need and he could have been a great resource for me. But he tended to just stand by the hood and criticize and even – on one memorable occasion – to shout at me, which I hadn't experienced since childhood.

'This place is fucking filthy,' he said on that occasion. 'You do realize that? It's a fucking mess. Christ. You pair are so fucking disorganized.'

I was doing some cell work under the sterile hood. Or trying to. It is impossible to concentrate when somebody is shouting into your ear like that. This was early on and I think he had come up with the intention of laying down the law, showing me who was the boss, which I've never had any time for, especially as I have always been a conscientious and diligent worker. I had a 96-well plate in front of me but my hand was paralysed over it because Solter was staring at it, standing at my right shoulder with an enormous Starbucks coffee in his hand. I think the coffee had gone straight to his head. His whole body was practically shaking from it.

'I mean, how do you expect to get any work done like this?' he continued. 'I mean, where are your protocols, even? What about the fucking expendables, even? Is this where you keep them? Christ. What about when the animals arrive? How do you expect to do in vivo work in this place? The animals will all die of dysentery or something. That's not fucking much use. Is it?'

I stared at him, a little taken aback. It was only later on that I started to appreciate him in more of a theatrical way and to become amused by him in general, but that wasn't yet the case as he stood there jittery from his enormous coffee and spitting out the first words which appeared in his head. On and on he went.

'This is not difficult. These are real fucking basics. Basic organization. You hear me? If you have a question, ask. Don't just sit up here scratching yourself. There's no problem if you don't know anything, but there is a major fucking problem if you don't ask. No excuse for that. So fucking ask, OK? And make a list. That's the only way it will work. Order whatever you need. Just make a fucking list. Christ.'

And he took another swig from his giant coffee.

I put down the pipette I was holding and turned around to face him.

'I'm sorry, David,' I said, 'but I'm afraid I really can't

concentrate with all of your shouting.' His eyes widened as he stared at me over the rim of his paper cup which he had lifted once more up to his mouth.

'I'm going to go out now for a cigarette,' I said and took off my sterile gloves. 'Perhaps we could sit down and talk about it later, discuss your concerns and your criticisms. I think that would be very helpful to me, actually. I might learn something that way, which I am very open to. As you know, I'm very new to this type of work.'

I stood up off the stool and noticed, I think for the first time, how short he was. I found myself towering over him and he had to back away to give me room to come out from under the hood. He didn't say anything else, so I put on my coat and left the lab to go down and sit on the smoking bench (thank God I was still smoking then), looking out at the endless traffic on First Avenue, which I could stare out at all day as if it was the ocean.

They had stopped singing 'Happy Birthday' by now and were doing some hip hip hurrahs, which you rarely hear nowadays. Again Solter was leading the way, still miles off key. The freezing mist emanating from the liquid nitrogen vat grew more intense on my skin, as if the insects were taking bigger and bigger bites out of it. I had to remove several carousels before I eventually identified the correct metal box in the vat. It had my name on it. I took it out, then replaced the lid and removed the gloves and left them there, on top of the vat, for the next person.

I went back to the lab and took the samples out of the metal box and wrote down all the numbers which were written on their side. That way I would be able to match them up with the clinical information contained in the medical record. Each one had a seven-digit medical record number. There were several samples for each patient. I took five of the samples and thawed them. Then I suspended them in some PBS and centrifuged them. After discarding the supernatant I suspended the pellet of cells in complete medium. I put the mixture into the cell culture flask and left them on a shelf in the incubator.

Deep came over to me.

'T-t-t-t-t-t-there was s-s-s-s-s-someone looking for you,' he said.

'Who was it?' I asked.

'A g-g-g-g-girl,' he said.

'What did she look like?' I asked and the ridiculous thought entered my head that it was my wife, which of course made no sense. All the same, you'd never know with Yvonne.

Deep shrugged his shoulders.

'S-s-s-she went . . . i-i-i-i-i-into the office,' he said.

I walked quickly through to our office at the end of the lab. There was a Post-it attached to my computer.

'So, postdoc,' the note said, 'this is where you hide. Hello. Maybe see you later around. Not on the bench, though. I try to give up smoking. Send me email or SMS.'

I removed the Post-it and stood there for a minute. Then

I did something that I never do. I smelled it. Don't ask me why. Of course it didn't smell of anything. I read the note a few more times, then I placed it on my desk.

I I

I saw her this morning.

I was in my apartment at the time, looking over at the hospital and trying to produce sounds out of my trumpet. I had some time to kill before I had to go over to the paracentesis that Jorge Seabat had emailed me about last week. He didn't give me a specific time but I know from experience that Jorge is slow to get going in the mornings. You see him in the Atrium or the canteen, chatting away to someone, or at the centre of a large, sociable group. It seems that he needs to have about four espressos before he does an ounce of work. None of his procedures happen before ten or ten thirty at the earliest.

I saw the girl from my window as I glanced over at the hospital. It is like looking over at an enormous doll's house, different scenes visible in each tiny compartment, but all variations on the same theme. Marya was in the room directly across from mine, sitting on a chair next to the bed. She may have been translating for somebody although I could not see the other person, who was most likely in the bed and not visible in the window. She was wearing the same yellow jumper as before and leaning forward with her elbows on her knees. She had sat like that out on the bench too. It is sort of a manly pose, on account of the elbows. They stick out a bit.

It was her yellow top that my eyes latched onto first, as if they were already searching for her by themselves, which would not surprise me in the least. Where women are concerned they have an independent agenda, alert in their sockets, like chicks in a nest, necks extended, beaks open, always hungry and waiting to be fed. When I saw her I stopped playing my trumpet and moved over to the left-most window of my three-windowed studio apartment to get a better angle. I leaned into the glass. Between us in the inter-vening space the wind was twisting and turning over on itself like one of those Chinese dragons that they use to celebrate New Year. You could make out its shape from the dead leaves carried on its back, stripped from the bony trees below on 64th Street. During the summer there is a canopy of bright and vivid green below me and I can't see the street. Nowadays it is easy to see it and the people walking on the sidewalk or emerging with their heads down from the side entrance of the hospital, pressed into the earth by the elements and holding onto their clothing as tightly as they can.

At that moment the door of the room Marya was in opened and the room filled up with white coats. She got up and moved quickly around the bed and out of sight, perhaps to get into a better position for translation, at the head of the bed. The senior doctor who was leading the ward round came over and stood with her back to the window ledge, her hands behind her. She had white hair and looked like Dr Harding, who I worked with initially when I first came over here, but since she didn't turn around I couldn't be sure that it was her. Whoever it was held the group's attention. Intermittently she moved her hands around in front of herself as she spoke. At one point all the other white coats laughed. They were younger, junior doctors or medical students. After a few minutes the main doctor disappeared from view, presumably to go near the patient and examine them. The faces of the junior doctors were focused downwards as if they were being shown something important. Perhaps certain physical signs were being elicited on the patient's abdomen, how to percuss the liver or palpate for the spleen, which is tricky and something medical students always have difficulty with. You have to roll the patient onto their side and position both your hands correctly. The spleen bobs down with deep breathing and glances off the side of your hand. The senior doctor became visible again, although she still had her back to me, and the entire ward round preceded her out of the room. I stood for a few minutes but the girl did not reappear in the window. A nurse came in and lowered the blinds, which they virtually never do in New York. It's as if they believe that nobody out there is ever likely to be watching anyone else. I replaced my trumpet on its stand and put on my white coat and left the apartment.

When the lift doors opened on my floor Cillian Deasy was standing there, already inside. He looked up from the floor and saw me.

'Look who it is,' I said smiling.

'Hi,' he said.

I walked into the lift and we shook hands and then stood and grinned at each other for a second. I hadn't seen Cillian for a while. When we came over here first we were in the same fellowship class and used to see each other on a daily basis, though we were never exactly good friends. The door was slow to close and Cillian immediately leaned over and pressed the button for the lobby even though it had already been pressed. He hit it a couple of times. The doors closed slowly and we descended. Once more we stood facing each other and grinning. We are more or less the same height.

'Nice tie,' I said to him.

He looked downwards at himself. I noticed that he was also wearing a very nice fitted dark suit. He looked as if he was dressed for a job interview, which was always a possibility with Cillian, who is very much a career person. I even saw him chatting away to Solter a few weeks ago, his face animated and attempting to please; or 'licking up' to him as we used to say in school years ago, and to which Solter would be particularly susceptible.

'I'm giving Grand Rounds to the paeds branch,' he said, by way of explanation for the tie he was wearing, which had cartoon characters on it. Certainly it did not go with the suit.

'Really?' I said.

'Yeah. I emailed them to see if they could get me on the agenda. Might as well, y'know? Good for the ol' CV.'

'Right,' I said, genuinely impressed.

I often meet Cillian like this, sometimes with suitcase in hand, on his way to the airport to network at some conference; or even – as was the case on one occasion – back to Ireland for some planning meeting with government ministers on the future of the Irish oncology services, dressed to impress, as he was now, shoes gleaming and his hair gelled back like a 1950s ad man.

The lift stopped again a couple of floors down but nobody got on. Cillian bent over and hit the Lobby button a few more times. It seemed to take forever for the doors to close.

'How do you know Solter?' I asked him. Cillian looked at me, taken aback a little.

'I saw you talking with him the other week,' I added, just in case he was about to deny it, which I would not put past him. 'It was on a Tuesday,' I said, '. . . at about eleven o'clock, outside the institute.'

'Who? David?' Cillian said. 'Oh yeah. We're working on a project. I was advised to try and work with as many people as possible over here . . . But it turns out that his father knew my father. They were fellows together in Chicago years back when Dad was over here.'

'What project is that?' I asked him.

'It's nothing. Just a retrospective analysis he wants me to do. Donkey work, basically, but good for the CV, y'know.'

'What are you analysing?' I asked.

'Nothing very interesting,' he said. 'It's something to do with the surgical database.'

Whilst Cillian is ambitious – transparently so, almost

translucent, in fact – his ambition is essentially social. His main concern is to get a good position back home on a public contract affiliated with one of the universities, with scope for private work, perhaps, and which after a few years might result in a professorship. For him the science is incidental. It would make no difference to him if he was practising law or architecture or engineering. Which is completely fine, of course. The main thing is that I've heard he's a good doctor and seems to be decent enough.

'Any word from home?' I asked him.

'You mean in general?' he said. 'No, not really.'

'Did I see your name in the paper there?' I asked. 'About some committee?'

'Oh, you mean the minister's task force thing? Yeah. What a joke! I didn't have to do much, though. Got a trip home out of it which was the main thing.'

The other thing about Cillian is that he worked with my wife a few years back, during his intern year. She was his boss, in fact. And it seems that they got along very well because they kept in touch and even went out socializing the odd time, usually as part of a larger group. Cillian and I had never met in Ireland. But since meeting each other for the first time over here neither of us has ever brought up my wife's name in conversation. In the months after my separation from Yvonne I saw them myself from a distance on one or two occasions, at Legs on Leeson Street, for example, a hole of a place that we all used to go to every week, or in one of the bars on Dawson Street. They would be sitting in some corner, Cillian nodding his head and Yvonne talking endlessly and conspiratorially into his ear, saying God knows what. There may have been even more to their relationship, I don't know. One or two people have alluded to it in my presence, cryptically.

'How's things otherwise?' I asked him.

'Ah yeah, all's well, y'know. Really good, actually.'

'Siobhan is well?' I asked, referring to his wife, a tall redhead who has never been the friendliest whenever I meet her out on the street or in the lift.

'Yes, yes,' he said but with some hesitation or awkwardness, 'yes, she's fine.'

Neither of us said anything else until the elevator landed on the ground floor and we emerged and went our separate ways.

When I knocked and then entered through the door of the procedure room, Jorge Seabat was already there and in position, his back to me. He was wearing scrubs underneath a white coat.

'There you are,' he said, looking back over his shoulder, 'just in time. We're about to get started.'

In front of him was a middle-aged woman. She was facing the wall but turned her head to look at me when I came into the room. Her shoulders were draped with a blue-green gown, the same colour as Jorge's scrubs. It covered her front and hung back down over the examination bench, gathering around her and lapping in waves on the floor. It made her look enormous. Her back was bare and white. It was a dignified posture, her chin up proudly, like an historic personage being dressed elaborately by courtesans. Something Velazquez would paint.

'This is the doctor I was telling you about,' Jorge said to her. 'He's going to collect some of the fluid we drain and study it, like we discussed.'

'Hello,' I said to the patient.

'Sure,' she said, looking directly at me, 'no problem.'

Her face was puffy but even from a few feet away you could tell her skin was thin as rice paper, and laced with a friable-appearing vasculature. Steroids, I thought to myself.

I moved over and stood by the door, out of the way. On the counter I placed my small case and lifted off its lid. The nurse assisting Jorge stood by the trolley, ready to open more equipment if needed. She was an older Asian woman who I hadn't come across before. From my vantage I couldn't really see what Jorge was doing. I could just see his back and his profile and the fact that he was focusing on his hands, one of which was spread open on a patch of the patient's bare skin. His body blocked out any view of the woman apart from the back of her head and a small area of her lower back.

'Little scratch here,' Jorge said, 'this is just the local.'

The woman's shoulders heaved a little, up and then down. He turned back towards me to a small trolley that stood beside him and upon which were laid out various pieces of plastic tubing, 20- and 22-gauge needles in plastic wrapping, two syringes, four vials of local anaesthetic (1% lignocaine), various dressings packs and Betadine antiseptic in a bowl. He moved quietly and quickly. He is good, Jorge, he never has any difficulties with these procedures. With one gloved hand he removed the needle from the tip of the syringe and placed another needle on top of it. He turned around then with his elbows close to his sides and his arms splayed, one of them holding the syringe.

'Right,' he said, 'I'll just give a little more now . . . That should be fine . . . Great . . . And now I see some fluid.'

'Good,' said the woman.

'Yes, that's the tricky part done,' Jorge said. 'Should be easy from here.'

'Where does it come from,' the woman said, 'all this fluid? I do wonder.'

Jorge removed the syringe which now had some pink pleural fluid in it. He placed it in the small sharps container on the bottom rung of the trolley, then took up another syringe. The nurse opened a small vial of local and held it upside down. Jorge stuck the needle into it and withdrew the contents. The nurse threw the empty vial into the bin beside her. Jorge then turned back towards the patient.

'Mmm,' he said, 'well, we are, what, eighty per cent water, I suppose.'

'But it wasn't there before,' she said. 'It's like I'm melting.'

'How much do you want?' Jorge asked me.

'The usual,' I said.

'Like you're melting. Right,' said Jorge to the woman as he administered more local, which the patient seemed not to even notice. 'I haven't heard that analogy before. That's a good one.'

He reached for a fifty-ml syringe off the trolley and attached the needle to it and turned back towards the patient's back. I moved towards the trolley and held out one of the plastic containers. When Jorge turned around again the syringe was full. I twisted off the top and held out the container for him as he squirt-filled it from the syringe. I held my head and eyes back in case of splashes. It was straw-yellow in colour. I replaced the top on it then and twisted it closed. He turned around and repeated this procedure, filling the syringe once more. I took a label from the patient's chart and placed it on the front of the container of fluid. The container was warm in my hand. I opened the case and placed the container inside it.

'Thanks very much,' I said, projecting my voice in the direction of the patient.

'No problem,' she said.

'Thanks, Jorge,' I said as I was leaving the room but he was already connecting up some plastic plumbing that he would use to remove the rest of the fluid.

I closed the door after me and stood with my back against it in order to allow a group of people to pass by. It was a small group who I had also seen on a few other occasions in recent weeks, wandering slowly around the hospital. There was a gaunt, elderly man in their centre pushing his IV stand, leaning on it like a staff. He had a grey beard and was wearing pyjama bottoms and a white vest. An elderly woman walked beside him, holding onto him. Younger adults and some children followed, presumably the children and grandchildren of the elderly couple. One of the adults was carrying a baby. They walked in silence, looking around, appearing lost, like a tribe wandering across a desert.

I started to walk towards the elevator when I heard my name called out loudly from the other end of the corridor. The voice came from the direction in which the lost tribe were headed. I knew straightaway that it was Dr Harding, my old boss, even before I turned to look in that direction and saw her walking towards me, a group of white coats fanned out behind her. It was the same ward round that I had seen a little while earlier in the room across the way from my apartment, when I had spotted Marya. I realized that now. The white-haired physician leaning back against the windowsill had indeed been Dr Harding.

She shouted my name out again, and waved her arm at me. I stayed where I was.

Dr Harding had been my supervisor and mentor when I first came to New York, that is until I stopped working in her clinic after only a couple of months and decided instead to move into the laboratory. At the time – and probably still – she considered that to be a strange decision, especially at my age. You can be slaving away in the lab for years before you get anything out of it in terms of publications, and so it is really for younger people, in their twenties. But I was adamant about it. I didn't want to work in the clinic any more and you could say that in general I wanted things to slow down. Over the last few years, and especially since I met my wife, I had the impression that everything had picked up speed; that each day was simply a means of getting to the next one and then to the one after that. It wasn't only because of how things were with Yvonne. Work was also a constant onslaught. Coming home in the evening was like returning from battle, mildly traumatized, the night a time of near dread as you faced into another day of it. Moving into the laboratory struck me as a good way to break this pattern. It forces you to take a proper look at whatever is in front of you, to allow your attention to be completely held by it, your gaze to go deeper than it normally does. Therefore, despite Dr Harding's misgivings – which she can easily express without saying a single word – I insisted on the transfer, even if it also meant exchanging her relaxed style of supervision for the more hysterical version that Dr Solter engages in.

I stood and waited for Dr Harding and her group but the gaunt elderly man stopped her. It appeared that they knew each other and he started to introduce her to his family. I was relieved about this because just then I wasn't in the mood to meet Dr Harding. Talking with her can be an exhausting experience in itself, for which you have to be prepared, almost having to work out in advance what you are going to say. Otherwise she is likely to draw out all sorts of things from you, which is her gift. When Dr Harding stands peering at you with her arms folded and her large, pale eyes locked on you, you find yourself confiding in her all your fears and concerns, even if you did not realize that they were your fears and concerns until they started spilling out of your mouth. God knows what I would have blurted out to her now, possibly something to do with my wife.

I raised my hand in greeting and went quickly into the gents which were directly opposite, pushing open with effort the heavy door, having to lean my shoulder up against it and give it a good shove. The cold tiled silence of the bathroom was an instant relief compared to the exposed avenue of the corridor. I stood over the sink and splashed some water on my face, staring at myself in the mirror, the water like beads of sweat on my skin. Regardless, I needed to use the bathroom anyway.

When I first came to New York I used to attend Dr Harding's clinic three times a week, reviewing her patients just before they went in for whatever weekly or biweekly treatment they were to receive in the day ward. After talking with them and examining them I would call Dr Harding on the phone and tell her what was going on with them, what their various complaints were and the results of their blood work. She is pre-retirement, Dr Harding, and a little burnt out, I think. Whenever I called her there would be classical music playing in the background. If there was any major issue she would jump in her car and come down from her office on the main campus which was a couple of blocks from the clinic, or even occasionally from her apartment, which was on Second Avenue. She had her own driver and was seemingly very wealthy. Cillian told me she had an elevator that opened directly inside her apartment, although I have no idea how he wangled an invitation up there. But it was seldom required for her to come down to clinic. She trusted my judgement, even if I myself was frequently doubtful or in two minds. Dr Harding herself had no problem accepting this as just the way of things. Generally she would listen soundlessly on the end of the phone to me until I had finished before saying 'Carry on then, carry on' and hanging up the phone a little abruptly. Dr Harding is English and still has more than a faint accent, despite having been in New York now for thirty or forty years.

When I finished in the gents I put my white coat back on, scrubbed my hands and walked out the door. I was stunned to find Dr Harding and the entire ward round waiting for me outside.

'Well hello there,' said Dr Harding when I opened the door. 'How are you?'

I stood in front of them and the door nudged me in the back as it swung closed. I moved a fraction forward. Dr Harding was leaning against the wall opposite, at the centre of the group of lab-coated medical students who were fanned out on both sides around her like enormous white wings.

'We were about to go in to see if you were all right.'

Everyone laughed. Dr Harding always did have a sly sense of humour.

'I was hoping you would explain to the medical students here what you were doing back there.'

I looked instinctively back at the toilet door.

'Not in there!' she said and everyone laughed again, harder this time, which annoyed me.

'In the procedure room?' she continued. 'Where you came out of before. I presume you were collecting more samples for that study you're doing.' She pointed at my case. 'I think the students here would find it very interesting. Why the fluid?'

'Of course,' I said, and I proceeded to explain it to them, the rationale behind my research protocol, and also the methodology: that I would centrifuge the fluid to obtain the cells, then extract the DNA from them and measure telomere length, that I would try and correlate that with certain clinical parameters. I went on then to briefly talk about the role of telomerase in cancer development, how it maintains telomere length and contributes towards cell immortalization; I finished by saying that I would also attempt to grow the cells so that I could then plate them or implant them into animals in order to measure their growth kinetics and their sensitivity to various drugs at different concentrations both in vivo and in vitro. The students looked back at me with blank faces. I don't think they understood or were listening to a single word. They looked completely bored.

'There you have it then,' said Dr Harding, 'thank him, everyone.'

'Thank you,' they said in an unenthusiastic chorus.

I turned away and started to walk off the ward in the opposite direction, towards the elevators. Again I heard my name called out.

I stopped and looked around. Dr Harding was walking towards me.

'I'm sorry for that,' she said. 'Ambushing you. It's just that I'm trying to show the students as much as I can on these teaching rounds, you see.'

'No, no that's fine,' I said.

'I do hope you're keeping well,' she said, still approaching. 'Why don't you call up sometime to say hello?'

'Yes, I'm fine, thanks,' I said.

'Really?' she said, and with her arms folded, she planted herself in front of me and looked directly into my face, locking onto it the way missiles are programmed to. Of course I looked away. Very few of us can withstand that sort of thing, although the Americans aren't bad at it. (The Irish in particular are awful at it.) And even fewer can do the actual looking itself, especially in the manner that Dr Harding does it, which is not merely eye contact, but more of a full facial opposition, her face like a satellite suspended down in front of you, capable of unscrambling a wide range of signal, even if it's a signal you didn't know you were broadcasting – in that frequency range perhaps that only dogs can hear, but silent as far as other humans are concerned. No doubt we all emit them, these continual, persistent, distress signals essentially. They are betrayed on our faces and in our frightened looks as we walk about the place wondering what will happen to us next. Dr Harding uses this technique on her patients as well, who love her, but are also terrified of her and the glare of the silences she allows – which are all-encompassing like the tunnel of a CT scanner, similarly missing very little – and at the bottom of which they may find certain unwanted truths that she might suddenly foist upon them, which she has a tendency to do, some new piece of news about their disease or prognosis, which they are happy not to think about today and just want to push off until tomorrow or next week or next month.

'And how's the laboratory working out?' Dr Harding asked.

Over her shoulder I could see her medical students loitering halfway up the corridor. One or two of them were messing about. The majority had their mobile phones out and were staring down into them.

'Good,' I said, 'yes, good, I think it's working out.'

'I'm glad to hear it,' she said. 'Dr Solter keeping you on your toes?'

'Yes, yes,' I replied.

'That's good, that you don't miss the clinic, I mean. No regrets then?'

'None,' I said, probably a little too firmly, and she squinted her eyes at me slightly, as if she was trying to enhance the glare of her examination, turn it up a notch or two.

I had decided to leave Dr Harding's clinic at around the same time that Mrs X – who was a patient of hers – died suddenly out on the street. The two events weren't related, at least not directly, although it did come as a shock at the time, not just to me but to the nurses and secretarial staff also. I had seen her in clinic just a few minutes earlier and had basically given her the all-clear. Her blood work and physical exam were fine, she had no specific complaints, apart from a very slight fluttering in her chest, 'as if I swallowed a butterfly,' she said. 'Did you?' I asked, and she laughed. Mrs X had a good sense of humour, we got on well. 'I think I would have remembered that,' she said. Then she hopped off the couch and headed in to the day ward. So it came as a complete surprise when the call came up to clinic shortly afterwards telling us that she had collapsed in the middle of First Avenue as she tried to cross it, in front of all the cars which reared back on their hind legs like frightened horses. I find it hard to imagine her collapsing. Mrs X was much too ladylike for that. I picture her instead sort of climbing down using her hands.*

Her mobile phone was found on the ground beside her. Her son's name was displayed on it, whom she must have been trying to call. He used to come with her to all her appointments, but not that day. He had instead gone to get a new pair of glasses. I feel bad for him on that account. He probably thinks his mother would still be alive if he had come with her, and he may be right about that; it's impossible to know, of

* When the call went up to clinic we all rushed down, myself and a few of the nurses. The crash team were already there, unaccustomed to working outdoors. I kept my distance, hanging back a bit, expecting someone to point at me with their fingers of blame, which in fairness nobody did. I leaned against the wall staring at Mrs X's shoes which stuck out from under the crash team. They were bright red, like Dorothy in *The Wizard of Oz*. Then the paramedics arrived to take her in the ambulance, even though she was most likely already dead, to restore some form to the situation, the correct form of what is to be expected, someone dying or being pronounced dead in an emergency room and not out in the middle of the road, even if it was just twenty yards from the hospital entrance, and thirty yards from the bench where I take my breaks. I've paced it out. She didn't make it very far.

course. The larger truth was that she was going to die sooner rather than very much later, as her disease was at a very advanced stage. And the whole thing could not have been avoided or predicted. The autopsy proved it. But I suppose it is normal to think that you could or should have done something different, even if there was nothing specific or especially significant that could have been done.

'It's such a different thing, laboratory work,' Dr Harding said to me now, her medical students getting increasingly restless behind her, but out of earshot.

'A different career, almost,' she continued. 'Certainly different to clinical work. But I do hope you didn't let what happened put you off. With Mrs X, I mean.'

'No,' I said, blinking under the heat of her probing gaze, 'of course not.'

It is true, though, that I think about them often, Mrs X and her son. I'm not sure why, perhaps because she was the last (I transferred into the lab the following week). But while it's true that I still feel bad for them, she was very sick. Even the fact that her death was dramatic was nothing that I hadn't seen before. There had been more dramatic ones.* And at the end of the day, despite what you might sometimes think, you can't really be blamed for it. You were always only trying to help, even if it didn't feel that way a lot of the time.

---

* My first week as an intern back in Dublin, I saw a man with a bulky neck tumour collapse without warning. He'd been whistling, on his way to the shower. The tumour had eroded into his carotid artery, and it exploded like a mini silent bomb just under the jaw. Blood pulsed from it in a jet. It painted the ceiling and the far wall and even some of the other patients in the six-bed ward in a bright arterial red.

'That's good,' Dr Harding said. 'That's very good to hear. It was really a blessing, what happened.'

'Yes,' I said, 'a blessing.'

Dr Harding stared at me and then repeated it to herself. 'A blessing.'

With that, she nodded her head and then abruptly turned away. Another thing I now remembered about her. The abrupt turn away. The switching off of the full beam of her attention, leaving you a little bereft, wanting more of what only a few seconds ago, you were wary of and did not want at all.

When I got back to the lab Deep was sitting at his half of the bench, his head on the counter resting on his sweater, which he had removed. He was fast asleep. I went over to the sterile area under the hood and switched on the fan, then I took the container of fluid out of the case and left it there. I had to walk past Deep to get to the fridge. When I opened the fridge door he woke up and stared at me as if he was seeing me for the very first time. The pattern of his sweater's creasing had imprinted itself on his face. He didn't say anything and neither did I. We can go for days like this, ignoring each other for no good reason.

On the shelf of the inner door there were a few bottles containing various solutions – PBS, FACS buffer – otherwise it was mostly empty. I took out the PBS and went back over to the sterile area. I placed the container in the centrifuge, making sure it was balanced, then I adjusted the setting to spin the fluid down at 1,200g for seven minutes at four degrees to isolate the cells. After that I took out the container and removed the supernatant using the vacuum suction. With the PBS I washed the pellet then resuspended the cells and incubated them in ACK buffer for erythrocyte lysis for fifteen minutes at room temperature. I filled two culture flasks with medium, then I distributed the samples into the flasks and replaced them in the fridge.

12

My brother Donal texted me today. It's his birthday next week and he wants to know if I am flying in on the Thursday or the Friday. If it's the Friday I might be too tired for the party so therefore I should come in on the Thursday. That would be better.

The text annoyed me. Donal knows full well I'm not going to be there for his birthday. I've already sent him his present and my mother has explained things to him. It was the same last year and the year before. Donal can be cute like that. It's his way of making me feel guilty about it. So I didn't respond to his text right away like I normally would. I know he'll be staring at his phone until I do so. I'll text him later.

Donal is thirteen years younger than me. Growing up we had our issues – as they're so fond of saying over here – and I remember with guilt being embarrassed about him during my teenage years. In my defence, none of that lasted long and at home we were always mostly fine, although I would have liked a brother with more interest in football. It was on Donal's account that I was involved in my one and only physical fight, in response to someone's predictable taunts which made me as enraged as I have ever been. The really strange thing was that the other boy had a sister with cerebral palsy. Who knows what was at the root of his rage? Perhaps it was directed at the other boys watching us fight and who used to also taunt him; or alternatively at the biological events themselves which had happened years earlier to his sister (and my brother) and had for both our families the size and scope of major history. Either way I got the clear sense that his fury was not really directed at me, as he burrowed into me, pulling my hair so that afterwards my entire scalp stung. Our fight lasted a while. We scuffled to a snotty standstill. We tore each other's anoraks. The boys watching drifted off, bored, before the end. Then we walked home in the same direction, him twenty yards in front the whole way.

Sometimes it stops me in my tracks, the awareness of how far from the jumping-off point I've ended up; not just geographically, although that quickly becomes the dominant fact. Not that there was anything storied in between, no wars or murdered relatives, no paedophiliac uncle or macheted mob; none of the things that seem to scar so many and which you only have to pick up the newspaper for two seconds to read about. I have no destructive memories, no particular experience of cruelty or even that many unkind acts, either felt by myself or witnessed; just a regular life, containing the thousands of decisions you make to end up wherever you end up, most of them so minute that they weren't decisions at all but acquiescences to the stronger guiding forces of continuity and least resistance.

Last year, when Donal got sick, I travelled home in an

unplanned manner around the time my alien visa was due to run out and I had to go and get it renewed in the US embassy in Dublin. I came across a real arsehole behind the thick glass. Younger than me but entirely bald. Ugly metallic glasses. It should have been a formality but he kept asking me the same questions over and over. *What are you doing in America? Why aren't you here? This is your home, right? This is where you're from. We have people in the US who can do what you're doing. Why are you there and not here? Enlighten me, please.* His interest and concern might have been touching if it weren't for his contempt. He kept flicking my passport around with the back of his hand, even at one point bouncing it off the thick glass that separated us. I stared at him, at a loss. He had caught me at a low ebb. Donal was not out of the woods completely. It was also just a day after I had met up with Yvonne in the canteen for coffee. The official stared back at me, his disembodied voice blaring out of a small speaker down to my left. His face had so much certainty in it. Try telling him what it is that's confounding you. Try telling him that you're trying to get to the bottom of things, anything, a scientific truth. That it's the only thing you think you can get your arms around. My own reflection was in the glass. It looked back at me as if it too wanted answers. Eventually he stamped my passport. He was just putting on a show, one of the more visible of the guiding forces to which you must acquiesce.

When I was young I was fatalistic, more than the average, especially for my age. I can clearly recall the terror that I would experience at school if – on the bus in the morning – we happened to pass an ambulance heading in the opposite direction. I would be convinced they were heading to my house, and nothing could distract me from this possibility. I would sit at my desk, barely keeping back the tears, waiting for the principal to appear at the classroom door with the tragic news. After school I would run home and I'd not be happy until the front door closed behind me. Those evenings didn't move an inch then. They were impenetrable. The hours were as thick as lymph. I felt safe, at least until the next day. Eventually we find ways to hide those feelings, distract ourselves from that anxiety which doesn't take much to rear up and make itself known. One thing a patient told me once has stuck: 'We only have to make it to tomorrow. If we keep doing that we'll be fine,' she said. It shouldn't be too difficult; it's always only a few hours away.

I took my phone out of my pocket and gave in to Donal. It's harder to win these little struggles with an ocean between you.

'Sorry bro,' I texted, 'I'll Skype you on the day. You're gonna love my present, boss man!'

13

The elevator doors opened and there she was.

'Postdoc!' she shouted.

I stood for a second and then entered the lift, standing between her and two other people, a man and woman. Marya started to introduce me to them so I turned around. Mr and Mrs Petrov. An older Russian couple. I put out my hand. Marya spoke to them in Russian and the man stared at me, then shook my hand. The woman looked down at the ground.

'I explained to them that you were also one of the doctors here,' Marya said, '. . . and see, you're not so terrifying.'

'Glad to hear it,' I said, and Marya translated that also but her translation seemed a lot longer than was necessary. Again the man simply stared back at me. He was short and bald and wearing a big overcoat. The woman on the other hand didn't look at me at all. Her manner was rigid and she was dressed very formally, as if she was going to mass. Marya put her hand on her arm but the woman just looked down at it.

'I'm showing Mrs Petrov and her husband around,' Marya said, turning back to me. 'She just checked in. She's having operation. Big operation, actually. Day after tomorrow.'

'Right,' I said, grinning back at them.

The lift door closed and we descended. Marya seemed pleased to see me, as if I was an interesting sight on the guided tour she was giving. I was relieved because I had emailed her the previous day suggesting that we meet up, perhaps get a coffee or go out to dinner. But she never responded and I was afraid that I had been too direct or brazen. I intended to give her another day before trying again.

'Where are you going?' she asked me.

'The basement,' I said.

'Why basement?'

'I have to get some supplies.'

'For what?'

'There's a procedure now,' I said, 'that I have to go to . . .'

Marya turned and translated what I had said to the Petrovs. Again she mustn't have done it literally because she spoke for a while, using her left hand for emphasis. Mr Petrov nodded and said something back to her.

'What kind of procedure?' Marya asked me. 'Mr Petrov wants to know. Back in Russia he was surgeon. Now nothing. Now he work at Home Depot.'

I looked at Mr Petrov. It wasn't hard to picture him as one of those old-school surgeons who are on the pernickety side and who love to strike fear into the students and junior doctors on ward rounds.

'I don't know,' I said. 'It's either a pleural or abdominal paracentesis. They didn't tell me.'

Marya translated what I had said, saying the medical

terminology in English, and Mr Petrov quickly spoke to her again.

'He wants to know why,' Marya said.

I took a deep breath and then gave the exact same explanation to Mr Petrov that I had given to Dr Harding's students the other day, Marya translating as I spoke. He didn't bat an eyelid. If anything he seemed unimpressed, and muttered something to Marya.

'He says they did the same thing back in Russia,' Marya said. 'Years ago.'

Mr Petrov smiled at me. He was clearly enjoying himself. His work at Home Depot must be a daily hell. He spoke again in Russian to Marya.

'What are the surgeons like here?' she said. 'He wants to know.'

'They're excellent,' I said, perhaps too quickly. I looked at him. 'Your wife is in good hands.'

He smirked a little and spoke in Russian.

'He says that's what the last guy told us,' Marya said to me.

She turned and spoke to them. Her tone seemed to vary between being warm and giving out to them or berating them, especially Mr Petrov. His face reddened a bit. I noticed that as she spoke she frequently leaned in and touched Mrs Petrov on the arm, trying to engage her, although she was getting very little reaction. The poor woman seemed terrified, continuing to stare into a no-man's land that only she was able to see.

'Did you get my email?' I asked Marya when there was a pause in the conversation.

'What?' she said, a little flustered or uncertain, although this didn't last long.

'Yes, of course,' she said then, a little wearily. 'Internet is not like regular post, you know, that sometimes you get and sometimes not.'

I looked at her but she avoided eye contact. I could sense Mr Petrov looking at us now with interest.

'Anyway this is us,' Marya said, and she seemed relieved. The lift came to a stop and she said something to them. The doors opened.

Mr Petrov shook my hand again, then he led his wife out. I went to say something to Marya, but she turned around and spoke first and I didn't at first catch what she said.

'See you tomorrow at Grand Rounds,' it sounded like, but I wasn't sure.

The door closed and the elevator continued without interruption to the basement. I got out and looked around for the supply room, which I hadn't been to in a while and is always hard to find. Ordinarily I would have simply ordered the supplies I needed online, but the procedure was last minute and I didn't have time to wait for their delivery.

I had a hard time finding the supply room. I made a wrong turn and had to retrace my steps back to the elevator. You have to be careful down there. You can very easily get lost, wandering for an eternity through its nondescript and endless corridors. The hospital is like a giant tree in that regard, its roots spreading out on all sides, taking over more than the entire city block you see above ground. I passed a line of silent men wandering with their heads down, pushing vats of steaming laundry. They looked like they were press-ganged into it, stolen from a foreign land. Eventually I found the supply room, which was next to the industrial laundry where the men had come from and where they dispose of the hospital's waste matter, sterilize the reusables, surgical equipment and soiled linen – the stuff off beds, but also what surgeons pull over their heads as they emerge from operating theatres. The non-perishables. All the time a constant loud hum of industrial noise could be heard emanating from some deeper, inner central point. The generator, perhaps.

When I got back up to the procedure unit and knocked and entered the room I was surprised to find that the patient sitting up on the examination couch in his hospital gown was the Chinese billionaire I had met a few weeks previously. His face lit up when he saw me and he greeted me like a long-lost friend. The only other person in the room was an Asian woman sitting against the wall. She stood up and started translating into English what the gentleman was saying to me, expressing on his behalf his relief and immense gratitude for my coming to see him and help him and study more of his fluid so that cure could be found. All the time the patient smiled enthusiastically and gave frequent small bows. As the translator was speaking the nurse came in behind me wearing scrubs and carrying several sterile kits which she placed under the trolley then stood beside me.

'He wanted us to call you,' she said to me, when the translator had stopped speaking.

'But I already have his cells,' I said.

'I know,' the nurse said, before turning away.

I looked at the patient, who was still smiling broadly at me. He had lost a fair amount of weight in the weeks since I had last seen him. He was also a little jaundiced in the eyes. After a while Jorge came in. He seemed to be in a hurry and the procedure was done in no time. I collected more of the patient's fluid despite the fact that I wouldn't be doing any additional analysis or studies on it. Then I said my goodbyes and left.

14

Marya was at Grand Rounds this morning. I spotted her as soon as I entered the enormous auditorium, which is just off the main corridor of the hospital, running along the centre of it like a vein. Unfortunately it was too late to move up anywhere near her. Solter – who was chairing today's session – had already taken to the podium to introduce the speaker, tapping on the microphone with his finger and saying 'Does this thing work? Hello hello, can you guys hear me?' I took a seat at the back and watched her from afar. The place was packed to the rafters.

Technically of course she shouldn't have been there. Grand Rounds is just for the medical staff, but who was going to complain about it? You do see it from time to time, visitors drifting in off the corridor, following the crowd, wondering where everybody is headed. Sometimes even the odd patient wanders in, wearing their pyjamas or even pushing a drip stand, hoping to find out what miracle drug we're holding back on them. They generally leave after a few minutes, bored.

Marya wasn't bored. She took notes just like at the bracka lecture the other week. When Solter left the stage after his lengthy and self-important introduction, he went down and sat beside her. I noticed him steal the odd glance in her direction and I admit that I felt a little jealous. The reason Solter was making the introductory remarks was because the speaker – an elderly professor from somewhere in the Midwest – had been his mentor. Solter did his postdoc under him, at the University of Michigan or perhaps Wisconsin or St Louis, I'm not sure which exactly. The old professor knew how to play the nice guest. Throughout the talk he mentioned Solter's name several times, causing Solter to perk up in his seat and even on occasion to turn around and smile back at the room. He seemed like a decent old man, the professor. I hope he wins the Nobel Prize like they say he might. There was certainly a large crowd to see him as he is very famous in the field, and even outside the field a little. As I say, the place was packed to the rafters.

After the lecture was finished, Marya, who had left the hall before me, was standing waiting for me in the corridor as everyone filed past her. I hadn't realized she had known that I was there.

'Coffee, postdoc?' she shouted out to me as I emerged from the hall, still some distance from her. People turned around to look at me.

'Sure,' I said, walking up to her. 'Where?'

'Canteen, of course,' she said. 'But give me one minute, OK? I need first to go briefly upstairs.'

She turned and hurried off in the stream of other people headed in that direction. I stood for a moment looking after her before heading along the north corridor.

She took ages to join me. Ordinarily I would not have waited so long. In the meantime I had two awful coffees. As I came back to my seat with the second one I was surprised to see the elderly professor from Grand Rounds bring over a tray to near where I was sitting. The professor chose the same table as me, a long one that would seat twenty, but in this case there were just the two of us. The canteen was practically empty, as it always is, even during lunch hour. There was just the odd other person seated here and there around the room. I recognized the family in the corner as the same lost tribe I had seen the other day with Dr Harding, the patriarch amongst them still attached to his IV stand. In the other corner a group of therapists – either OTs or physios – were sitting around a table, a prosthetic leg in front of them. A man wearing a suit sat with them and he seemed to be doing most of the talking. Every now and then he would pick up the leg and demonstrate a manoeuvre with it, flexing it at the knee or the ankle.

Up close the professor seemed even more ancient than he had earlier when he was giving his talk. It hadn't been so apparent when he was at the podium, waving the laser pointer in the air, although when it came to rest on the screen the red dot had trembled badly. Up close he looked a great deal frailer, particularly given the unforgiving light where we were sitting, in front of one of the enormous bay windows that face out east onto York Avenue and at that time of the day are filled with the mid-morning sun. I noticed that his hands visibly shook. He was wearing a nice grey suit and green tie with a matching pale green handkerchief. He even had on a waist-coat, which you rarely see nowadays. It made me wonder who was at home waiting for him and had helped him get ready, laundering or ironing his shirts, now waiting for him to return, or if he had arrived at that point where there was no one at home to help him get ready. He had a number of sun spots on his face, which only the elderly get, black ones on cracked but tanned skin. He was certainly well past retire-ment age, but that is pretty much the norm over here. In America they keep you shovelling at the furnace until you are worn out completely. He was struggling with the little tub of butter, trying to open it with his trembling hands, and I was worried about his eye because of the way he held the knife with the point of it aimed towards his face. I couldn't help but feel sorry for him, which is always the way with the elderly when you see them defeated by some everyday thing, even if it's the sort of thing that you yourself have trouble with from time to time.

'That was a great talk, professor!' I said over to him.

But he didn't hear me and I looked around self-consciously. I debated saying it again as he continued to struggle with the butter.

The professor's talk was about telomeres, which are all the rage these days. He had been working on them since the late 1970s, his major insight being the discovery of the activation mechanism of telomerase in cancer cells, the basic telo-mere concept having been originally discovered by Barbara McClintock in 1941. (She won the Nobel Prize in 1983 for it, working mainly on maize.) McClintock had wanted to find out how a cell knew that it was time to die rather than continue to divide further. After fifty or sixty cell divisions that is what ordinarily happens, as if the cell becomes burnt out. Instead of dividing itself in two – to give rise to two daughter cells – the cell enters the senescent state and simply ceases, without reproducing. Its lineage stops with it. It is the end of the line. This phenomenon is known as 'replicative senescence' or 'the Hayflick limit', in honour of Leonard Hayflick, who was the first to publish the observation. Senescence is quite beautiful under a microscope. The cells become engorged, satiated, porous, lit obesely by the bright colours of the immunohistochemistry like a stained glass window.

The question was, what told them to do this? How would an individual cell know that they were the fiftieth or sixtieth iteration, that theirs was the generation designated not to reproduce but to enter the senescent state and simply die out altogether, leaving no generation behind them to carry on? How would any of us know that we were the marked or predestined ones, the end of the line, and in a manner that was written into our DNA; that our generation was the one to cease and that we were the ones who were supposed to lay our heads down without reproducing; to not just die but to die out?

In other words it was a medical riddle, something that could perhaps be solved by cleverness – as opposed to something that was simply part of the vast unknown, as so much was back then. It's easy to forget how recent our knowledge is. A hundred years ago they were still decades away from discovering the structure of DNA. The entire community of scientists was essentially standing on the same beach where Newton imagined himself as a boy playing on the strand 'diverting myself in now and then finding a smoother pebble or a prettier shell than ordinary, whilst the great ocean of truth lay all undiscovered before me.'* There wasn't much to see, just a great mass of unknown things compacted beneath its silent surface. Only occasionally could there be sensed the slow movement of distant shapes, some of which were almost mythical in dimension.

There has been nothing linear about the progress since 1953.† They can map the entire genome now in minutes. The problem these days is almost the exact opposite one – of too much information. We don't know what to do with all of these raw data points which we generate on a daily basis and rush to put on PubMed. There are no vast dark shapes any more, nothing mythical. They have been replaced by a rapid surface motion of many things, little particles, a multitude of

* Ironically, though, by the time he wrote that nice line old Isaac had lost the run of himself a little, had started looking away from his ocean of potential truth, moving instead from physics to an interest in witchcraft, sorcery and the occult. Fortunately, the importance of his earlier discoveries – gravity, the laws of motion, etc. – ensured his reputation, and you don't hear much mention of the other stuff. Even his biographers mostly ignore it.

† Specifically 25 April when 'Molecular Structure of Nucleic Acids: A Structure for Deoxyribose Nucleic Acid' was published by Francis Crick and James D. Watson in *Nature* 171; 737–8, and which ends with one of the most modest statements in history: 'It has not escaped our notice that the specific pairing we have postulated' – the double helical structure of DNA – 'immediately suggests a possible copying mechanism for the genetic material.'

phenomena, darting in a Brownian motion, only a minority of which can be explained or put in context.

(Not that you will find anyone jumping up and down about it, how much progress has been made. Particularly if you have a job where you are reminded all the time that there is a way to go yet. Mrs X collapsing out of the blue on First Avenue in front of all those startled cars; or that small boy in his pyjamas I saw the other day in front of the elevator, a yellow tube coming out of his nose. His parents were trying to bring him down to the radiotherapy suite but he didn't want to go. He was only a small lad but he put up a hell of a struggle. When the doors of the lift closed his persistent screams were still audible, even as they descended below our feet. It was as if he'd been dragged down there by demons. We all stood in silence afterwards, rooted to the ground, avoiding eye contact with each other. Newton's ocean may have been darker than the one we're looking out on, but it is the same body of water.)

The Hayflick limit or replicative senescence, however, had the appearance of something which could be worked out with the tools available at the time. The question was how a cell would know not to reproduce but simply to cease. Some manner of generational clock must exist within a cell which would measure elapsed cell generations rather than absolute time. According to Weinberg* this hypothetical 'generational clock' would need to have the following theoretical proper-

* *The Biology of Cancer*, Chapter 10, p. 369.

ties: 1) be synthesized early in the development of the cell so that it could start the count straightaway, and 2) be present in high enough concentrations within the cell so that each progressive dilution of it (by a factor of two, every time the cell divided) would still allow it to be present up until the sixtieth odd division, at which point it would drop beneath the critical level and trigger senescence. The problem with this theory was that it was mathematically impossible. Nothing can withstand sixty successive halvings of itself. The solution to the riddle came to Barbara McClintock when she noticed under the microscope DNA segments (comprised of repeating nucleotides) at both ends of the DNA strands, like – again according to Weinberg – 'the plastic aglets at the ends of your shoe laces'. She called them telomeres, derived from the Greek nouns *telos* meaning 'end' and *meros* meaning 'part'. The end parts. As cells divide the telomeres get successively shorter. It takes roughly sixty divisions for them to whittle away to nothing. When that happens the frayed ends of the DNA strands become exposed. The DNA strands stick to each other end-to-end and are useless. Karyotypic disarray occurs. Mayhem. The cells die, their mortality dangling at the end of these progressively shortening telomeres.

To achieve immortality cancer cells need to escape this mechanism of their death. They rebuild their telomeres using an enzyme called telomerase*. The telomeres become longer. The cancer cell can then divide indefinitely, propagating itself

---

* Discovered by Carol Greider, who won the Nobel Prize herself for it in 2009. Her achievement was even more remarkable on account of her dyslexia.

even beyond the sixtieth cell division, growing into a tumour, which is just a descriptive term for a matted collection of cells, the size of a marble or a golf ball or an egg, or even a fist or a head or a football, or – alternatively – the size of a million tiny nodules, each one much smaller than a marble, some no more than specks, but dotted throughout the lungs in an infinite array like the sky at night, particularly when seen against the air-filled lungs which appear black on the monitor of a CT scan.

Marya had seemed fascinated by it all throughout the professor's talk. She'd taken notes and sat forward in her seat. Even from where I was sitting I could tell her face and entire bearing were straining to absorb everything. I'd half expected her to ask a question. But nobody asked any questions, perhaps because the professor had gone on a bit as he approached the end and started to ramble. His age had become appreciable. He'd got his last few slides mixed up and then stopped abruptly without any conclusion slide. People had coughed into the silence and the microphones – which stand in the aisles for you to go and stand at in order to ask your question – had remained idle. The professor had peered out at the darkness of the auditorium – his hand over his eyes, shielding them from the spotlights – and he'd seemed to be disappointed by this, unsure what to do next.

'Great talk, professor!' I said a second time to him now, as we sat across from each other in the canteen. But again the professor didn't look up. He was still focused on the little tub of butter which I also have trouble with. You need to break off the plastic tip and then use your nails, which is a problem for me because I have the bad habit of biting mine. He seemed intent on it, so much so that again he didn't hear me.

Just then I spotted Dr Berger, one of the hepatobiliary surgeons. He was standing at the entrance of the canteen, near the till, and was looking around with his hands on his hips. When he saw the professor he nodded and his face opened out into a smile, which it always seems on the verge of doing. Berger is a very jovial sort. He started to walk in our direction.

'Professor!' Berger shouted out in a loud voice when he was twenty feet away. The professor looked up straightaway and turned around. There was no ignoring Berger. He put the butter down and wiped his hands on a napkin, and made an attempt to get up.

'Ah!' he said. 'Dr Berger!'

Dr Berger is a popular figure around the place, a large, fat man originally from Iceland who laughs a lot but apparently is not a safe surgeon. That is what they say. Back when I was a clinical fellow, I never heard any of the other doctors ask for him to see their patients. If they wanted to refer somebody for a surgical opinion or a consult they always specified Jacobson or Dement. They never said not to call Berger, but they never asked for him specifically. It is also well known that Dr Berger will operate on just about anybody. He will take on any case, even patients who have very advanced disease and who really shouldn't be anywhere near an operating room, but who are driven there by their need to do something, anything, in the belief that intervening is always better than doing nothing, a belief which Berger shares. In that way Berger is without doubt fully Americanized, in accord with the creed that is so strong over here, a creed stronger than Jesus, even, whereby every problem is fixable, even biology, that there is an answer to everything and you can always do something and that something is always better than nothing.

'Professor! Why are you sitting here all alone?' Berger boomed. 'Please, don't get up,' he said, and he put his hand on the professor's shoulder and practically shoved him back down into his seat.

'We were expecting you upstairs but you disappeared!' he continued.

'Ah yes,' said the professor, 'I'm sorry but I thought there was time. I thought I'd come here for some tea first. I hadn't had breakfast at the hotel.'

'But we have some refreshment for you upstairs, professor, in Surgery Branch. It's a Grand Rounds tradition, you know. We always have a little reception for the visiting guest. Dr Solter will be there too. He has gone to look for you, in the library, I think. But I knew where you would be, professor!' Berger said laughing, and here he grabbed his own belly with two hands and moved it around. 'Yes, I knew where you would be all right!'

Whilst Berger is popular, he needs to be a little more careful, I think, as he is prone to making inappropriate comments, especially where women are concerned. This technique works well enough in Europe, but not over here. I've heard him in queues at the Starbucks or in the canteen remark aloud and in a jokey way how short a girl's skirt is, or how he had four girlfriends last month and they all dumped him on the same weekend, or how he would never get married, never, and why would you do that anyway, you're stuck with the same woman then for heaven's sake. Once in the canteen I saw him go up to a girl who was sitting with a friend. The girl's blouse was halfway up her back and her trousers were a little low, exposing a pink G-string that Berger just couldn't resist. He went over to the girl and put his hand on her shoulder. I don't know what he said to her but she shifted her position and quickly adjusted her clothing, pulling down her shirt to cover her exposed back and underwear, while Berger walked off laughing to himself.

'Anyway,' he said to the professor, 'I am to call Dr Solter as soon as I found you. Come, everyone is waiting, including Dr Jacobson, who is very eager to meet you again, and there are a lot of pretty girls up there, professor. I guarantee it!'

As he spoke Dr Berger pulled out the chair beside him so that he also could sit down. He pulled the chair way back from the table to give himself plenty of room and then he sat on it, at an angle to the old man.

'Ah yes, Dr Jacobson,' said the professor. 'How is Dr Jacobson these days?'

Berger wasn't listening to him. He took out his mobile phone and pressed the face of it, before holding it up to his ear. As he did so he looked at me and gave me a friendly nod, smiling, as if we were sharing an in-joke at the old professor's expense. He raised his hand and gave me a wave. He must have seen me around, Berger, just as I had seen him around, even though it always surprises you to think that other strangers recognize you. We tend to think that everybody else is a permanent fixture in your world, but that you are invisible in theirs.

'Hello, David? David?' Berger said loudly into the phone, apparently to Solter. 'I've found our friend. We can call off the search party,' and he winked at the professor, 'he's in the canteen, just like I told you. Yes, yes, I will bring him upstairs.'

He closed over his phone and stood up.

'Come on, professor,' he said, 'why don't you take your tea, but leave the toast and all this, and we'll go upstairs.'

'All right,' said the professor, like a child. 'In any case I was having an awful time opening these little tubs of butter.'

'Yes, professor, I say so,' Berger said, 'in fact, I insist,' and he slapped the professor on the back. The professor tried to stand up but he could only do it slowly, using the back of his chair for support. He didn't have a stick but he looked in need of one. Dr Berger stood with his hands on his hips and watched him, still with a grin on his face. He could have easily helped the professor with an arm under the elbow or the armpit, but he didn't. Eventually the professor got to his feet.

They were on their way out of the canteen when Marya finally appeared. Berger seemed to know her. He opened both his arms out wide as she approached and then made a ridiculous ceremonial bow in front of her. She couldn't help laughing. He introduced her to the old professor. And then

Berger did something as unexpected as it was blatant. He placed his hands on Marya's shoulders and shook her a little. Then he pulled her towards him and whispered into her ear, then kissed her on the side of her head and gave her a big hug.

'I see you know Dr Berger,' I said to her a moment later when Marya pulled out the seat opposite me.

'Ucccch,' she said sitting down, 'everyone knows him. Complete creep,' and she rubbed the side of her head where he had just kissed her. 'Always coming up to you, putting hand on you. Marya, Marya, tell me, how are you? How are you? Stare into you, into your face, y'know? Make deep eye contact, just like all the Americans. Uccch!'

'I don't think he's an American.'

'He is now, whatever. Acclimatization, you know? Be careful, it might happen to you.'

'You too,' I said.

'No chance. For Russian it is impossible. Except for my brother. But he is unusual case.'

'Do you go to Grand Rounds every week?' I asked her.

'First time, actually. I hear something on NPR about this famous professor and then I see sign that he is coming. Anyway I had nothing else to do. But it was good. Now I know what you all talk about when you get together in room behind closed doors. I even take some notes!' and when she said that she lifted up her pad, which was covered in scribbles.

'Were you able to follow it?' I asked her.

'More or less, gist, you know? Not all bar graphs and things but big picture, yes. He was pretty cool, actually, the professor. I hope he wins Nobel Prize like they say in introduction he might. But you know, I can't make up my mind, postdoc.'

'About what?'

'About you guys. Doctors, scientists, whatever. You all know a lot, right? Tons of stuff. But at same time it seems, like no offence, that you guys don't know very much. At end of day. So it seem anyway. I mean, the professor, it was all this stuff, you know, about yeast and fungus and virus and then he talk about genetic mouse and this and that and blah blah blah and he show picture and graph and picture and more graph . . . really tiny, tiny stuff, y'know? Miniature . . . but at end of day he was like . . . might cause this . . . or may be involved . . . but most of the time he was like, we don't know, we don't know, we think, we think, is possible, is possible. When are you guys going to come out and say, yes we know? Finally. We have done the miniature. Now we know. No maybe any more. No is possible any more. We just know. And we fix.'

'We're getting better,' I said, 'but yeah, there are always more questions.'

Marya laughed.

'Very deep, postdoc,' she said, 'now you sound like rabbi. You should grow white beard. I see it, actually.'

She laughed again. Our attention was then briefly drawn to the hospital clown who was sitting not far from us and had gotten up and was bending over to tip his toes. The clown is a familiar presence around the hospital. He works mainly with the paediatric patients. He's always blowing up balloons for them and twisting them into shapes. He seems to be quite moody, though. A lot of the time you see him out the back of the hospital smoking, standing beside the old man with the sign asking for St Michael to appear, as if there was something he was also protesting about. Marya and I looked at him as he stood back upright and gave his back a good stretch.

'By the way, how did you find me?' I asked her. 'The other day? I got your note.'

'Not so easy, postdoc. Nobody knows you, I'm afraid, no offence. But in the end I ask security guard did he know any Irishmen working there, in that building.'

'The Jamaican one?'

'How should I know? He was black, anyway . . . or sorry, African American, whatever! He describe to me one person and I know that it was you.'

'How did he describe me?'

'You really want to know? He told me there was this one guy who was either Irish or Scottish and very tall but also very serious and always he look at ground. And I say, "Yes! That's him!" Then he tell me which floor you are on. So I go. And that creature you share the lab with?'

'Deep?'

'Oh my God, he's so strange, not even saying one word, you know?'

'He's OK,' I said. 'We get on well. How did you get in without a swipe?'

'I ring bell, of course. Then the . . . eh . . . creature, he answer like thirty minutes later, and of course then he just stand there, you know! Like he never see woman before! It was obvious which one was your desk. I know from the picture of the sax guy on the computer.'

'John Coltrane.'

'Whatever.'

Neither of us spoke for a few moments. Marya took out her mobile phone and looked at it, before starting to talk again. The clown was still stretching over by the wall. He had his hands on it and was bending over trying to really work on his calf muscles.

'But the animals, postdoc!' Marya said. 'When I see them I feel so sad for them. I run out of there then. Don't worry, I'm not some crazy, but oh my God! I stand and look down for a while. They have no clue, you know? I mean, this is it for them, right? One of them in particular didn't look so well.'

'That was probably Henrietta.'

'Henrietta?'

'I've given a few of them names. It's maybe a little stupid.'

'Like Henrietta Lacks, you mean?

'You know about her?' I asked.

'Of course. She's famous. We even read about her in school, back in Russia. And there was also book recently. I read it, actually. So you have her in your lab? That's pretty cool. Is she responding to treatment?'

'I think so. Stabilized anyway.'

'Cool. I should call up again to you one of these days . . . Maybe you'll be actually doing some work this time, so that you can make proper introduction to the famous Henrietta. What about the rest of them?'

'What about them?' I replied.

'Do you ever cure them?'

'Sometimes. But it's easier to cure mice.'

'Easier than what? Human?'

'Yes.'

'Why?' she asked quickly.

'I don't know,' I said.

Marya looked at me but didn't say anything. Over by the wall the group of OTs or physios at the other table stood up and the man in the suit shook hands with each of them. He picked up the leg that was on the table and put it under his arm and they all walked out together. The clown was now sitting down again, his back to the wall and his legs up on the seat beside him. He looked in a bad way, actually, as if he was really hungover.

'Then what?' Marya said to me.

'When?' I replied.

'After you cure mouse?' she said. 'You let them go or what?'

I looked at her and shrugged.

'But seriously?' she said.

'Seriously,' I replied.

'They die anyway? The mouse?'

'Yes.'

Marya said nothing. She closed her pad and placed it in her bag, which she had hung over the back of her chair. I asked her did she want me to go and get her some tea or coffee but she just shook her head. She leaned back in her chair and seemed to have lost a lot of her energy.

'By the way,' I said to her, 'how did it go with that woman from last week? Did you go and meet her doctors like she asked? The Russian patient from that talk we went to?'

'Her? Yes, of course.'

'What happened?'

'I go there like she ask but arrive late. They come and go already, big crowd, it was ridiculous.'

'How so?' I asked.

'Uccch,' Marya said, and she sat forward, regaining her energy. 'She just there on bed, y'know, but no make-up, nothing, just woke up. Her hair everywhere. Mess. Still half sleeping. Can you imagine? They don't even give her time to put on dressing gown! When I get there they finish already, and are at other patient bed, but still in the same room, it was multi-bed. And when I go over to her she's like . . . in a stun, you know?'

'Stunned.'

'Not even crying.'

'What did you do?'

'I shout out to them, hey, come back here, explain, you'know, explain. They stop and all look back at me, big crowd, all wear white coat . . . So I go up to head guy and say to him: "Hey, she didn't understand word, you know, of whatever you guys say. Go over it one more time so I can explain to her, but this time slowlier. She has like no idea, no clue!"'

'What did they say?'

'It was so stupid. This woman, she have cancer, OK, in the liver and the lungs and in the bones. The doctor then, he take up this consent form again for clinical trial and he go through everything, you know, but too much, he is like, the drug could do this, this, this and this, it might do this, it might do this. Blah blah blah. It might kill you. It might make you bleed. And I have to translate this shit, can you imagine?'

She was staring at me with her mouth and eyes and even the palms of her hands wide open as if she was challenging me to imagine it or defend it.

'No, I can't imagine it,' I said, even though this wasn't strictly true.

'Of course,' Marya continued, 'I don't translate word for word but only some . . . Your kidneys might fail, your lungs too, et cetera, et cetera, blah blah blah. He go on and on, and she was like, yes, but will it work, this drug, you know? Is there point, doctor?'

She stopped again and looked at me in that exasperated manner.

'I mean? WTF? Y'know?'

I returned her gaze to show her that I also was in disbelief at what she was saying. But at the same time I could also see it from the other side. It is an awkward thing to speak through a translator. I've done it myself a few times. There is a built-in delay that makes things both harder and easier. Harder to explain things properly, but it's also easier because you are less connected to your own words, and therefore less responsible for them. The slight delay allows you to stand back and watch the effect of your words on the patient's face as the translator relates what you have just said, as if you are now removed from the process, absolved of any blame and whatever distress that has been caused.*

'So,' Marya continued, 'she say it in English the woman, and I also ask, will it work? Is there point? That's what she want to know, not this other stuff. Guess what he say?'

'What?' I said.

'He say we just have to take it one day at a time. Can you believe? He just shrug shoulders! One day at a time! Like easy for him to say, no? Oh my god, I want to slap him! Goddamn, lie a bit, you know! For cry out loud. Lie! Say yes, good chance. No guarantee but good chance, you know? At least keep up hope, you know? Not this NONSENSE! Uuuuccchhhh, doctors, they're so stupid! No offence.'

The girl sat back on the chair then, a little breathless after telling her story. I sat back also and looked over at the canteen entrance. A man and woman came in with the child who I had seen put up such a fight recently going into the elevators. He seemed relaxed and happy now, even though there was

---

* I read a profile a few months back about a B52 bomber pilot who flew in Vietnam. He had no problems with PTSD. He didn't think it existed. The plane's main strength lay in its ability to fly very high in the abstract silence, out of harm's way, and also out of range of the sights and sounds and screams far below. There is no doubt that things are easier that way.

still a yellow tube coming out of his nose which was taped to the side of his cheek. The child was wearing his pyjamas, which were covered with aeroplanes. His head was completely bald and he was holding in his right hand a helium balloon which they are always giving out to the paediatric patients. The clown goes around with them. It made me turn around and look over to where he still was, his feet now up on the chair beside him, his head resting against the wall. It looked like he was fast asleep. Marya was looking at the little boy. She turned to me and frowned as if to say how shit. I gave a useless shrug. As if on cue we both stood up. I went over to leave my tray on the trolley and we walked out of the canteen in silence.

We were in the small corridor lined by paintings when I grasped hold of her elbow to make her stop.

'You never answered my email by the way,' I said.

'What?' she said, even though I knew she had heard and understood. It wasn't the first time I noticed that she did this. We had the corridor to ourselves.

'Well?' I said. 'What about it?' We had both stopped walking and were facing each other. There was nobody else in the vicinity. Behind her was a large painting of a nude figure. It is the only decent painting which hangs there. The girl didn't say anything.

'It's a Russian restaurant,' I continued, 'the one I mentioned. I was reading about it. Ballerine, I think it's called. In the LowerEast Side?'

'Yes, I know it. Very expensive, postdoc. Trendy also, you

know? Anatoly Schevchenko's place, actually. Ex-Kirov. You know him?'

'No,' I said.

'You know him. I guarantee. All the time on television. Date movie star. Advertise watch. Car also, I think. If you see you know.'

'Well? Maybe on Thursday then?'

'Ha!' she said, and her face reddened a bit. 'I don't know, I don't know.'

'Why not?' I said, stepping slightly forward.

'OK,' she said, 'OK. If you can afford. Why not?'

'Yes, I can afford,' I said, and I looked at her, making a conscious effort to maintain eye contact, just like Dr Harding does. We were standing so close that I could have easily kissed her without taking another step.

'It's a date then,' I added firmly.

She looked at me very briefly and then she looked away.

15

I got an email from my wife. When I saw her name in my inbox I was surprised and did nothing but stare at it for a minute, wondering what she might want. Yvonne and I haven't been in touch for a while, and we haven't seen each other in person since last winter when Donal got sick and we met each other in the hospital canteen. Afterwards we agreed that we would stay in regular contact but then we didn't.

Her email, when I opened it, was cheery. She seems to be getting along fine and I was pleased and also not pleased to hear this. I suppose it is natural to want the other person to be suffering a little; and also to want you back, which I had thought more likely if I left the country for a period of time. But it hasn't panned out that way and I get the impression that she has 'gotten on with her life', as people are always saying, and as if there was any alternative. I don't know what I was expecting to happen. More and more I fear that the right thing might well have been to stay put and dig myself in, the way soldiers do when they are getting it from all angles. You can be too philosophical about things, too able to accommodate or contextualize them. Then when you leave you think everything has frozen in time back there and that you can always return to change things, your mind now finally in sync with what is happening in front of your eyes and able at last to work at normal speed and absorb things the way other people seem to be able to without any difficulty. Whereas beforehand the majority of things seemed to be passing far too quickly – or so it seemed anyway – like the images on a screen of a film that has been sped up slightly, but whose main messages are subliminal and largely beyond your grasp.

Yvonne and I were married for just over three years before we separated. During the last twelve months together we underwent IVF to try and have a child, which wasn't success-ful. There are seven embryos still in a freezer in the clinic in London. I think about them often. If we are never to get back together I suppose they should be destroyed, but I haven't been able to bring myself to suggest that to Yvonne and she has never suggested it either. At the start of the process we both had all the tests for infertility and nothing specific turned up. My sperm count was down in the twenty-fifth percentile, but still well above the threshold for fertility. In her unkind moments it was something Yvonne liked to remind me of, that by definition it was less than the majority. We each had our unkind moments. Even her father would make the odd joke about it, or allude to it in some none too subtle way. I got the impression a few times that he was tempted to have his own tested just for the bragging rights. I never got on with my father-in-law. He is a well-known orthopaedic surgeon in Dublin, with a small celebrity practice – the Irish rugby team, et cetera – in addition to the run-of-the-mill private one, and he's a vain old philanderer. Yvonne is an only child.

Yvonne and I had known each other peripherally for a decade before getting together. Both of us had been on the medical scene for several years, which is to say that we both worked as senior house officers and then registrars in the various Dublin hospitals, sometimes for longer than a year in one and occasionally even returning to work in the same place for a second or third time. Because there are certain pubs associated with each hospital and because everybody ends up in the same one or two wine bars on Leeson Street every Friday (and sometimes even Tuesday, Wednesday and Thursday also), the scene becomes small and familiar. As contemporaries moved on and got married we were the last two standing, so there was an inevitability about the whole thing, particularly as we both approached forty, her approaching it sooner than me by two years. She made up her mind about it. She made all the moves, right down to stopping the taxi at a petrol station on that first night back to her place to send me in to buy a packet of Durex. She was surprised that I didn't have any.

We got married quickly. She had made up her mind and I thought, this is it, this is what other people do all the time, so why not? You can be too open to things, too able to acclimatize; it is not always a survival skill. Neither of us were the marrying type, she less so than I. To my surprise, though, I found that marriage suited me, apart from certain limitations that it places on you. It sounds sentimental but I enjoyed being married. People view you with less suspicion. And in the early days I looked forward to coming home in the evenings and listening to Yvonne, who was a complete chatterbox and a very good storyteller regarding her day, bringing to life all her little dramas (which were considerable in number). Yvonne is pretty, a small blonde, although she does wear too much make-up. It gives her face a mask-like quality when she smiles.

We only did one round of the IVF and the embryo didn't take. It was cast out in her first period, which came relentlessly and remorselessly – just as it had done apparently every month without fail since the precocious age of eleven – bang on schedule, like a tide that can be charted and depended upon by others. She cried and I felt very sorry for her that night, as I did on that day of every twenty-eight-day cycle of that first year when we were still trying the natural way and she would rush to the bathroom in the middle of the night and I could hear her crying amidst the small rustling of a packet of tampons being opened. It is a difficult thing not to be able to do, have a baby, especially as it is something that even the stupidest and most incompetent are doing all around you, apparently with not much effort at all. It made us both feel like failures, as if the entire world had been set a task and we were the only ones who couldn't accomplish it. Practically every week, a text or email from some friend or acquaintance or work colleague would arrive announcing their own good news, which would send Yvonne to bed in tears, but only after she had responded to the text message or email in the way demanded by politeness.

At the end of Yvonne's email she mentioned that she would like to talk to me about something, if I could give her a call. I read that part several times. It was the casual tone which made me especially wary. There was a studied quality to it. Then I went back over the whole email looking for any hints or insights. It is always hard to put a halt to the imagination and stop it going straightaway to the best and worst scenarios. Your body doesn't know the difference. I had to tell it to breathe slower, the pulse to bound less. I replied saying that I would call her.

Going home in the evening I had to take a detour up 65th Street on account of roadworks which wouldn't allow me to go directly home. I was walking with my head down and when I looked up I saw Marya ahead of me going in the same direction. I was debating whether or not to jog up to her when I realized that she was with someone, a man in a suit. They were walking side by side, not particularly talking to each other. The man was stocky and had dark red hair that had been gelled. I pulled back before I was right on top of them and stood in by the wall and watched them as they crossed First Avenue. When they got to the CVS pharmacy on the other side Marya turned to the man and judging from their body language they started arguing. Both of them used their hands a lot as they spoke. Marya put her hand up to her forehead in exasperation. The man stepped forward and took her in his arms. She resisted for a minute but then they embraced.

I didn't want to see any more so I turned and went back

the way I came. I walked slowly, confused by what I had seen but trying to stop myself from analysing it too much. But still there was that heaviness you get with disappointment. I was physically exhausted and in a mental daze from having spent the whole day in the lab. Today was Day 30 of the experiment. Per protocol there were a lot of blood samples that needed to be drawn. But also the email from Yvonne was never far from my thoughts. Everything around me seemed both louder but also further away than usual, as if the different strands of noise were easily distinguishable and competing with each other to be heard. I walked on, looking for a crossing point. The workmen were still hard at it despite the lateness of the hour. They had made a deep trench which ran the entire length of the street between First Avenue and York. It hadn't been there in the morning. A silent JCB stood exhausted in the middle of the street, its bucket resting on the ground, its teeth sore. The trench must have been six foot deep. It was a few feet from the kerb, not far from the tree line. The roots of the trees emerged through the mud of the trench, long and slender like the tendons of tall people, as white as bone.

Once, I was giving bad news to a woman. Her husband sat beside her and he took it much worse than she did. I remember there was a potted plant in the corner and he kept staring at it even when I spoke to him directly. For some reason a section of the plant's soil had been removed and you could see its roots exposed. It looked like a machine had taken a scoop out of it. The husband buried his head in his hands and his wife tried to comfort him, patting him on the shoulder and saying, 'It's OK, Tom. It's OK, love.' When he lifted up his face again it was red and swollen. He went back to staring at the base of the plant and its naked exposed roots. I thought he was going to say something about them but he didn't.

16

Mr Miyagi is dead. When I came into the lab this morning I found him lying on his back in the centre of the cage. He was cold and stiff, rigor mortis having already set in, which happens much quicker in mice than in humans. I stood for a while looking down on him. He was almost comical in his appearance, his four little legs sticking straight up in the air, just like in a cartoon. None of the others seemed particularly bothered by it. In fact they didn't appear to notice him at all, continuing to run about the place like normal. Even Henrietta was unperturbed. She was as free in her movements as I had seen her in quite a while.

I picked Mr Miyagi up using some kitchen roll and examined him closely. There was no outward suggestion of trauma. Certainly there were no bite marks that might have come from the other animals, or any signs that they had ganged up on him. Likewise there was no blood on his coat or on his face, which was frozen into a small grimace.

I brought him over to the dissection table in the corner of the laboratory where Deep and I have a small station set up beside the bio-disposal unit. Deep uses it on his drosophila, having to wear a special lens system for the micro-dissection required for them. Now and again he also uses the dissection area for mice which he occasionally keeps, but only for very quick experiments that last a few days, a week or two max. The mice never last long with Deep. On the wall is a sign that says 'IF you use it CLEAN it'. The sign appeared about a week or two after I moved into the laboratory (and even before I had done any animal dissections). The idea of Deep going out to a shop and buying it makes me smile every time I look at it.

I put Mr Miyagi down to one side and sprayed some bleach on the board and gave it a good wipe. Then I set him down in the centre of the board. For some reason he reminded me a little of Mrs X. Probably because of the way the tissue paper was pulled right up to his neck like a shroud, and also the facial expression, that blankness that you get with death. Hers was the last sudden and unexpected one I had experienced. All the deaths since have been predictable down to the day and hour. I planned them in advance, working my schedule around them so that when the protocol called for them to be sacrificed I could take my time about it and not have to rush.

I will have to replace him in the experiment, I realized, in addition to performing the autopsy – or necropsy, as it is called in the case of a non-human. It will be important to establish the cause of death, just in case the experimental drug I am testing has had any lethal off-target effects that could not have been predicted based on the drug's mode of action. It was the same with Mrs X, who also required an autopsy, although in her case it was because her death occurred outside the hospital and the list of potential causes was extensive. Autopsies are never as conclusive as you would think. The majority of the time the findings are non-specific, the cause of death hard to pin down. There may only be evidence of generalized organ failure and widespread tissue death or inflammation, but without an identifiable stimulus or pathogen. It's like coming across a burnt village in the middle of nowhere, every inhabitant and piece of wood charred black. All you can say for certain is that there had been a fire there or some other cataclysmic event. Alternatively you might encounter the exact opposite – as was the case with Mrs X – where everything looks pristine and it is almost as if there was no cause of death, but rather the body appeared simply to have ceased of its own accord and for no good reason.

Mrs X's autopsy was performed on the same day that she died. I was called to see her beforehand as she lay in the morgue in the basement, the white sheet pulled up over her, just like it was for Mr Miyagi now. I had to see her for bureaucratic reasons, in order to fill out some forms. Specifically I had to complete documentation verifying the absence of a pacemaker, which would otherwise have caused problems during the cremation. The man from the morgue wouldn't take my word for it over the telephone that she didn't have one. When he called me I had already returned to my apartment and was sitting on the floor in the corner of my room, still shocked by the suddenness of what had happened to her and which you never get used to, no matter how inevitable things are. (Mrs X's major organs were heavily involved by her cancer. Her liver in particular had what is termed a 'large tumour burden', as if it was a working animal, unable to support the weight of the disease.) Nevertheless I was thrown totally by it in a way I had not been before. I felt nauseated and even vomited once in the sink of my bathroom. Then I went into my room and pulled over the blinds and made the air dark around me. I sat on the floor leaning against the wall, sitting the way migraine sufferers sit, as still as possible. About an hour went by when my pager started going off, its shrill noise like a needle inserted into the darkness, bursting it. I removed the pager from my belt and stared at the bright numbers which showed up on it. I ignored it, but it went off repeatedly, three or four times in quick succession, the same number appearing on it each time. When I eventually got up and rang the number the morgue attendant answered.

'Thank you for calling back,' he said sarcastically.

I said nothing and just waited for the voice to say more.

'This is the mortuary here,' it said. 'I need a signature on a Mrs X who just arrived. You need to come and sign the cremation verification form, confirming the absence of a pacemaker.'

'What?' I said.

The man sighed loudly into the phone.

'I need a signature stating that she doesn't have a pacemaker. You need to do an examination, to verify. It is a prerequisite for cremation. If she does have one and is cremated there will be a small explosion. Now we wouldn't want that, would we?'

'But she doesn't have one,' I said, 'she doesn't have a pacemaker. There's nothing wrong with her heart.'

'Yes,' he said, 'I'm sure it is quite pristine. Nevertheless, it is mandated by New York State law. A signature and medical verification. Thank you.'

He hung up.

Twenty minutes later my pager went off again.

'Are you coming?' the man asked.

'Yes,' I said.

I put the phone down and headed back over to the hospital, entering through the ER, and going down in the same freight elevator that they would have brought Mrs X down in after she was pronounced. There's a direct connection between the ER and the morgue. The ER was carrying on as usual, packed and full of activity. I recognized one of the nurses who had just a little while earlier been out on the street working on Mrs X, trying to resuscitate her in the middle of First Avenue. She now had a coffee in her hand and was sitting on a desk at triage with her feet on a chair, talking and laughing to a fireman dressed in his full regalia. He had his helmet on and a large axe in his hand. He looked like a pretend fireman on his way to a costume party.

The freight elevator moved at a centimetre a minute. When I got down to the mortuary I found the attendant sitting in a small office, reading a newspaper. A kettle was boiling on the counter. He looked up and said my name when

I appeared in the doorway. I nodded and he stood up and I followed him into an adjacent room, stopping suddenly as I entered it.

It is always a confusion to the senses when you see someone dead. No matter how many times you see it, and especially if you knew the person when they were alive. On the one hand they look as if they could simply open their eyes and sit upright, pull back the white sheet and swing their legs over the side of the trolley. In that instance you can easily understand the incomprehension of a dog or small child who you hear about or read about now and again waiting beside their dead owner or parent for hours or even days, expecting them to arise at any minute, not understanding why they don't. But at the same time, as you stand there stunned by that initial sight, it also looks as if it was never a possibility for them to arise and it is now barely credible that they had ever been alive or that they had ever opened their eyes. Both scenarios seemed so for Mrs X, that she was about to open her eyes and that she had never opened them, her features instantly familiar and also unfamiliar as she lay on the trolley, a slab of white wax, her sternum bruised from the inadequate CPR, the ribs no doubt broken underneath, her face without an expression that was recognizable.

I approached her body and performed the examination the attendant wanted, placing my hands on her cold skin, moving my palms over her upper chest wall. Her skin was so cold it felt damp. The attendant stood at the doorway and watched me. He wore a tweed cap and a large cardigan which bulged from underneath his dirty light blue coat. There was definitely no pacemaker, which it was easy to verify by palpating Mrs X's sternum and the infra-clavicular areas on both sides. I did it slowly and methodically, more methodically than was perhaps necessary, feeling also that I should have been saying something, maybe even chanting softly in Latin as my hands moved across her cold skin.

I removed my hands from her and held them outwards, away from me.

'You can use that sink,' said the attendant.

I went over to the corner and washed them.

Afterwards I went into his office and signed the form in triplicate. The attendant lit a cigarette, which is completely against the rules, of course, but he was probably safe enough down there.

When I examined Mr Miyagi's organs I found that the cancer hadn't actually progressed very far. He had a little bit of peritoneal involvement and also a few liver lesions, but nothing major, certainly not enough to explain things, why he had died prematurely. Day 32, to be exact. He barely made it one-third of the way. Even the liver lesions were more on the surface than in the substance of it. There was evidence of some tumour necrosis, indicating a degree of response to the drug, and I was pleased to see this. I got the digital camera and took photographs of it. I also dissected the necrotic tumor and placed it in formalin. I will ask the pathology department later to make thin sections of it to mount on slides. His lungs did have some fluid in them. When I took them out and weighed them they were heavier than you would expect. I don't know what the cause of death was. He may have had a pulmonary embolus. Possibly a heart attack. In any case I don't think it was cancer related.

I put Mr Miyagi's lungs and liver back into his small body and buried him in the yellow bio-disposable unit, slipping him off the dissection board between the lips of its lid. I found myself doing it slowly and with some solemnity. As he slid off the board it reminded me of a sailor being buried at sea. I felt like I should say a few words. But I just bowed my head and stood there. I don't think sailors are buried that way any more.

17

I tried calling my wife today but she didn't answer and I did not leave a message.

I used the computer in the office to call her, even though I had to wake up Deep, who was fast asleep in front of his own screen. I shook him a couple of times and asked him if he wouldn't mind giving me the room for a few minutes. It took him a while to process my request before he shuffled out to check on his drosophilae next door in the laboratory. I shouted 'Thanks!' after him.

There was no answer from Yvonne, except for her voice-mail. I tried her again a couple of times, all the time looking up at Deep's blown-up photo of a drosphila on the wall which stared down at me with its small, angry face, its teeth bared.

I don't know what my wife wants, but it makes me uneasy. Yvonne is a great one for resolution. She is always wanting to draw a line under things and not leave them hanging. To her that is the worst thing you could do; whereas I am perfectly fine having a bit of time enter into the equation, allowing things to breathe and expand, while at the same time keeping them in amber so that their possibility is preserved. Given the choice I would take uncertainty over certainty every time.

Generally you are better off when things are not resolved at all. You only have to ask any one of my previous patients that. It is rarely in your interests.

I noticed with surprise that Yvonne still has the same answering message as before, which I remember her recording. It was early on in our relationship when we were both still on our best behaviour. She had just bought a new phone and spent the evening rehearsing the message. She wanted it to sound 'breezy' and on the verge of laughter.

'Hi, this is Yvonne, but I'm just not around at the moment. Do leave a message and I'll try to get back to you, promise!'

I was amused at the time because she literally spent an hour at it, recording and re-recording it. Yvonne was always known as an extrovert, someone loud and good fun, and here I was getting a glimpse of the effort that went into it. It was like watching an opera singer go through her scales in the dressing room before stepping out. And now when I heard the message I could easily see myself sitting in the background of her voice, looking on – as I did at the time – with amusement and affection. The ridiculous thought came to me that perhaps if I shouted loudly enough into the phone I could get through to that person, my former self. But even if I could I wouldn't have known what to say. I don't think it is necessarily true that you get any wiser.

Given that I had gone to the trouble of banishing Deep from our small office in order to get some privacy, I thought that I might as well call home.

My mother was there on her own, which was probably just as well. It meant I could talk to her a little, without my father or Donal present, who are distracting in their separate ways. They had gone up Annaverna, my mother told me, a family tradition, hiking to the transmitter on its peak along the S-shaped track that you can see out of our living room window and which is emblazoned across the mountain's chest like Superman. I found my mother a little distracted, though, turning every now and again to listen for the sound of Donal and my father's return.

'They've been away a while,' she said. 'It's just that it's getting dark. Maybe they stopped off somewhere. He might have taken Donal in for a mineral, into Fitzpatrick's, maybe. Anyway, we're not to worry.'

But I could tell she was worried. There comes a time when all there is to do is worry. My father has been increasingly forgetful recently, or so she says, I haven't noticed any difference. He has always been a little forgetful.

'I told him not to take the child up that mountain,' she continued, working herself into annoyance. 'And it raining. But do you think he would listen? He spends too much time at that book. His brain is going doolally because of it.'

The book she was referring to was about the poet Yeats. My father is retired now but was an engineer by trade, something to which by nature he was never really suited. Rather, his passion was literature and Yeats in particular. For the past ten or fifteen years since retirement he has been working on a book about the poet – part biography, part analysis, or so

I gather from his descriptions of it – which he intends to self-publish. He used to say that it was for his future grand-children but he doesn't say that any more.

'Anyway, son,' my mother continued, putting on her glasses and focusing on the computer screen, 'what's new with you?'

'Nothing much,' I said, before filling her in a little on some day-to-day issues: work, a paper I just published, the garbage chute being broken. My parents love to hear about the mundane stuff and I've learned to give it to them. They are proud of the fact that I am working over here in this world-famous place, but at the same time they don't fully understand why I don't come home and hang a plaque outside a private practice and get on with things.

'Yvonne's been in contact,' I added, after a slight lull in the conversation.

'What does she want?' my mother shot back quickly.

'I don't know,' I said, 'perhaps it has something to do with the embryos. She's forty-four now.'

My mother said nothing and I knew that she was deciding which outcome would be less desirable, for Yvonne to have one of them as a child or for her to destroy them.

'It's not right, son, the marriage is over,' she said then.

From the beginning my parents didn't like Yvonne, even my father, who would find something redeeming to say about Stalin. The first time I brought her home to meet them she was on her best behaviour and talked continuously, which she did whenever she was nervous and out to impress. She hardly even stopped to put food in her mouth. I thought the visit had gone well at the time. However, when I next went home for the weekend I noticed that my parents were reticent, not asking after her or even mentioning her.

'You didn't like her,' I said to them.

Eventually my mother spoke.

'She's trouble looking for a home,' she said, my father sitting damningly silent beside her.

'I'm sorry, I don't want to hurt you. It's not her fault, her father has destroyed her,' my mother continued, having heard all about him through golf club heresay. 'That was no up-bringing for the girl.'

Even though my parents both came to the wedding I don't think my mother in particular ever considered us married, because it occurred in a registry office and not a church. It was a very muted affair. Yvonne's father had just left her mother for the umpteenth time to shack up with one of his theatre nurses. It was a real struggle to get the old fool not to bring her along. My mother thinks that everything is genetic – she may be right – and was convinced from the very start that our marriage never stood a chance. The fact that we needed to try IVF probably underlined this in her eyes. My mother is very religious even though she herself doesn't think so and is always giving out about the Catholic church.

Neither of us spoke for a minute, which is a long time on Skype. Her attention kept going to the front of the house where she was listening for the sound of my father's key in the door. I thought that she looked tired, although it was hard to get a good look at her on account of their poor internet reception, which I must remember to get fixed for them the next time I am home. They probably need a new router.

'Here they are now,' she said, 'we'll say no more about her to your father. It'll just annoy him.'

The door opened and Donal came in first and then my father. My mother shouted at him, saying that he should not have gone up the mountain on a day like this, it raining from the heavens, and that he was to go outside and take off his boots because he was getting mud on the carpet; but it wasn't hard to hear the relief in her voice. Donal ran up to the computer screen, sitting down in my mother's chair after she got up and went next door following my father.

'I scored a hundred points in Kinect,' Donal said.

'A hundred points?' I said. 'That's nothing. I scored a hundred and fifty the other day.'

'No, you didn't!' he said. 'You don't even have an Xbox.'

'I do,' I said, 'they give them out for free in America. Only they're much better ones over here. They have lasers.'

Donal squealed with laughter.

Donal never liked Yvonne either. In her defence it was not because of anything she did, and it wasn't for the want of trying. She simply never knew how to approach him or talk to him, coming at him directly and waving her arms about as if she was on the attack. When Donal saw her coming he would go and hide. On that first weekend when she visited he had a tantrum and refused to leave his bedroom to come down for dinner, which he virtually never does any more. Perhaps I should have paid a little more attention to his reaction. You could do a lot worse than follow Donal's instinct on things, using them to guide you the way some people use a weather vane. For sure he understands more than you would think, and there is generally a good reason for why Donal doesn't understand the things he cannot grasp. For example he does not for the life of him understand why I am in America. Although he may not express it exactly in this way he would be completely baffled by someone not wishing to spend every waking hour with or close by the people they dearly love. Yes, you could do a lot worse than take Donal's comprehension or non-comprehension of things as your guiding principle in life.

By the way, they don't have Down's syndrome in America. You could walk the sidewalks of New York for a month and not come across a single case of it. I remember that thought occurring to me abruptly one day when I was in Time Square, after I had just arrived in the city and was wandering aimlessly along its thronged sidewalks, captivated by the giant TV screens and entire building fronts of light screaming their presence at me. Donal would not have survived here, I thought suddenly, as I was being pressed from all sides, surrounded by the masses that congregate there and for whose imperfections there is no prenatal testing. They would not have allowed him to be born, I thought. They would have searched him out in the womb, thrashing the long grass and beating on their drums with their blood tests and ultrasounds and amniocentesis needles, trying to make him reveal himself.

'Mam!' Donal shouted out now, turning towards my parents who had just come into the room together. 'He doesn't have an Xbox, isn't that right, Mam, tell him! He doesn't have one, so he doesn't!'

'Don't listen to that fella, son,' my mother said to him, 'they don't have them in America. Only here. We're way more advanced than them.'

My father was eating an apple and came over and stood beside my mother. I said hello to him and he waved at the screen. I asked him how he was and he said, smiling, 'still fastened to the dying animal', a perennial Yeatsian quote of his. 'And holding on for dear life too,' he added, laughing. My mother shook her head and looked upwards. The two of them then listened in the background to mine and Donal's routine, which rarely changes, and hopefully won't for another while yet. My mother told my father to fix himself up a bit as his top two shirt buttons were undone and then they faced towards the camera, their images flickering on account of the poor internet connection, forming and reforming.

18

On the subway down to Houston Street the mood was subdued, as it frequently is down there, even for the crazies who you can pick out easily. The carriage was crowded and we stood packed tightly against each other, open-eyed and fearful. The bright carriage moved through the darkness, imposing a blankness of the mind and soul melding with the white noise of the thin-walled train as it rattled through the ancient, dank tunnels. Patterns on the walls caught the light and passed like memories.

When I first came to New York I spent a lot of time in the subway, as a means of exploring the city and getting to know it, but also as an end in itself.* I read in the travel guide

---

* On one occasion I also took one of those open-decked bus tours, just to get my bearings, and which was better than the subway for that purpose. I was on a tour going through SoHo, stuck in traffic, when I spotted the Irish actor Stephen Rea walking along the street. The tour guide saw him also because he said: '. . . and if you look to your left you will see the actor Stephen Rea who you may recognize from a film called *The Crying Game*, which was a big movie a few years ago. I think it won an Oscar . . .' Stephen Rea stopped to look into the window of a closed-up shop, cupping his hands over his eyes and trying to get a good look in through the dark glass. Behind him, our double decker busload of tourists crammed over all on one side, our cameras trained on him. A reminder that in New York there is always someone liable to be watching. It's what religious people must feel when they look up at an angel-filled sky, confident that they are being kept under constant view. Not all of us are recognizable from tour buses, however. The bus moved quickly on. We were in no position to pass judgement. Stephen Rea could have been about to break into the place for all we knew.

I bought in Dublin Airport that going on the New York subway is one of the most existential experiences on earth. It sounded hyperbolic but I have noticed it to be true. Even the crazies tend to be well behaved down there, becalmed like the rest of us by the white noise as the train passes through the black tunnel. You can't but feel a fondness for everyone or remember that we all share the same basic predicament. Even the Wall Street types draw sympathy, looking like little boys outfitted in the disguises of grown men. We all stare ahead and are quiet.

This evening a group of young deaf people sat at one end of the carriage. There were six of them, three on either side, five girls and one guy who was very thin. I stood near them hanging from the overhead rail, watching as they spoke in sign language to each other. They appeared to have a system in place, each taking their turn. Whoever wanted to speak next waved their hand in the air and the rest of the group focused all their attention on that person. It was the most civilized thing I've ever seen. Their faces were eager and alert and full of expression as they became physically the message they wanted to transmit. Their hands and fingers danced in front of them as if they were holding in their palms small birds rapidly opening and closing their wings. I stood amongst several others and we stared at them, hanging from the metal rails, allowing our arms and the metal to take our body weight. You could tell I was not the only one captivated by the language they spoke through their hands and which seemed beautiful and ancient.

Marya was already there waiting for me outside the Rocks Hotel on Clinton Street down in the Lower East Side. The restaurant we were going to was in the ground floor of the hotel. There were lots of other people in the vicinity, either on the narrow footpaths or just standing around. Unlike midtown, which is perpetually bathed in light, the Lower East Side is barely lit at all and you have to make an effort to separate individuals from the mass of dark forms roaming up and down the sidewalk or congregating in packs like wolves. When Marya saw me in the distance she started coming towards me. Outside the hotel entrance was a red rope and a line of people going around the corner.

'You have reservation?' Marya shouted out to me when we were still ten feet apart. 'We cannot go otherwise!' She seemed annoyed. Her tone was accusatory, impatient, as if she had been waiting a while for me, even though I was on time.

I walked up to her.

'Hello to you too,' I said and kissed her on the cheek. She pulled back a bit and even in the darkness I could see her face blush. She looked beautiful. Her lipstick was red and she was wearing a grey woollen dress that was very tight to her body, with black leggings and boots which came up to her knees. She had clearly put in a lot of effort.

'They say reservation only,' she continued. 'In fact they laugh when I say it, that more than likely we don't have.'

'Relax,' I said. 'Of course I have a reservation. Come on.'

I put my hand on her back and we started walking towards the hotel.

Seeing the crowds outside, though, I was relieved I had phoned earlier. I hadn't thought it necessary for midweek. But in my experience it is those small incompetencies that women hate more than almost anything else. Especially as they make such an effort themselves to get ready, whereas we just have to just turn up, more or less. And conversely, if you do get the details right they are usually pretty impressed despite themselves. I always thought the clincher with Yvonne had been on that first night going back to her place. Earlier, coming out of the nightclub on Leeson Street, there were the usual hundreds of revellers fighting over just one or two cabs. I walked into the middle of the road and rapped on the driver's window of one taxi that already had four people in the back. I offered the driver an extra fifty euro and he kicked them out, much to their annoyance, and Yvonne's admiration. That was the night she insisted upon the contraceptive pit stop.

'I like the name,' I said, as Marya and I approached the revolving door of the hotel. Over the doorway was the silver outline of a ballerina in flight. 'Is it Russian?'

'No,' Marya said.

Inside, the lobby was very dark, barely lit, with black marble everywhere. Even the thick carpet was black and your feet went down into it. You could tell that money had been sunk into the place. There was a bar to the left that was surprisingly empty and a door to the side of it that led towards the nightclub below. We walked on towards a large archway at the end of the lobby where the restaurant was situated, behind tinted glass with images of dancers etched into it. A hostess was standing at a little lectern which had a small light on it and a cord hanging down, just like the reading lights they have in the main public library on 42nd Street, guarded outside by the stone lions. We checked in with her and she brought us inside under the archway, neither of us speaking as we were being led along.

The restaurant was only half-full. There was a DJ set up in the centre, surrounded by a narrow moat, but there was barely any music coming from his sound system. The tables were glass and did not have any coverings and the seats were a very shiny metal. The entire side of the restaurant was an enormous sushi bar with perhaps a dozen Japanese chefs behind it, all wearing black T-shirts. Perhaps I had been mistaken about it being a Russian restaurant.

'Your waitress will be with you in a minute,' the hostess said, seating us in the centre near the moat, which I could see was filled with water and had a current to it. Our table was near that of another couple, including an older blonde woman who was wearing a tight and revealing black dress and who blatantly sized me up and down with her eyes as I stood waiting for Marya to sit. Her companion turned to see what she was staring at. He shook his head.

'Let's get some cocktails,' I said, after we were sitting. I opened the menu. Marya didn't say anything.

When the waitress appeared I ordered a champagne

cocktail but Marya said that she wasn't going to drink for now. I ordered a selection of sashimi for starters and then we sat and faced each other. She really was looking beautiful. On her right deltoid I noticed a small birthmark, or possibly it was a bruise.

'So,' she said, 'this is the treatment, is it, that you give to every woman?'

'No . . .' I said, looking at her in all seriousness, before adding: 'They're all a little bit different.'

She laughed despite herself.

'In any case there's no mystery to it,' I said. 'We all want the same things.'

Her smile vanished and she looked down at her menu. She didn't seem in great form. Perhaps it was nerves. I looked around the room.

The couple sitting across from us made a small commotion, causing us both to look over. The man was gripping the woman by the wrist and was muttering to her fiercely under his breath. The woman stared into his face, unfazed and full of antagonism. She was much older than him. A wine glass lay broken on the floor beside them. A waitress came almost running to their table and the hostess appeared under the archway and looked over at them.

'So,' I said, turning my attention back to Marya. 'Did you have a busy day translating?'

'Ucch,' she said. 'I don't want to talk about that place. I get so sick of it sometimes . . . How can you stand it, to work there?'

'You're the volunteer,' I said.

She didn't respond, but instead took out her phone and checked it.

'I suppose it's kind of just where I ended up,' I said, answering her question, but mainly just to keep the conversation going. At the same time my attention was drawn to the moat that surrounded the DJ's station. The water was lit underneath and I noticed that there were fish in it, fleshy orange ones, like large, meaty goldfish.

Marya put her phone away.

'Me also,' she said. 'Kind of where I end up.'

'Anyway,' she added. 'We should talk about other things . . . where life happens. Not there. Other places . . .'

'Like the bitch,' I said, laughing.

'Sure,' she said, but she was looking over at the other table. I looked also. The man had let go of the woman's arm and she was giving a round of applause to the busboy who had come to sweep up the wine glass. She was clearly wasted.

'How did you learn your English, by the way?' I asked, turning back to Marya. 'At school?'

She shook her head.

'At school we do German, French . . . No. English I learn from television. MTV. Pop song. Radio. Hollywood film. Now internet, blog, whatever.'

'Do you still have family over there? In Russia?'

She shook her head again. The question seemed to irritate her.

'A little bit. Cousins,' she said.

'Are you still in touch?'

'Why?' she said. Her face was flushed.

'Just being nosey, I suppose,' I said, smiling, but again she didn't laugh and seemed tense.

'Are you OK?' I asked her then.

'Fine,' she said. 'Maybe under weather a little bit. That's all.'

'Here, have some of this,' I said and I pushed my enormous cocktail towards her.

'No,' she said. 'I don't want.'

The waitress came back with the starters on tiny plates and we ordered small additional plates of nigiri and some sushi too. I asked her about the place. It seemed that it was a sort of Japanese tapas place. The Russian connection was just with the owner. Marya said I could order for her so I asked the waitress to make a selection based on what was good. I also ordered a jug of sake but Marya said she didn't want anything to drink. I ordered it anyway.

'How's Henrietta, by the way?' Marya asked me.

'She's OK,' I said. 'Not great. Stable, I suppose.'

'Still she just sit in corner, not move?'

'Sometimes she's a bit more active,' I said. 'Although not so much the last few days. But she's OK . . . One of the others died, though. Unexpectedly,' I continued. 'I discovered him on Monday when I went in in the morning.'

'Why unexpected? I thought that they all die?'

'Yes, but this was sudden.'

'Sudden how? Like heart attack?'

'I don't know. The autopsy didn't really explain it.'

'You make autopsy?'

'Yes,' I said, and Marya stared at me.

'Do you always make autopsy?' she asked then.

'Yes,' I said.

'What about in human? Do they also make autopsy in human?'

'No, not always,' I said.

'When? When with human?'

'Only if it is very sudden and unexpected,' I said.

Marya didn't say anything for a while and simply used her chopsticks to move the food around. She didn't eat much of it and she only drank a little from her water glass. There was a long period when neither of us spoke. Luckily, the woman at the other table continued to create more scenes and distractions for us both to look over at. At one point she stood up and starting shouting out something indecipherable to the Japanese chefs behind the large bar. I think it was a speech of appreciation. She held up a piece of her food from her plate and started waving it at them.

'Shut up,' her companion hissed at her, trying to grab her, 'shut the fuck up!'

Only one or two of the chefs had stopped to look at her. The rest of them continued working.

'Henrietta you must kill, right?' Marya said after the woman had stopped shouting and sat down.

'Yes,' I said.

'No matter what? Even if cure?'

'Yes,' I said.

'When?'

'Day ninety.'

'When was day one?'

I thought about it for a moment. 'About five weeks ago,' I said, '. . . when I started the treatment. Today was day thirty-five.'

Marya looked down at her food again. I took a big drink of the sake.

'That's just the way it is,' I said in a resigned voice as I filled up my glass again. Marya looked up sharply at me but didn't say anything.

Neither of us spoke then for a while. Even our drunken neighbour was quiet. I had forgotten how artificial dates were, sitting full frontally across from the other person like that. It's hard to think of a more contrived situation, one where you have to wear such a large mask, covering as much as possible, with the exception of when you are at work, perhaps, seeing patients and projecting your knowledge of the future. It made me think of the disco I used to go to as a teenager, when the slow set came on and you would do laps of the place looking for a girl. Then, with barely any preliminaries, you would just plant your mouth on her. It's hilarious now but at the time it was the most serious thing in the world. The first date I had with Yvonne I barely said a word. She was a torrent of speech on the other side of the table, as if she had taken amphetamines. (Close. She told me much later that she had met with a colleague beforehand and drunk two gins.)

'Are you OK?' I said to Marya. 'You seem tired. Why don't you take a day off?'

'Not so easy, actually,' she said. 'To take day off.'

I wanted to ask her who that was she had been with the other day, but at the same time I was in no rush to hear the answer. My eyes went to the bruises on her upper arm. They looked like the marks fingers would make, gripping or holding firmly. A boyfriend with fists, perhaps. I heard that Russians tend to have volatile relationships.

'Who was that you were with the other day?' I said. 'The day before yesterday, crossing over First Avenue. Around four or five p.m.'

Marya looked up at me and then smiled, for pretty much the first time of the evening.

'Ah, postdoc,' she said, 'you were keeping watch on me. Like KGB.' And she laughed and her face went a little red. But then it seemed that she purposefully didn't answer my question but instead left it hanging there between us, and just then the waitress came over and asked us if everything was to our liking. I said it was and she was about to walk off when Marya asked her what time it was, despite the fact that her phone was on the table in front of her. The waitress took out her own phone to answer her.

'Do you have a curfew?' I asked when the waitress had left. 'A midnight one, like Cinderella?'

'No,' she said, 'but I don't want to stay out too late. Excuse me,' and she got up quickly from the table and went in the direction of the toilet.

She was gone for ages. I sat back and looked around the restaurant, which if anything was emptier now. The couple beside us were eating in silence and I was able to take a long look at them. They were certainly a strange fit. The woman was a lot older than the man, and was still fairly knocking back the wine. She also had an enormous milky cocktail in front of her which she sucked from now and again through a straw. At one point she took out her phone and started waving it at him.

'Take one, take one!' she started shouting. 'Take a picture!'

'Stop it!' he hissed at her under his breath.

Just then Marya's mobile phone lit up. She had left it on the table before going to the bathroom. I turned the phone around so that I could see the screen. Somebody called Uri was calling her. It vibrated loudly and rang out soundlessly but then straightaway its face lit up again, the name Uri once more flashing on it, vibrating even more aggressively this time. After one more truncated attempt Uri gave up.

'Go on. Take a picture, will you!' the drunk woman was shouting out still. I looked over at them. This time the man reluctantly accepted the mobile phone from her and took a photo. He seemed resigned rather than annoyed. The woman then took it back and turned the lens of her phone towards him and made it flash and he held his hand across his face like a celebrity in front of the paparazzi.

'Stop it!' he hissed at her again under his breath. 'Put the fucking thing away!'

I was also taken in by its lightning. When they look at the image later they may wonder about me, glowering out of the ether back at them like Jesus in the Turin shroud.

Eventually Marya returned from the bathroom.

'Are you OK?' I asked. It looked like she had splashed water on her face and her cheeks were very flushed. It occurred to me that she had been crying.

'Yes,' she replied, sitting down again. 'Like I tell you already, I just feel not so hot. Sudden onset virus. Influenza maybe. No big deal.'

'Someone called for you,' I said.

'Really?' she said, and she picked up the phone and looked through it quickly.

I debated asking her outright who Uri was. She may be in a bad situation, which apparently goes on far more commonly than we think.

'Ucch,' she said, after listening to the voicemail. 'Some people are ridiculous!' she added and then she laughed. 'They never leave you alone!'

The conversation continued a bit stop-start after that. Marya asked about Yvonne and I found myself telling her about our marriage, even a little about the IVF treatment we went through, despite the fact that it was the last thing I wanted to talk about. At least it seemed of interest to her, although that too passed and she looked beyond me into the distance. I asked her several questions about her life back in Russia but she gave only minimal answers and seemed irritated. It began to feel like I was interrogating her so after a while I gave up. We talked a little about the college system over here and how much of a racket it was but even then she was half-hearted about it. When the waitress asked us if we wanted to see the dessert menus Marya said no and got up to go to the bathroom.

She was gone again for a long time. I ordered a coffee and asked for the bill. This time she'd taken her phone with her and on coming back stood outside the toilets talking on it. It looked like she was arguing with whoever was on the other end. The drunk woman to the right of us was now looking at me, perhaps wondering what the story was, Marya plainly visible up by the toilets talking loudly into the phone. She raised her glass to me. She was even older than I had thought, well into her sixties or even seventies. I raised my glass in reply. It was obvious that she had had a lot of plastic surgery to her face; she had that particular look that is almost but still well short of being attractive. Her breasts had no doubt been augmented and were pushed up over the edge of her clothes. You couldn't help but admire her a little. Another interventionist, I thought, smiling back at her. Another who subscribes to that ethos that you can always do something, and that something is always better than nothing.

'I must go,' Marya said, when she finally came back to the table. She picked up her bag from the arm of her chair.

'Wait,' I said, 'let me just finish up here, I just need to pay the bill. I can drop you home in a taxi. Even to Brooklyn, I don't mind.'

'No!' said the girl, raising her voice a little. 'I must go!'

She looked at me and said 'I'm sorry,' a little quieter. Then she leaned over and kissed me on the cheek before walking off quickly. Her lips were moist and cool.

When I came out of the revolving doors of the hotel she was standing across the street trying to hail a taxi. She saw me and appeared to redouble her efforts. I crossed the street and went over to her. She stepped off the footpath practically in front of an empty taxi. As she opened the back door of the taxi she looked up at me.

'It's just bad time right now. I should not have come out,' she said. She went to say something else but stopped and closed the door. The taxi drove off.

I went towards Houston Street. There were large numbers of people out and about and the sidewalk was a shrieking animal with a thousand heads, each one of them emitting noise. Walking along the footpath I felt like I was forming part of it, another of its many mouths. Someone sprinted down the centre broken line of the street half-naked and cars beeped and the animal I was part of cheered. I got to Houston and stood for a while trying to hail a cab. Midtown was lit from the inside, its black skin sparkling. It appeared to be floating upwards like an enormous spaceship. The avenue was a depthless plane of oncoming headlights.

Eventually I got a taxi and specified to the driver to take the FDR even though it would have been far quicker to go up First Avenue. He grumbled about it but then acceded. I sat back on the leather and exhaled, looking out at the silent night and the silent other cars materializing out of the middle distance going by in a futuristic gliding manner. The skylines – both Manhattan's and Queens' across the black East River – glowed silently in the lit bare frame exteriors of their constituent buildings, which stood against the darkness like blocks of petrified flames. Above them the dark-fisted clouds made space impenetrable, revealing no sign of the sky full of stars which by all accounts are already dead or dying. If there are any new ones they haven't reached us yet. I pressed my face close to the glass. Everyone should take the FDR at night at least once before they die.

19

Yvonne is pregnant. There was an email from her today. I got it at lunchtime when I went to the internet cafe beside the hospital, which is more of a launderette than a cafe. I had left my lab coat in to be cleaned. As I was waiting I sat down and logged on to the only computer.

'I had hoped to tell you in person,' she wrote, 'but given that you haven't bothered to call me I've no choice. I'm pregnant. I suppose you should know about it. Don't worry, I don't expect anything. My father is going to support us.'

I read it several times but the meaning didn't change. I stared at her words until the glare hurt my eyes. My time ran out and the screen defaulted back to its home page. A voice shouted out behind me. People waiting. The voice was a million miles away. *Yo, buddy. People are waiting*. I got up and walked to the door. Another voice. The Asian owner. He was holding my lab coat on a hanger. It was an astonishing white. The brightest thing in the entire shop. I made some gesture and walked out of the shop without the coat. I started walking down First Avenue, vaguely aware of where I was going, moving slightly from side to side, as if several winds were pushing me, fighting over me. Every so often I stopped and looked straight up at the sky. The cars whooshed by. They were very loud and far away.

After some time I found myself by the East River just up from the Queensboro Bridge. There's a low wall there at around 56th Street and a quiet area with a bench, which was empty. Thick streams of water were coming out of the bridge from recent rain. They slapped loudly onto the concrete as if the bridge was an enormous pissing metal dog. I sat on the bench, but couldn't sit still. Every now and again I got up and went to the wall as if I was going to vomit over it. I looked down into the East River. There were so many thoughts occurring to me at once I could practically hear the little popping sounds as they formed on the surface of my brain. Each time one of them came close to definition I lost its thread. Every few minutes the whole process started up again. I stood up and went to the wall.

She must have used one of the embryos. That is the most likely explanation, especially given the wording of the email, which I tried to remember now but couldn't except in snatches. I should have printed it off. I was angry at myself for not having done so. Perhaps I had read it wrong. I should have printed it off. I yelled it soundlessly into myself, futilely. Like a falling man in the middle of nowhere.

I don't know how long I stayed there. The day was overcast and then it darkened. After a while I stopped pacing up to the wall. I was exhausted. The cold didn't bother me. I sat on the bench looking out. Barges passed in silence. Small ships, several of them, indistinguishable from one another, not memorable at all. No crew visible. I can look at water all day long.

She must have used one of the embryos. I would have previously signed all the necessary consent forms. I hadn't unsigned them at any stage. The Centre would not be aware of the separation, and probably wouldn't have cared. We had used a place in London, even though the whole thing is now available in Dublin. Yvonne was paranoid about coming across anyone she may have worked with or been involved with, some previous subordinate, an old SHO or intern, turning up to insert the IV line prior to any one of the numerous invasive procedures that they put you through.

Very likely all of this was with her father's encouragement and blessing. Her email as good as said so. It is inconceivable to people like him that their lineage should end. I will have to watch out when it comes to the name. He will most likely stick his oar in there if it's a boy, and probably even if it isn't. Chances are he'll want the same name and surname as him with, heaven forbid, a roman numeral appended.

The thought of it caused me to laugh out loud like a crazed man. The cold was bothering me. I stood up and went over to the wall, slower now, more collected. There was a strong current to the water. It was thick and black like petrol.

A scene comes back to me: it's the night of her first miscarriage. Yvonne is sitting on the floor of the bathroom in her nightdress, a thick drop of blood visible on the skin of her bare ankle. I stand over her, leaning awkwardly on the sink. Yvonne's breath is amplified by the bathroom acoustics, my silence just as amplified. There are still tears on her face but she has stopped crying. The toilet has stopped flushing but the pipes are regurgitating loudly as they always did in that house.

I feel self-conscious, awkward, a million miles away, my elbow unnecessarily on the sink marble. It is a useless posture, which seems to say it all to me now.

'We're incompatible,' Yvonne says.

I look down at her. The blood on her ankle has formed into a clot.

'We're incompatible,' she says again, firmer this time.

I don't say anything and I can tell she has thought about this before. It is also clear to me what she means. She is not being figurative or abstract. She means it literally. That our bodies are biologically incompatible. Chemically. Physically. That together we are inert.

My response is shameful. Essentially it is silence. I look down at my shivering, devastated wife and I offer her nothing, not even reassurance.

The last time I saw and spoke to Yvonne in person was that time just over a year ago when my brother Donal got sick. On the Monday morning I got a call from my mother telling me that Donal had pneumonia. He had already been in the local hospital a few days, apparently. They hadn't wanted to worry me. But now he was too sick and needed to be transferred to the respiratory unit in St James's in Dublin where Yvonne was working at the time. I headed straight for JFK and was very lucky to be able to get out of the country. It was during the record snowfall. The snow went almost the whole way up the dumpsters in the alleyway out the back of our building where we leave out our trash. When it cleared in the following weeks the corpses of dead rats in their hundreds were revealed, strewn along the alleyway. Over the ensuing months the garbage trucks ironed their corpses into the fabric of the concrete.

When my mother rang it was the first time in my life that I panicked, I mean with all the physical symptoms that go along with that, finding it hard even to catch my breath, a tightness in my chest. I could barely sit still in the taxi out to the airport, the entire time feeling a shapeless and non-specific rage directed against myself. Mostly I felt exposed and also foolish, how prone you are to chance when you live far from home and you have no close family – or any family – near at hand. It's artificial, of course, in that you're always exposed, all of the time, without the respite of a single second. You just become acutely aware of it at certain unbearable points in your life. Because of the snow I was lucky to get back to Dublin at all before they closed JFK, which they almost never do. I went on standby, hanging around the departure lounge until I finally got on a late night flight. On the plane I drank three Scotches, terrified about Donal, and the state that he might be in on the other side of the night after we had ploughed through the thick Atlantic blackness and emerged into a patch of morning blue. (Night is as much a physical barrier for planes, like passing through a stretch of dense water.)

When I arrived in Dublin I went directly to the hospital

from the airport. Donal was better than expected, the antibiotics having finally kicked in. Although Yvonne wasn't taking care of him directly she must have seen his name on the census and had called in to check on him. Poor Donal must have thought he was a goner for sure when she appeared by his bedside. Apparently he screamed as if it were the devil himself who had come to make his introduction. My parents thanked Yvonne for calling in and she left.

'He never liked me. Your brother,' she said later that morning when we met in the canteen.

'That's not strictly true,' I replied, and Yvonne looked up at me from her coffee, partly in hope. She couldn't stand the idea of anybody not liking her, even if it was somebody with an intellectual disability, as they call it now. (I think, I lose track of the currently acceptable terms. Donal himself couldn't give a rats.)

'It just takes a while with Donal,' I said. 'He is always strange with newcomers. Especially women. He doesn't know how to approach them.'

'Well, his big brother never had that problem,' my wife said, as quick as ever, despite the fact that she was post-call and had no doubt been up most of the night. I didn't reply even though it wasn't true, what she had said.

We talked for about an hour on that first morning, interrupted by her pager going off every few minutes, and which she largely ignored. In actual fact it was pleasant talking with her. We were both exhausted and this probably took away whatever angst or tension that might otherwise have been present. There were silences which neither of us rushed to fill, and this was a welcome change from the conversations I was getting used to having in New York – on dates – where you would both rush to fill in and cover over with words the slightest pause or gap of silence, as if you would both seize up and die otherwise. Essentially we acted like the middle-aged married couple we legally still were, and it made my mind wander a little and to question what might be still possible or desirable. We talked in general terms, careful to avoid any specifics. Mostly I told her about the mundane nature of settling into New York and my work. She was especially curious to know about Cillian and Siobhan, asking whether I saw much of them and how close I lived to them and how they were generally getting on with living in America. I got the impression that she didn't care much for Siobhan.

At the end, as we took our leave of each other, she even mentioned the possibility of visiting New York, which she had been to years earlier, with her mother on a shopping trip.

'Yes,' I said, 'you should come. I'll show you a good time.' Even this seemed a little too much and we left it at that.

One nice thing that used to happen each night in our marriage: Yvonne would cling to me, not with her arms as would be normal, but with her hands, taking fistfuls of my T-shirt, and even digging into me a little with her nails, like a small monkey or baboon. It was very surprising the first night she did it but I quickly came to look forward to it each night – her holding on to me as if for dear life – so much so that I would make an extra effort to short-circuit whatever fight or argument we were having that evening, just so she would cling to me in that manner, as if our mattress was a piece of debris out on a black swollen sea and we were all the other person had.

Donal recovered quickly from his pneumonia, but he remained in hospital for another week. I commuted up and down to Dublin, spending the nights back in the family home, which is a couple of hours away. I didn't see Yvonne again for the rest of the trip. I spent the week mostly with Donal, and mostly playing video games, which he is completely addicted to. I got him some new ones but we still played for the most part his old ones, which he much preferred. He especially likes the ones where there is not too much in the way of direction or reading and where it is more intuitive and you can just get on with it, and on which he easily thrashed me every time. Nothing gives him greater pleasure.

The rest of the time I wandered Dublin, as I now do New York (minus the subway). I didn't meet a single person that I knew – even on Grafton Street, which I must have traipsed up and down a hundred times. It made me feel even more of a tourist in what used to be my own city, although I didn't mind that. It is neither a good thing nor a bad thing, but just adds its own particular colour to everything.

I got up from the bench and started to walk back in the direction of my apartment building. My body was stiff and cold from being out so long. I was exhausted, and I walked slowly. It was not dark but the cars coming towards me had their headlights on. I stared into them. Their lights passed like a surprise over my body, painting it, like a wounded man who raises his hand to find it covered in blood. The many strands of thought were still there but they had slowed and I knew that if I wanted I could identify them. But I didn't bother and instead I walked on, exhausted but also aware now of a different feeling. It was hard to put a finger on it exactly, but it was something closer to excitement. I laughed out loud. I walked quicker. I realized I had a big grin now on my face and that made me laugh again. The prospect of fatherhood. It is one of life's experiences. Why wouldn't it happen to me? I crossed over the wide avenue, pausing in the centre of it. Downtown was a mile of traffic lights all on red. At that point in the evening when the buildings are black but the sky is still light, is there any more beautiful sight in New York?

When I got back to my apartment I tried Yvonne's number. I must have tried it twenty times in quick succession, but each time it went straight to her voicemail. I really wanted to talk to her. Even the patients across the way in the hospital would have been able to see that, from the way I paced around the room with the phone in my hand. As usual a few of them were lined up along the link corridor, which is a sort of Bridge of Sighs connecting the main central atrium to the wards out the back. The able-bodied ones always congregate there in their dressing gowns. They are bored and anything on the move is worthy of interest. No doubt they followed me with their eyes as I marched around my apartment hanging up the phone and redialling, hanging up and redialling, hanging up and redialling.

*

Two months before we are due to leave for New York I am sitting on the step of our back porch, the sliding patio doors open, looking out at the rain. My wife comes into the kitchen. All afternoon she's been in our bedroom, where I myself haven't slept in weeks. I am aware that she didn't come home last night. The kitchen door closes and I can hear her walk towards me. I can sense her standing behind me but I remain staring out at the garden, which is woefully neglected, the grass thick and weedy. There is even a thistle patch. The rain strengthens.

'I'm not going to America,' Yvonne says.

I turn around. Her chest is moving up and down rapidly, but the rest of her is perfectly composed. It makes me think of a small animal that has been maimed. It is the only evidence of her distress. That and the fact that she's been crying, which is appreciable despite, or perhaps because of, her make-up. She is dressed to go out. I start to speak but she cuts me off.

'I can't do this.'

I start to speak again but she stops me by closing her eyes tightly as if any words I speak will be physically painful to her.

'I. Just. Can't,' she says again, her eyes still closed. She opens them but doesn't look at me.

'I need more. Christ. It's like being married to that, for fuck sake.' I follow with my eyes to where she is pointing at the bare kitchen wall. I start to say something and this time she doesn't stop me, but nothing occurs to me that is not automatic so I end up saying nothing. Yvonne shakes her head

165

and then gets her car keys from the drawer and walks out of the kitchen. I turn around and face back towards the rain. Over the next few hours of sitting there, the light darkening, the rain not letting up and getting thicker, I try to decide if what I am feeling is mostly relief.

A patient once told me that I was good at giving bad news. He meant it sincerely and also as a compliment; which was pretty big of him considering the circumstances of his reeling world. His wife's face was melting in the corner of the room. At one point he looked over at her and gave her a big thumbs up, before turning his attention back on me. I bumbled and flailed around for the right words and all the time he had the same faint smile on his face, even encouraging me a little ('go on, it's OK' he said, 'it's OK') like a teacher urging on an effortful but talentless student. Eventually I hit on the right words – ones that gave a fair appraisal of things while at the same time allowing a role for uncertainty and even holding this out as an alternative to hope.

'I like the way you put that,' he said when I had finished, leaning back a little on the examination bench, as if I had said something that he found clever and interesting but did not particularly relate to him. He was wearing a tank top and his face and shoulders were red from sun and a side effect of the pills he was taking.

'You're good at this, I see,' he said chuckling. I half smiled and looked at the floor. He had already told me about his faith in the Lord and I was always pleased whenever I heard that. It makes things easier, turning down the heat of the spotlight beam a notch. That flailing and bumbling were genuine, of course, but also intentional. If all you have are words the very least you can do is act it out a little.

Yvonne was always looking for things that had an 'effect' on me, meaning really what explained me. A favourite line of thought for her was the role of Donal in shaping my ... what exactly? Personality, outlook, patience, which she considered coldness, distance, objectivity. And then of course there was my work, which carried for her a morbid fascination, especially late at night, post dinner and wine, both of us sitting on the ledge of our porch smoking, watching the rain splash on the grey patio. Neither of us liked to smoke in the house.

'But it must be so depressing,' she would say. 'Oncology. I mean, how can you sit there listening to people and talking to them when you know ... I can't imagine it ... I just can't imagine it.'

I wouldn't mind but Yvonne herself was a hard-nosed vascular surgeon. Albeit, most of her work was elective and on the minor list, leg ulcers for example, or yanking out the varicose veins on the legs of her consultant's private patients. She did see the odd emergency (a ruptured triple A or some motor vehicle disaster that she would be called down to casualty for), but they occurred at light speed compared to the slow traumas I would witness over the space of months and even a year or two, evolving CT scan by CT scan in front of my eyes and across my office desk, which I took to piling high with medical journals like a barricade and which seemed to get bigger as time passed. Leaving work it did sometimes feel that I was stumbling off a battlefield, somewhat stunned, or 'in a stun' as Marya might put it, staggering from side to side, my eyes too widely opened, having seen too much, like that scene in *A Clockwork Orange*, where Malcolm McDowell's eyelids are pulled back by metal hooks to bare his retinas to the full brunt of what was in front of them.

But I never liked this line of conversation, and at this point I would get up and go looking for another bottle of wine to open or a cigarette or a glass of water. Illness makes for oddly insubstantive discussion. There is too much density there across the desk in front of you, hunkered down and looking back at you from under its lids and across your barricade of journals. There's no cleverness can shift it. No analysis. It was already the case that I increasingly came to dread those days when I knew that bad news was on the agenda. Well in advance, it came to seem as if somebody placed in front of my field of vision a large opaque object, something with the dimensions of a breezeblock or a concrete slab, jet black, dense and immovable, but offering nothing, without function or usefulness. And then afterwards you'd feel not quite guilt exactly, but more a sense of being complicit, or at the least being perceived that way.*

---

* And why shouldn't you be perceived that way? They attribute their good results to you, shaking your hand with gusto and looking you in the eye, high-fiving you or even hugging you with tears of relief. Therefore it stands to reason that they would also curse you when the result is not so good, hate you even and wishing with all their breath that it was you in their place. After all you are the next best thing, the tumour's representative on earth, the one who talks about it all the time, finds it all so fucking interesting and worthy of study. Christ, you even make a decent living out of it.

It was also the case that part of me was always keenly aware of that five per cent absurdity in those situations – where one human sits across from another and advises him on his mortal issue. Like two drowning men consulting one another out on the vast ocean, the water swelling under you both, benignly for now. Because of course whilst it may be true that the person who is sitting across from you in the white coat may know more than you, he is also human in case you have forgotten. He may already have his own tumour growing inside him, rearing itself up to its full noticeable height, or have a heart that is being strangled slowly in a vice grip of hardening arteries; which makes it even more strange that we make him the doctor and you the patient and that you both sit on opposite sides of the desk that way and you ask him what will happen and he tries to tell you or comfort you and you look for assurances about tomorrow and he tries to give them to you. We are all human, we are all in the same boat, there may not be a tomorrow for him either. You might as well drink up, was my viewpoint. And that we surely did, generally getting through two bottles of wine and sometimes even three, Yvonne consuming the greater part. The nights generally ended in a fight, Yvonne on the attack.

A teacher once told my parents at a parent-teacher meeting that I was a 'fan of distraction'. His class was boring and I used to stare out the window. I can still recall the scene I looked out on, just some pipes going up the side of a wall. A small, irregular shape of sky above it. The teacher was a nice man, from the west of Ireland, who was, I think, a little intimidated by me because it was his first time teaching the honours stream and I was the only A student. He may even have resented me but that 'fan of distraction' comment was as far as he went in that direction. My parents weren't sure if it was a criticism or not. My father loved the phrase. He used to put on an English accent and say it to Donal: 'Are you a fan of distraction, Donal?' he would ask. Donal would laugh hysterically. After a while it became a stock family joke, whose origin we couldn't immediately remember. But thank God we're all fans of distraction. If not then you really are in trouble. The prospect of what lies ahead would drive you mad. The uncertainty as well as the certainty. That schoolyard scape I used to stare out at. If I close my eyes I can reach out and touch it.

But looking back on it now the teacher must have spotted what it was that would drive Yvonne crazy years later. That when it came to her, I seemed to be always looking out of the window. He must have seen the beginnings of it, because I admit that it got worse. Either way it strikes me as good a reason as any for wanting everything to slow down, allowing you to put from your mind that hyperawareness of time passing that you acquired at some point and which is not very useful to you. It strikes me also as good a reason as any for wanting to go into a laboratory, so that you can really look things squarely in the eye without backing off even one inch because your gaze is deeper, more penetrative in there.

After trying the usual way for months to have a baby, Yvonne got more and more preoccupied, quiet, withdrawn and defeated – none of which was like her. The months went by and we continued to try and nothing continued to happen, Yvonne becoming slightly frantic all the time, and the more that nothing happened the more frantic she became. This feeling was just beneath the surface, but always detectable. You didn't need to be Dr Harding to detect it. Our efforts became a parody of sex, until that stopped also. I stayed away as much as possible. Sometimes instead of driving straight home I would go to Sandymount and walk on the damp strand and look over at the twin cylinders plunging into the blue or black sky. I would lightly close my eyes and remain as still as possible, as if something large had me in its grip and I was waiting for it to forget about me. And sometimes it did forget about me and its grip went limp and I stepped out of it and walked around and out towards the retreated sea and it was so quiet you could imagine the large, grey clouds making creaking metal on metal noises as they collided with each other in slow motion. Heading back to the car was to feel the fist return for me and gather me up, a feeling that is not all bad. I only have it the odd time here in New York but occasionally I look out for it and would even welcome its return.

During one early ultrasound Yvonne's sonographer said something about her womb being retroverted with a fibrous strand down the centre of it. Yvonne immediately set about researching operations to fix it, even though it couldn't have been relevant. While she became more frantic I remember sort of shrugging my shoulders, standing even further back from her, as remote as anything you can imagine. I couldn't get it into my head that this was it. There was no higher being to scream it into my face. That this is your life so get the fuck on with it.

It was Yvonne who wanted to try IVF. I was ready to move on, I would have been OK without trying it. She worked at the hospital pretty much through the whole process, taking only the odd half-day off and continuing with the ridiculous one in three or even one in two call that the surgical registrars do. She took one week off for the initial laparoscopy but even then got called in on the Friday because her consultant wanted her to cover for him. He wanted to go skiing earlier than planned on account of an air traffic control strike that was threatened. Yvonne couldn't really drive and could barely walk so she did the coverage in-house rather than by phone, spending most of the day and entire on-call period in bed in the doctors' res. Luckily none of the swollen aortic aneurysms wandering silently around Dublin decided to burst that day and it was quiet. In the evening I brought her some chicken soup and a salad roll from the Spar across the street from the hospital.

'Yvonne!' I shouted into my mobile phone, when it sounded like she had finally picked up.

'Yvonne? Hello, Yvonne?' I repeated, suddenly desperate.

But there was no reply other than the static silence at the end of the phone.

I hung up and then rang back straightaway but it went directly to her voicemail and it was then that I relented and left a short message.

'Yvonne, call me,' I said. I left my apartment and my mobile phone number even though I was sure she already had them.

I closed the door of my apartment after me and took the lift up four floors, then walked to the corner room at the end of the corridor. I was reasonably sure I had the right door and knocked loudly on it. When Cillian Deasy answered I could see the alarm on his face.

'I need to get through to Yvonne,' I said. 'I know that you are friends.'

Cillian didn't say anything and for a moment he just stood there. Then he stepped back against the open door and said, 'Come in.'

Their apartment is much nicer than mine. For starters it is not a studio but a one-bedroom, meaning that the person you invite in isn't immediately confronted – as they are in my apartment – with the spectacle of an enormous bed and its inescapable implications as soon as they come in the door. In addition, given that theirs is a corner apartment it has good views of the cityscape, which was now beginning to glow and flicker as darkness fell. The East River was a plane of silver. They must also get lots of light in the morning, whereas my own apartment has no river views and gets just twenty minutes of light at around 8 a.m. or so when the sun manages to squeeze between a distant crack in the Manhattan skyline. Also their apartment does not look directly across at the side of the hospital. They are not confronted with its unremitting stare.

Cillian's wife Siobhan was standing in the kitchen but she was putting on her coat to leave. She nodded slightly at me.

'I'll be back in a while,' she said to Cillian, but it seemed that she was cold towards him too.

I turned my back on them to give them some privacy as they took leave of one another but in the reflection of the window I walked towards I could see that they did not kiss and whatever look she gave him caused him to shrug his shoulders and show his empty palms as if to say, 'I don't know why he's here, it has nothing to do with me.'

I turned around when I heard the door open and then close as she left. There were packed matching suitcases on the floor beside it.

I moved closer to the window and looked out at the view of the East River. I could still see Cillian in the ether of the glass. He hadn't moved an inch and was staring at me. I turned around and faced him.

'I won't be much help to you,' he said.

He had come over towards me and was standing in the centre of their living room area on a thick, overgrown carpet which almost completely buried his feet, which I noticed were bare. The ludicrous thought came to me that if it came to a physical fight between us I would have the advantage over him given the heavy boots I was wearing, which could do serious damage to his exposed toes. I moved over and sat down on the sofa without being invited. Cillian backed away and sat in an armchair, although he was now some distance away. We would almost have to shout over at one another.

'I know that you know more than you should,' I said to him. 'About Yvonne and me.'

He looked back at me with no reaction.

'But I don't blame you for that,' I continued. 'You can't help what people tell you, especially if the other person is persistent about it, always hammering away, beating on the drum.'

He still didn't say anything.

'And anyway,' I continued, 'some people have that facility, that makes other people want to tell them things. All they have to do is stand there and say nothing and people for some reason want to tell them everything. Maybe you're a bit like that,' I said, although I doubted it. It occurred to me just then that I would love a cigarette.

'We almost never discussed you,' Cillian said quickly, almost pleading. 'It almost never came up. She mentioned a few things. Not much.'

His denials made me feel that I was threatening him in some way. But that was ridiculous, I had nothing to threaten him with. Apart from my good winter boots, of course.

'Anything about fertility issues?' I asked.

There was a trace of a quick smile at the corners of his mouth. It was so quick I would have missed it had I not been on the lookout for it.

'I knew it,' I said. 'So she told you about the IVF? What about in more recent times, has she done it recently? Another round of it?'

His eyes opened slightly, as if he couldn't believe we were

having this conversation. I could scarcely believe it myself.

'It's really none of my business,' he said. 'Why don't you ask her?'

'I can't get through to her. She's not picking up the phone for some reason. Or returning my calls. Is there anyone else?' I asked. 'Do you know? Has there been anyone else recently, somebody new?'

He said nothing for a few seconds but just stared at me, bolder now, more confident.

'No,' he said. 'Nobody new,' and his gaze lingered on me.

Neither of us said anything for a while and it felt like a long time.

I stood up to leave.

'If you're talking to her, tell her to call me,' I said.

He stood also, and we both walked towards the door. For some reason, whatever tension there was seemed to have dissipated and all I felt was a tremendous tiredness.

He opened the door for me.

'Is Siobhan going on a trip?' I said to him and tapped my foot on one of the two packed suitcases that were up against the wall. They looked expensive, Louis Vuitton, I believe.

'No, not really,' he said.

'I guess I'll see you at the Concept meeting tomorrow,' I said. There had been an email sent around earlier that afternoon about it. Cillian was scheduled to present at it.

'Yes, yes,' he said quickly.

I walked out into the corridor and he closed the door after me.

20

Henrietta has an eye infection. When I arrived at the lab this morning I noticed that the sclera on her right side was inflamed. The white was streaked red and there was a copious discharge coming from the eye. It stained the tissue paper underneath her. I picked her up and examined her closely, cleaning the eye with some baby wipes. The lid was also swollen and half closed over. The capillaries were a ripe meshwork, blood-red against the white. I had to pry open the sticky lid with my fingers. But that seemed to bother her so I replaced her back on the floor of the cage and simply stood looking down on her.

The infection could be a side effect of the investigational drug I gave to her. The company brochure said that in some of their internal experiments there was evidence of immune dysfunction. They weren't very specific about it but when I rechecked the manual they'd given me it appeared that the onset of the symptoms was delayed. There was a wide range, the earliest case occurring one week following drug administration. Henrietta is already at Day 40, almost four weeks after the last dose of drug on Day 15. Alternatively it may have nothing to do with her immune system and be related instead to the underlying genetic defect which I had introduced into Henrietta back when she was at the blastocyst* stage. The gene she is lacking may have some consequences that we don't know about yet. That is the main purpose in building a mouse: to isolate and therefore define the function of whatever gene you have deleted. Paradoxically it is by leaving out a gene that you learn more about its function than when it is present. If the animal dies in utero you know that the missing gene is essential for development and that its absence is lethal, or as they delicately put it, incompatible with life.

Even as I stood there I could see that Henrietta's discharge was already reaccumulating. The eye was practically pasted shut again within a minute. She looked miserable and wasn't moving at all, remaining very still in the corner, in contrast to the other animals who were in continuous motion around her. One of the younger pups in particular was full of energy, running around the small enclosure. At one point he came over to Henrietta. Their mouths touched and then he was off again. With her good eye Henrietta stared up at me, fitfully blinking.

I took a swab to send to micro for culture and sensitivity. Regardless she is going to need antibiotics. I logged on to the computer and put in a stat order for them so that they get here today. Once I had done that I went back over to Henrietta and cleaned her eye again with the baby wipes and

---

* Blastocyst = A thin-walled hollow structure in early development of the embryo. The outer layer of cells gives rise to the placenta while the inner cell mass gives rise to the tissues of the body.

then repeated this several times. It wasn't long before I had gone through the entire packet of baby wipes and decided to go to the CVS pharmacy to get some more. Before I left I separated Henrietta from the other animals. I could have just lifted her out but instead I lifted them out, one by one, and put them into a separate cage. None of the others had any signs of infection. Their eyes are OK.

Outside on First Avenue it was raining like it was the final deluge. I held my lab coat over my head and jogged over to the Tower of Babel. They have made great progress with its superstructure these past few weeks. Still, it is mostly a shell, a glassless, wire mesh, the ribs exposed through vacancies in the scaffolding. At its base above head-height a perimeter platform of planks shields pedestrians from falling hammers. I ran under the platform for shelter. Beside me was a woman with a stroller. She was giving out to somebody on her mobile phone. I looked at the little boy in the stroller with more interest than I normally would. I wondered how far along Yvonne was with the pregnancy. She never specified in her email. The little boy in the stroller had a dinosaur in his hand. It made me think forward a little. If Yvonne has a boy I would tell him about the subway escalator at 63rd Street and – who knows – perhaps even take him there. It is very long and makes loud groaning noises. At night especially it is notice-able against the tiled acoustics of the always empty chamber. A chorus of groans as if the escalator is struggling with the burden of your weight on its back. The sound is eerie, as if there is a herd of sick dinosaurs underneath it. We stood under the platform for a while, the boy's mother on the phone the entire time still arguing with the person on the other end. Then the deluge stopped and it brightened a little and I was able to cross the avenue.

The old woman who works in the CVS is usually a sour old crone but today she was in great form, chatting away cheerfully to the customers ahead of me in the queue.

'Boy or girl?' she said to me when I got up to the register and placed the packet of baby wipes on the counter. I stared at her until it dawned on me what she was on about.

'Girl,' I said, and handed her my debit card.

21

It came as a bit of a surprise this morning at the Concept meeting to discover that Cillian has left for Ireland. It was strange that he hadn't mentioned it when I spoke to him just yesterday, even when I had tapped the packed suitcases which stood by the door of his apartment, assuming they had belonged to his wife. Apparently he had arranged for Cindy from Solter's lab to stand in for him.

Solter didn't know about the last-minute change either.

'I thought the Irish were up,' he said when he appeared in the doorway of the conference room and saw that Cindy was standing by the computer, dressed to the nines in a leopard-skin blouse and short black skirt. She was trying to get her presentation to project onto the wall behind her. The elderly chairperson – Dr Kotz – was up with her trying to help but I doubt if he was of much use. Both his hands were joined behind his back and he was peering down at the computer as if wondering what sort of new modern object it was.

'Cillian had to go to Ireland,' Cindy shouted out from the podium, without looking up from the computer. 'He asked me to do it at the last minute.'

Solter – still standing at the doorway – looked over at me

as if I might provide additional information, which of course I couldn't.

The Concept meeting is held in the Nathan Institute in one of its upper conference rooms. You get great views of the East River from it but somebody always lowers the blinds and we sit in darkness, staring at the PowerPoint presentation on the far wall of the long, narrow room like the Neanderthals in Plato's parable. There are never enough chairs for everyone. In the centre of the room is a large mahogany table covered by a pane of glass stained by the spilt orange juice of a million breakfast meetings. All the senior staff sit around it, Solter typically at the head of the table despite the fact that Dr Kotz is the permanent meeting chairperson (although he is old and semi-retired and ineffectual, and the position is largely honorary or even charitable). Chairs line the walls and the clinical and postdoctoral fellows sit there, myself among them. At the back of the room some medical students and the odd ambitious nurse stand.

The point of the Concept meeting is pretty much as you would assume. You present your Concept, your Big Scientific Idea about curing cancer or treating it, or – as an old boss of mine in Ireland used to say – knocking it back a good bit. You flash your hypothesis in addition to background information and the statistical design up on the far wall on the giant screen, and you stand on a small podium, your projected thoughts beside you framed by the screen like the speech bubble of a cartoon character. But your presentation is not supposed to be entirely conceptual or hypothetical. Rather it is supposed to be based on hard data, ideally that you yourself have generated in the laboratory, and an extension of your experimental observations. If it were simply an idea that you had to draw out of the air, it would be straightforward, even fun. You could easily come up with something.

Solter walked over and pulled out his usual seat. He nodded to everyone around the table. But when he finally sat down he slumped back in a very exaggerated fashion, the arms of the chair going all the way up under his armpits. He groaned dramatically as he did so and a few of the fellows laughed. He can be very theatrical, Solter. Dr Kotz left Cindy to her own devices with the computer and projector and came over and sat across from him at the big table.

'That bad, eh?' he said to Solter.

Solter swivelled his head in Dr Kotz's direction and squinted his eyes at him. He said nothing for a while, but just shook his head slowly. The fellows started snickering again. Solter sat forward then and extended his arm out over the table.

'This time yesterday morning,' he said, 'I was waterskiing on this,' and as he said it he opened out the palm of his hand and held it over the table, allowing it to hover an inch off the glass covering. We all stared at his hand, nobody saying anything, and followed it with our eyes as he moved it slowly palm-down over the glass.

'I tell you,' he said, staring at the back of his own hand, 'It was . . . Just. Like. This.'

We all stared at Solter's hand in silence, easily picturing

the glassy water and the clear sky reflected perfectly in it and the buzz of the motorboat and the fresh morning sun and the dense ring of trees surrounding the lake. There's no doubt about it, Solter would have made a good actor. He has that ability to command fully the space he inhabits, making you take notice of it, and him, as he expands out into every inch of it; whereas for a lot of us we just kind of sidle into the space we inhabit, commanding very little of it.

There was a flash of light and Cindy's presentation finally appeared on the back wall. The spell was broken. Solter pulled his hand back and the lake water disappeared. He sat all the way back in his chair again and turned to look at me.

'Why's he gone to Ireland?' he asked.

'I wouldn't know,' I said.

Cindy's presentation wasn't very good, although I was the only one who seemed to think so. Her concept was mundane, not innovative in any way. She wanted to add an anti-angiogenic agent to a PARP inhibitor, but there was no pre-clinical data in support of it, simply assumptions based on the supposed but completely disparate mechanisms of action of both drugs. Solter loved it, of course. *This has a lot of merit. And how do you propose to . . . ? One issue you may run into is . . . You also may want to consider . . . But apart from that I think you'll be able to . . . You could really learn a lot from this approach . . . blah blah blah.*

Like I said already, Solter is not a natural scientist. He has too much certainty spread out over too many things. Whereas a true scientist can be certain only about very few things and the starting point for any experiment is that you know nothing. (A lot of the time it's where you also end up.) The certainty explains his arrogance, which is a quality I've never understood whenever I witnessed it myself in a medical colleague either here or back in Ireland, and which is one of the qualities the general public probably associate most with senior doctors and consultants. It doesn't really square with how little we know, although it is probably less common now. For the most part I think it probably was not really arrogance at all but a sort of burnt-out fatigue at not knowing very much, or being able to do much, and yet still having the droves in your waiting room with their inexplicable illnesses turning to look at you with their expectant faces.*

In Solter's case his arrogance is at least entertaining a lot of the time, something to marvel at, the pure and impressive fact of it, as if it was a bird hovering over his head, a bird of paradise perhaps, performing – like Sylvia Plath's fingers in that Ted Hughes poem – balletic aerobatics, in some tropical sexual play of display, leaping and somersaulting, doing strange things in the air above his head. Either way it is not the hallmark of a true scientist, for whom the best quality to have is not stupidity exactly, but something that is much

---

* There was a story doing the rounds back when I was a medical student in Dublin. It may have been apocryphal but it involved an ophthalmologist who mainly did private work but once a week staffed a clinic in the public hospital. He famously came into work one day to find the waiting room full of public patients waiting to see him. He said good morning to the clinic nurse and went into his room. When the nurse went in to bring him to the first patient he was nowhere to be seen. The window was open and the curtains were moving with the breeze, suggesting where he had gone.

closer to that than cleverness, which at the end of the day doesn't get you very far. It serves only to help you anticipate the next question so that you can get your answer in quicker than the person next to you, and generally give the impression that you know everything already.

Solter is more of an operative, a mover and shaker, and good in a committee room where he spots opportunities and raises his hand before anyone else, or indeed his voice louder than anybody else; and he is on all the steering committees of all the international cooperative groups. And as I said, he had a lucky break to begin with given that he did his postdoc with the old professor from Grand Rounds who is for sure a genuine scientist and a shoo-in for the Nobel Prize, if he doesn't die first (no small risk given how frail he appeared when viewed up close in the unforgiving light of the canteen). So Solter was lucky with that, to publish with him, although even then his publications are not as impressive as you would expect. For somebody who is the genuine article your publication record should be a bit like a tree, with a thick trunk of articles condensed tightly around the minutiae of some topic. As your career progresses and you get more collaborators (including slaves like me who will do all the work and who then branch off into their own minutiae) you will find your name spread over many different but related article types, hundreds of them, so that the internet will be dotted with your name and so many of your citations and references that – on a PubMed search, at least – you will feel yourself to be as famous as a rock star. But with Solter it is almost as if he skipped the first part (the trunk) and went quickly to that second part where your name appears on a plethora of things into which you had very little input.

Cillian will also be a little like that, I think, in a couple of years. He is very similar to Solter in many ways, although an Irish version, perhaps a little more charming. Both are men of the world, good at the world, their minds moving too quickly for science, working on a different plane, the plane of the world as it exists all around you; whereas the mind of a proper scientist doesn't move very quickly at all. Instead they spend much of the time completely baffled even by the smallest of things. They want to question everything.*

I was therefore not surprised that Solter liked Cindy's concept. He was probably already beginning to think about how to get the funding for it and which of the cooperative groups he would pitch it to and generally set the ball rolling. Which is a different and necessary skill set in itself. The world needs its Solters too.

He turned and stared at me for a few seconds in silence.

'You don't agree?' he asked, catching me by surprise.

The whole room turned in my direction.

'Excuse me?' I said back to him.

* It is like that Yeats' poem 'The Tower', where he talks about pacing around the foundations of a house looking at the ruins and ancient trees surrounding him and he wants to 'ask a question of them all'. It is my father's favourite poem. He can quote the whole thing verbatim from beginning to end and does so at the slightest provocation. Many a bemused visitor to our kitchen down the years has sat as my father reams it off, wondering what exactly it was that they had said which jarred him into doing it. But it captures the baffled state quite nicely, I think. 'I would ask a question of them all.' By the sounds of it he would have made a decent scientist himself, Yeats.

'You don't agree,' he said, although this time it was more of an accusation than a question, despite the fact that I hadn't said anything at all. I hadn't even opened my mouth.

'I didn't say anything,' I said.

'You don't have to,' he said quickly.

It's true that I have one of those faces that can appear contrary, or certainly be open to that interpretation. Stop frowning, was a constant refrain I heard from my mother growing up, and which is very confusing to a child. How do you alter your affect? Especially if underneath it all you are as happy as Larry, or at a minimum, a good, healthy mix of both happiness and sadness, which I read recently is the defining quality of Brazilian music.*

'You don't agree,' Solter said, repeating his accusation. 'You don't agree with her concept. Please. Do enlighten us.'

In addition to him and the room I was aware that Cindy was also now looking at me and I didn't want to be an arse-hole and ruin her presentation – even if I did think that her concept was poorly conceived – and especially if it was something she had thrown together at the last minute. It was a decent thing for her to do, to step in like that. I'm not sure I would have done it myself. I also hadn't forgotten that there was a time when she had been very helpful to me, back when I was just starting out in the laboratory.

'You don't think it will work?' Solter persisted.

---

* Go and listen to Jobim if you don't believe me.

'It's not that I don't think it will work,' I said, with reluctance. 'It's just that I don't see any evidence why it should work.'

'But each mechanism is validated,' he shot back. 'Proven.'

'Yes,' I said, 'independently, but not the combination. I suppose I just don't see the rationale. Is this not just simply adding drug A to drug B?'

'If both work,' he replied quickly, 'then yes. Two is better than one, right? More is better than less.'

'Why?' I said.

'There should be an additive effect. Even synergy.'

'Why?' I asked, and Solter just looked at me without saying anything.

According to Socrates if you ask the question 'why?' five times in succession you will end up face-to-face with the biggest question of them all. But with Solter I had only gotten through two why's and we were nowhere near any fundamental truths. And the second 'why?' didn't really count, as it was essentially just a repetition of the first. It hadn't progressed out of it, or emerged from his answer. His eyes drifted over towards the Chairperson, Dr Kotz, who nodded back to him.

'All right then,' Dr Kotz said, 'in that case we should move on to the next concept.'

But there was no next concept, there rarely ever is. The meeting was over. Dr Kotz nodded at Cindy and smiled and said thank you very much and her presentation disappeared from the wall, as if the cartoon character had suddenly been shot in the head, its speech bubble collapsed. We filed out of the room in silence.

I was only just back in the lab when my pager went off. It startled Henrietta, who I was holding in the palm of my hand. She opened her eyes and grimaced at its piercing sound. I quickly reached to turn it off and gently stroked the back of Henrietta's neck until her eyes closed again.

Her infection is already worse. The discharge from the right eye is more purulent and the lid far more swollen than it had been even just a few hours before. It also looks like it might be beginning to spread to the other eye, although that eye does not look too bad yet. It still opens freely and is only a little bit bloodshot and oozy. This morning, before going over to the Concept meeting, when I performed my daily weight measurements I decided to leave Henrietta be. The whole time I stood at the sky of the cage looking down at her she barely moved. Her head rested on the floor, her mouth twitched, her body shivered.

I set Henrietta down on the floor of her enclosure and went into the back office to answer my page. It was Solter's secretary. She told me that I was to go to his office to speak with him.

'But I just saw him a little while ago,' I said. 'Up at the Concept meeting.'

'He says it's urgent.'

'OK, I'll be up shortly,' I said.

'He says it's urgent,' the secretary said again.

I put down the phone. Everything is always urgent with Solter.

I rang the switchboard and asked them to put me through to the vet. When I eventually got through to him he didn't seem too concerned about Henrietta's eye.

'It's probably viral,' he told me over the phone, 'given that both eyes are infected. If it was just the one eye then it would be bacterial.'

I told him about the antibiotics I had ordered.

'Antibiotics won't work,' he said, 'not if it's viral. Just keep it clean and it will blow over.'

'Will you come and see her?' I asked him.

'OK,' he said, 'but not right now.'

It sounded like he was out and about somewhere. There was traffic and street noise in the background and the wind trying to get into the receiver was like a wordless voice trying to interrupt our conversation.

'Make sure you separate her from the others,' he said.

'I already did that,' I said.

I decided to try the antibiotics anyway. I went out to the hallway to get them. There must have been ten packages for Deep, all of various sizes. It was only when I spotted them that I realized I hadn't seen him in several days. I stood still for a moment, a little shaken by the realization, not so much out of concern for Deep, but at how distracted I must have been not to notice his absence. I rummaged around the packages. Some of them had fragile stamped on them, but I didn't think there was any cellular or organic matter that needed special storage, for instance requiring placement in the minus eighty freezer like he had done for me a few weeks ago. The packages looked more like equipment, which can presumably wait for him to get back from wherever he is. I can't imagine where that would be. It is very unusual for him to be away even for one day, never mind more than that. The drosophila seem to sense that something is up. In retrospect their droning in recent days has been at a slightly different frequency, making it hard to concentrate. I have had to keep the office door closed but still the sound permeated through the fabric of the walls, as if the drosophila had escaped and were burrowing into the plaster. This morning I even went and stood in front of their green tank, staring in at them through the mesh that surrounds it.

When I got back into the lab I daubed both of Henrietta's eyes gently with a damp baby wipe, then held each of them open and dropped in the antibiotic ointment. I gave her an extra couple of drops in each eye just to make sure. Then I held her eyes closed and her head tilted back for a few minutes in order to allow the ointment to really sink in. Afterwards I placed her back in the cage. It was difficult to find a way to hold her so that it wouldn't hurt her. One of the tumours is beginning to ulcerate through the skin. So it was awkward.

'Hi, doctor, do you need any more fluid?'

It took me an instant to react to the voice, which came from a woman in a wheelchair. Her face was swollen and she was looking up at me with a wide open face. I had no idea who she was and I just stared back at her. We were standing in front of the main bank of elevators, waiting for them.

'You remember taking some of it?' she said.

'Of course,' I said, and as I said it her face became a little familiar and then I recognized her as the woman from a couple of weeks ago, who would have made a good subject for Velazquez. Her face was even more bloated, however. She was clearly still on the steroids.

'But no, I'm fine, thanks,' and I laughed a little.

Her face looked at me in earnest. There was an older woman standing behind the wheelchair. She was wearing impenetrable sunglasses, large, densely black ones which were more like a visor. She was carrying a green shoulder bag. The visor focused on me for a few seconds. I nodded at her and she nodded soundlessly back.

'Let me know if you need any,' said the woman. 'I'd sure like to get rid of some.'

'I will,' I said, instinctively looking down at her abdomen. It was now extremely swollen and could no doubt do with a drainage procedure. The older woman leaned over and picked something, a bit of fluff or a dead or dying insect, from her shirt. She was wearing an all-white thin silk tracksuit with a giant blue star and the word 'Venus' on the back.

When the elevator doors opened I let them go first, the older woman reversing in and pulling the chair after her. Others also got in. The doors closed again and we all stood and listened to the sterile jazz that they are always playing here, piping it through the entire building like an odourless soporific, not just through the lifts but through the phone system and corridors also, no doubt to soothe or anaesthetize the patients as they wander stunned from the CT scanner. In my opinion they should be blasting out Coltrane in a place like this, especially those final weeks and months of his career, after he got sick and knew the end was near and had to sit in a chair to produce those searing notes which are almost unlistenable to.

The patient rested her head back and closed her eyes. I noticed that there was an oxygen tank fitted to the back of her chair. The lift started to rise slowly. I looked down at her face in which it was easy to see the deterioration. There were telltale signs that anyone could spot – a clarification of the skull, for example – but also more subtle ones that you'd need to be a professional to notice – slight icterus of the sclera, spider naevi, some peripheral cyanosis on the lips, neck swelling related to the steroids – and which you get into the habit of looking for instinctively, after all the years of doing it on a day-to-day basis. If possible I would like to lose that skill.

The lift stopped at Diagnostic Imaging. A porter got on carrying a capped Styrofoam cup in a bucket of ice, rap music coming out of his cheap headphones, thankfully drowning out the elevator music. He got off at the next floor, Pathology, taking his cargo with him, no doubt some human part for analysis, his music following him like a swarm of metallic wasps about his head. We passed silently through and above Paediatrics before stopping at Five, which said OP5 beside it in a large, handwritten note Sellotaped to the underlying metal.

The lift door opened. I let the others get out first. The patient woke up and was a little disorientated. She had forgotten that I was behind her. The woman with her wheeled her off without saying goodbye and I walked behind them at a slower pace. The doors of the lift closed over behind us, leaving Kenny G or whoever it was, condemned – I would like to think – to going up and down in it forever like Sisyphus.

Solter's office door was open and his secretary wasn't about so I went straight in. He was speaking on the phone and when he saw me he bade me with his right hand to come in and sit on the very low chair in front of his enormous desk. I would say the chair is purposefully low and I had to crouch down quite a bit in order to ease into it. I wouldn't be surprised if he has a little platform on the other side where he sits. The surface of the desk was bare apart from a large white Mac and one of those small, annoying ornaments that swing backwards and forwards with gravity, never stopping once they get started. When he put down the phone he looked up at me.

'Welcome to my paperless office,' he said, even though I'd been to his office several times before.

But now I saw it truly was paperless, a new development. There wasn't a scrap of paper to be seen. He'd even gotten rid of his row of thick textbooks which usually stood on the shelf in a row behind his head like praetorian guards protecting his back. He was always neat, Solter, far more so than Dr Harding, for example, in whose office you could barely move for the stacks of paper, some of which would have yellowed from the sun and had no doubt been there for decades.

'I didn't know you were an environmentalist, David,' I said, and he laughed and I was relieved that he appeared to be in a good mood. The one-year extension I applied for some months back hasn't been approved yet.

'Sooooooo,' he said, and he leaned back in his chair, his hands behind his head, all the time maintaining eye contact with me. Then he didn't say anything but continued to simply look at me. I've noticed that Solter uses a similar technique to Dr Harding in this regard, or at least he attempts to: intense eye contact with lots of pauses and silences, although his silences aren't as persuasive as hers. Rather they make you wary, apprehensive, watchful of yourself; as opposed to Dr Harding's silences, which are non-compressive and enticing, like an open field on a warm, sunny day that you are driving past and which makes you want to get out of the car and go out and lie down in it.

In addition Solter doesn't have the right amount of self-possession to carry off the technique properly and make it effective. He is too kinetic, twitching and fidgeting and shaking his head, as if he's dying to get back to doing the talking or the shouting or the accusing which comes more naturally to him. With Solter, when he talks to you in a deliberate fashion like this, with the silences and eye contact, it makes me laugh because I imagine him employing techniques which he has picked up on some management course, rather than these coming to him naturally and blending into his personality down the years as in Dr Harding's case, who I couldn't imagine going to a management course even if it was to save her life.

He broke into a massive yawn.

'Tell me,' he said through the yawn. 'Where do you see yourself in five years? What is the plan?'

'My five-year plan?' I asked.

'Yes,' he said.

'Hmmmh,' I repeated slowly to myself, 'my five-year plan. That's a good question,' I added, as if to buy time, half laughing as I said it. It was typical of Solter to ask such a stock interview question, which tells you nothing worth knowing. Probably he had picked it up at the same management course where they told him about the importance of maintaining eye contact at all times and building little platforms on your own side of the desk so that you can tower over the other person and impress them, or even intimidate them, which of course he never manages to pull off either.

'I have no idea where I will be in five years,' I said after a pause, 'and if you happen to know, don't tell me.'

He laughed. At his back was a window full of direct sunlight. Every time he moved even slightly to one side I got it in the eyes and was blinded. I tried to mirror his positional changes, which were frequent as he's very fidgety.

'You don't have one then? A five-year plan?' he said back.

'No,' I said, adjusting my head again on account of the

sunlight, 'although I hope to stay around here for a little bit longer, if that's OK with you.'

I'm sure Cillian would have had a ready answer for him. Probably he could have given him the long-form version, the ten- or even twenty-year plan, right down to the month or day. And Solter himself of course could no doubt open up his paperless, online calendar and show you entire years that are shaded in and spoken for, which is certainly one approach. It depends on how much of a passenger you want to be as things unfurl (they can't be stopped anyway) or to what extent you wish to intervene in your own life, or – as they're so fond of saying over here – how proactive you want to be.

'Ha!' he said. 'But I'm curious. Are you not ambitious? I mean, you're my age, right, even a couple of years older? Do you want to be doing what you are doing now forever?'

'Probably not,' I replied, 'but that will take care of itself, I think, if you work hard, which I always do.'

There's no way they would understand it, but as regarding the more or less social type of ambition that Solter and Cillian have, I'm completely fine with just being a passenger, albeit an interested one who likes to look out the window and take it all in. Perhaps I get it from my brother Donal, who is of course an extreme case of passengerism, in that he has never had to intervene at all in his own life. (It is one of the only advantages, that and a very sweet nature.) And it has worked out well for him. He sees my parents every day and lives to a large extent still back in our idyllic childhood, which I had to leave after a certain age. And who's to say you can do better than that? When my parents are dead and the two of us sit side by side and tot up how many hours we each spent with them it will be not even remotely close between us.

'But,' Solter continued, 'if you plan it right you can go anywhere. All you have to do is set your sights on something. What you want to do. Then you go and do it. It's very simple, really.'

'I suppose that's one way of looking at it,' I said and I laughed at how earnest his facial expression was. He really did seem genuinely interested in all this, as if he was coming up against an ideology which never occurred to him had even existed: to go with the flow, working hard for sure, buffeted along by whatever currents you happen to drift into but with your eyes wide open.

Solter stared at me for a few moments longer and then he got up and walked over to the window. I thought he was going to pull the blinds down because of the blaring sun but instead he remained standing over there, turning around to look back at me. I could barely see him. He was just a dark silhouette in the centre of the light, standing with his hands behind him on the windowsill. It reminded me of that image of Jesus I have seen where he is standing with the entire sun behind him, Roman soldiers lying at his feet shielding their faces and their melting eyes. There is a mural depicting it in our local cathedral at home. I think it relates to an episode where Jesus moved the sun closer to the Earth to prove who he was, revealing, like Superman, the extent of his powers to the apostles.

'Do you know where I saw myself ten years ago?' Solter shouted out from the centre of the light, 'when I looked forward to this time, the age I am now?'

'No,' I shouted back, my hand shielding my eyes and feeling a bit like one of those Roman soldiers.

'Right. Here,' he said, and as he said it he pointed straight downwards with both index fingers towards the floor.

I assumed that he was being metaphorical and that he meant simply that he had planned on being a consultant physician, or head of a laboratory as he is now – obviously no small achievements – or else that he had intended simply to be working in this world-famous institution, that is number one pretty much every year on those ridiculous league tables they have and which also tell you very little worth knowing.

But that's not what he meant at all.

'This used to be old Kotz's office,' he said, still with his index fingers pointing downwards to the floor. 'I came to give Grand Rounds when I was finishing up my postdoc and afterwards old Kotz invited me up here for coffee. You may not believe it but he was a piece of work in his day. You think I'm bad? Jeeze. The fucking place would jump to his command.'

'Dr Kotz?' I said. 'I can't picture it.' And I really couldn't, especially when I thought of him as he was this morning, standing up by Cindy's computer with his hands behind his back, blocking out the light so that she had to say to him, plainly irritated, 'It's OK, thanks, but I think I've got it.'

'I came to see him,' Solter continued, 'and I stood at this exact spot and looked out this exact window – which was his window then – and I said to myself: I will stand here again someday and it will be my office.'

'Well, it is a nice office,' I said looking around, and I meant it sincerely. It had nice views of the river that certainly Dr Harding's office doesn't have. I wouldn't say that she is much of a planner either.

Most people are like me, I think. Solter and Cillian are in the minority, although it seems to be a rapidly expanding minority, particularly in places like New York where in many ways the future is as definite as the past and the present is at its screaming loudest. People come at you all the time with their opinions, their heads lowered and aimed at your chest like Zidane. You are even being invited nowadays – and sometimes forced – to look into their dreams, which are the size and shape of websites, bright and shiny like newborn deer's eyes. There is something almost touching about it. Whereas most of us are just happy to keep our heads down and not get in the way too much and to simply get through today and tomorrow and wait and see how things pan out after that rather than planning it all from a ridiculous distance of five or ten years, right down to the office you will sit in (on a small platform, behind an enormous desk) or stand in, looking out at a biblical sun hovering outside your window.

'Well,' Solter shouted over to me from the window, 'I was hoping that perhaps you may consider staying here for a while. In New York. Because we'd like to offer you a job. A staff position. Junior faculty.'

'Really?' I said.

I was stunned.

'As you know,' Solter said, 'we're all moving over to the new research institute.'

In actual fact I did not know this. It was news to me. Solter must have seen this in my face because he pointed out the window at the Tower of Babel which I now noticed was visible off to the left. It gleamed like a needle.

'We're reorganizing the branch,' he said. 'I'm heading up a new translational science division. Trying to translate our lab work into an early phase clinic.'

At the mention of 'translation' I immediately thought of Marya, who I haven't seen since last week and who hasn't responded to any of my emails.

'We're going to have a much bigger lab over there,' Solter was saying. 'I'm bringing over staff scientists, postdocs, epidemiologists, molecular guys, bioinformatics . . . Essentially everyone, a full crew.'

'Like Noah and his boat,' I said.

Solter stared at me and shook his head slightly.

'There's a lot of opportunity,' he said, 'is what I'm saying.'

He turned around to look over his shoulder at the rapidly approaching sun, which really did appear to be coming closer to the Earth. In fact it now seemed to be hovering just outside Solter's window.

22

Of the paintings they have hanging in the small, L-shaped corridor outside the canteen, the one on the far right is the best. None of the others are much good. This one is a nude, roughly painted with a knife, of an elderly woman, I think, but it could just as easily be a man. The artist wasn't interested in their gender, but in their decaying body. The figure is about to break into a scream or a howl. The dark parts of its body appear burnt, real blood used, you imagine, real bone fragments crushed using a mortar and pestle. Two weeks ago I stood in front of Marya here and thought how easy it would be to lean over and kiss her. That seems like a long time ago now. I haven't seen or heard from her since the restaurant. Similarly there's been no further word from Yvonne, not since her email last Friday. I stared at the painting. I can't make up my mind if they should have more or less of this stuff hanging up around here. Perhaps it is only the foolish well who need this type of reminder, like the rawness that fills your lungs when you breathe too deeply. A reminder that you are not here forever, or even for all that long; that it's just you and the dimensions of the bone muscle box you're born into, confined by, totally dependent on.

'You here for the special?'

When I turned around to the voice I saw that it was Jorge Seabat, the radiologist. He was carrying a tray.

'Yes,' I said, 'what is it?'

'It's OK. The usual. Turkey, et cetera. You on call, I presume?'

'No,' I said, 'I live across the road.'

'What? You're crazy! If I had the choice I could think of a million places,' he said. 'I mean, it's Thanksgiving, dude!' he added then, which I had completely forgotten about.

'You're not an American either,' I said.

'Whatever. It's Thanksgiving! Get yourself downtown or something!'

'Right,' I said.

'Hey, that reminds me,' he said, as he started to walk off, 'you still doing that study, right? Collecting the fluid?'

'Yes, Jorge, still doing it.'

'Tomorrow at eleven,' he said. 'Got another one for you.'

'All right, thanks.'

'Enjoy the turkey, dude!' he said, and he continued around the corner.

I stood looking at the painting for another while. Then I headed off.

23

Deep got married. When I arrived at the lab this morning he was back sitting in front of his computer, a million miles away, leaning forward on his elbows and staring into the depths of space. He has changed his screensaver again. The Orion nebula has been replaced with some other astronomical scape, far bleaker in its appearance but more realistic. It looks like the outermost edge of the universe. You can practically feel the sub-zero temperature on your skin. Deep didn't look up when I came into the room.

'Ah, Deep,' I said, 'I was just going to contact the police about you.'

'Why?' he said. 'I d-d-didn't do anything.'

I laughed. It was good to see him, I have to say.

'I mean because you had vanished,' I said. 'I didn't know where you were.'

He kept his back to me, staring into his computer.

'What's that?' I asked him.

'It's a b-b-b-black hole,' he replied.

I went over to sit at my computer and opened up my email. Still nothing from Yvonne. Over the past few days I've attempted to write to her. But each time I discarded the draft.

I started another one now but it was useless. It was hard to write anything that didn't quickly become a list of questions. And for most of the questions I had I was apprehensive about the answers. I wrote a message saying, 'When can we talk?' but even that I deleted.

There were two messages from Solter. He wants me to do another analysis on some frozen cells, from the same patients as before. Although this time he is more interested in NK* cell function, their frequency and absolute numbers. His second email said ASAP with about ten exclamation marks after it. You have to laugh. Deep was standing by my shoulder. It gave me a fright.

'In a-a-a-a-a-actual fact,' Deep said, 'I got m-m-m-m-m-married.'

'Really?' I said, turning my chair around to face him, but also to give myself some space. 'That's great. Congratulations.'

'It was in C-C-C-Connecticut. My p-p-p-parents arranged the whole thing. Would you like to see a p-picture?'

'Absolutely!' I said and I got up and followed him over to his computer. He sat in his chair and opened up one of his files. A girl appeared on the screen. She was standing alone in traditional Indian dress, wearing a red sari. It was the same picture he had had open a while back, with the door of the office closed. At least his parents had shown him what she looked like in advance. She was really beautiful.

---

* Natural killer cells. They are part of the innate immune system, meaning that they are amongst our most primitive and ancient defences. They are fairly non-specific, primed always to go on the attack, at the sight of any old red rag that is waved in front of their faces.

The next picture he showed me was from the wedding itself and it made me almost fall on the ground laughing. It was a picture of Deep sitting on a white horse. He passed over it quickly but I made him go back. In the photo Deep was wearing an elaborate gold-sequinned costume, and hunched over, grabbing onto the reins of the horse for dear life.

'I l-l-l-l-l-look ridiculous,' he said, and let out a sigh.

I went down to Solter's lab to get the cells that he wants me to analyse all of a sudden. I'm not sure what the big rush is; the cells have been frozen for over ten years. Perhaps he has heard on the grapevine that somebody else is thinking of looking into the exact same thing. His lab was a hum of activity. All the machines seemed to be on at full tilt and the postdocs were moving around the place all business, most of them wearing headphones and listening to music. You have to hand it to Solter, he really knows how to motivate a work-force. There was no sign of Cindy, whom I was hoping to run into. I wanted to make sure there were no hard feelings over her Concept review, which in any case got approved. I did a lap of the laboratory looking for her but she wasn't around.

I climbed the small ladder of the liquid nitrogen vat and, with the thermos gloves on, lifted the lid off. I moved quickly as the freezing mist engulfed me and nipped at my ears and neck. I removed the box I was looking for and took out the small vials of frozen cells, placing them in a small metal basin which I had prefilled with liquid nitrogen to ensure they didn't thaw out too rapidly. I replaced the lid of the vat and took off the gloves.

When I got back upstairs I took the samples under the hood, where I thawed them out in the water bath and then emptied the contents into separate red-top tubes, each containing saline. I spun them down in the centrifuge and discarded the supernatant, after which the cells were compacted into small, visible pellets at the bottom of the tubes. There were twenty-five samples in total. They all had the acquisition dates written on the side of the little plastic tubes, in addition to the medical record number, which I wrote into my lab book. The dates were all from over ten years ago – when the blood samples had been taken and the patients were alive and undergoing treatment. I recorded all the dates in my lab book: 11 March 2000; 13 June 1999; 30 May 2000; 4 Oct 1999, et cetera. Each date meant nothing to me; I had no idea where I was or what I was doing for any of them.

That thought was one of my wife Yvonne's constant preoccupations. She found it galling, almost repulsive, that there were whole tracts of time she couldn't recall. 'June 1989,' she might say. 'I have no clue what I was doing then. It might as well not have happened,' and she would go quiet, stunned by the realization that even a whole month could have been skipped and it would have made no difference. That you are liable to have no memory of it. You may not want to admit it but not much happens in your life from day to day, there aren't all that many significant days, and most of them could as easily not have happened. And even of the significant days there are only a handful of moments that you vividly recall. It was no doubt as a result of this type of thinking that Yvonne attempted to mark every day, plant a flag in it like a negotiated peak.*

I added some staining antibody to the cells and – after incubating them for forty minutes and washing them a couple of times – I left to take them to the flow cytometry machine, which is in a separate room on our floor. As I was leaving, Deep appeared at the door of the back office and shouted out to me.

'Are you going to the m-m-m-m-machine?'

'Yes,' I said.

'I'll come with you.'

'OK,' I said, remembering that he had previously asked me to show him how to work the flow cytometer.

I stood by the door and waited for him. Then we left the lab together and turned to the right and along the long corridor that points east towards the river.

As I prepared the machine – turning it on, opening up a new experimental layout, setting the data acquisition, adjusting the cytometer settings – Deep sat on a little stool by the computer and watched closely everything I did. He had

---

* One Friday we drove to Maynooth. She'd told me to pack a weekend bag. I assumed we were staying in an inn for the weekend, possibly Carton House which is out that way. But she pulled up at an airfield. She chatted familiarly with the man in the office. I had known vaguely that she had her licence. We went out to a small plane and climbed into it. She flew us to Normandy. Evidently she had done it many times. We stayed in a guest house where they greeted her like family. There was a picture of her and her father on the wall, with other previous guests.

brought a notepad with him and took notes with one of his biros. I primed the machine and labelled all the channels. Eventually I started the run and I sat down too, watching as the small mechanical arm sucked up each of the wells containing the cells. Instantly the cells appeared in swarms of different colours on the screen. Deep inhaled sharply when that happened. It is a striking sight. The cells were a teeming multitude of freely mobile luminescent dots lit up by the fluorescence and made to dance in their millions by the voltage in real time across the computer screen. They seemed to have sprung back into life, like a terracotta army released from their clay, so much so that it was easy to forget that the patients they came from were all long dead. I set the gate so that I could identify the population I wanted, based on their antibody expression. They glittered on the screen surface in a bright green colour. They looked full of energy as they buzzed in the gate I chose, feeling the light of the world on their faces once more. There must have been a million cells dancing across the screen at any one time. Deep leaned forward close to the screen, staring into it, utterly absorbed. He stopped taking notes. At one point, he turned to me and smiled.

Jorge Seabat walked past as I was standing in a line at the receptionist desk behind a group of patients and their relatives. I was waiting to ask which room he was in, but as soon as I saw him I left the queue and continued after him. He must have sensed my presence because he turned around and spoke to me.

'Hey, good timing,' he said, 'we're just about to get started.'

'What's the case?'

'Someone young,' he said. 'Breast cancer. Not our first procedure on her.'

As he spoke he pushed in the heavy door of the procedure room and then stood holding it open for me.

'After you,' he said and I said, 'Thanks.'

The room was very bright. Directly across from the door the X-ray viewer had been left on even though there was no film hanging up on it and the glare was unnatural and hard on the eyes. The nurse looked at me and I said hello. There was a patient in a gown sitting on the examination table. I saw straightaway that she was young. Her bare skull was bluish. She wore a white dressing gown, but underneath it there was a bright red T-shirt. She smiled at me and I stared back at her face, which was familiar to me.

'Hello, postdoc,' she said.

I stood in the centre of the room. From behind me I heard Jorge's voice, asking me to move because I was in his way, but his voice seemed very distant. He had to ask me twice or three times. Then I felt a touch on my arm. 'Sorry,' I said, 'sorry', and my own voice also sounded distant to me, as if it was a pre-recorded version of it. Jorge pulled over the trolley containing the sterile procedure pack, which was already opened. I leaned back against the sink.

'Long while no see, right?' said the girl.

I briefly glanced at her and quickly looked away. I didn't

know where to look but I didn't want to look at her.

The nurse tapped me on the shoulder to signify that I was now in her way. I said 'sorry' again, 'sorry', and went and stood on the other side of her so that she could access the trolley. She checked something underneath the trolley and expressed some frustration then walked out of the room. Jorge called after her and, taking off his gloves, he followed her. Marya and I were now alone. At my shoulder was a locked cabinet that jutted out from the corner. I leaned against it, allowing it to cut into my shoulder, so that the point of it went right to the bone. Marya was sitting on the edge of the examination couch, draped in a surgical gown. I did not remember seeing them exchange it with her dressing gown. There was an intolerable silence and I could tell that she was looking at me.

'I'm sorry about the other week, postdoc,' she said. 'At the restaurant. I should not have gone in first place. I felt shit, to be honest. All the day before. I knew. I knew that it all start again. I had been good before. But I know. I know sign, postdoc. Even before CAT scan. That's why I call my brother, be on phone with him so much, you know. GET BACK TO HOSPITAL he shout and scream at me over and over. I was scared, postdoc. Anyway, I'm sorry. You must have thought I was some crazy weirdo.'

Just then the door opened and Jorge and the nurse came back into the room.

'Now we're ready!' Jorge said aloud. The nurse was carrying some sterile packs and she placed them under the trolley. She then went up to the girl and arranged her gown by pulling it to one side, exposing an area of skin. Jorge concentrated on pouring the antiseptic into the sterile container. The nurse gave Marya a pillow to hold in order to increase the curvature of her spine as she bent over in the erect position, and Marya did so without being told. Clearly she knew the drill. Her exposed skin was pure white. It was the brightest surface in the room, even brighter than the X-ray viewer. With his feet Jorge pulled his stool up beside the girl and sat on it. He turned towards the procedure table and using plastic forceps daubed the cotton wool in the antiseptic.

'So I see you know each other,' Jorge said, speaking to Marya. 'He is going to take some of the fluid that I remove, if that's OK?'

'Sure, postdoc can have as much as he wants,' she replied and she smiled at me. I looked away.

Jorge cleaned the exposed area with the Betadine. The pure white skin turned brown. The edges of the surgical gown turned black from the Betadine also. Then he administered the local anaesthetic and Marya's back straightened a little but she didn't say anything. The familiar yellow fluid appeared quickly in the twenty-ml syringe. Jorge reached back for another, bigger syringe and inserted it, drawing out the fluid. I was glad that he didn't ask how much I wanted. When he removed the syringe from the body he turned towards me and untwisted the green 22-gauge needle. I went over with the two plastic tubs and collected the fluid, surprised as usual by the small warmth of the tubs. I took them over to the bench and tightened the lids. My hands were shaking. Jorge was speaking to Marya and she replied but I couldn't focus on what they were saying. It sounded like a foreign language. I put the two jars in the case. I said 'Thanks.' Then I went out the door without saying anything else.

I went through the heavy door under the sign that said EMERGENCY and entered the stairwell. It was cool in there. The air was damp and the walls were unpainted cement. Thick pipes came up at me through the steps and ran up along the walls. The steps were a severe sharp-edged metal and the gap between each one was substantial. If you fell you would split your head and the thick, bright blood would collect in shallow puddles. You would most likely lie there for hours or even days until some maintenance person came across you.

I began to descend, slowly at first then quicker. I fell into a rhythm, faster and faster, until that was all there was and all thought was banished. It seemed to take forever to reach the ground floor but I would have been pleased to continue on down and down. I pushed on the heavy bar of the emergency exit door and entered the lobby area where the security guards sit. They looked up when I came out. No one usually comes out that way, not unless there is an emergency, just as the sign says. Some of the usual smokers were standing to my left at the back entrance. The man with the sign: ST MICHAEL PROTECT AND SAVE US. Also the moody clown. He stared at me with his painted smile and blew cigarette smoke out his nose.

I stood and got my breath back. The rain and hail from earlier had stopped. The air had lost its violence. After a while I went back up to the lab and placed the samples in the fridge.

I spent the rest of the day in the subway, hiding in its dark catacombs like the early Christians. At West 4th I watched a man get trapped in the jaws of the doors as he tried to squeeze in. They opened and closed on him repeatedly as if they were trying to get a good hold. The rest of us watched without intervening. The jaws then swallowed him whole, spitting him onto the floor of the carriage. His momentum made him fall to his knees. From a small unseen speaker in the ceiling the voice of God rang out full of static: DO NOT OBSTRUCT THE DOORS REPEAT DO NOT OBSTRUCT THE DOORS REPEAT DO NOT OBSTRUCT THE DOORS.

The man got to his feet and raised a fist to where the voice had come from. He started shouting back at it. 'He can't hear you, man,' someone called out from behind me.

The man sat down.

I stayed down there for hours until it was dark. When the train got out to the outer boroughs and above ground I got off and then went in the opposite direction back into the city. A group of sports fans got on. There were hundreds of them, all in blue, getting on at different stops. I stood in their centre amongst them. We were all packed in. There wasn't an inch of free space. I felt the bodies all around me, pressing from all sides. When the train stopped or jolted we were thrown forward and then backwards together as if we were all part of the same organism, comprising its soft insides and protected by its outer hard shell as it scraped up against the black walls. The sports fans whooped and cheered as we roared into the blackness and I stood facing forward. They got off at Madison Square Garden and I got off with them. We stood in silence as the packed escalator carried our weight on its back. It felt good to be in amongst them walking up out of the subway and along the sidewalk. There were so many of us that some people walked on the avenue and cars had to give way. When we got to the entrance of the arena I hung around for a while. I considered buying a ticket to whatever event they were going to but then I didn't.

24

Henrietta's eye is back to normal but I fear that her general condition is worse. I saw this morning when I weighed her that her weight was down a touch compared with the mean of the last few weeks. I thought also that I could detect a slight limp. She seemed to be favouring her right-hand side. I stood for a good long while observing her as she moved about. Even though it is the weekend I'm glad I came in to check on her. Both days, actually. She was also more lethargic, less interested in her surroundings, although some of that is personality, present at baseline. Even when she was at her best Henrietta would generally stick to her favourite corner, nonplussed. If she was human I would say that she had a tendency to wallow. To mope about the place like a teenager, as if to say this is such a boring experiment, I'm so over it. Considering how many experiments she has taken part in she may have a point. I read on the internet that at one time they even brought some of the HeLa cells into space on the Shuttle. You can't compete with that. They wanted to see if the cells' growth rate was affected by the change in gravity. I don't think it was.

Notwithstanding her deterioration, there aren't any

specific indications of distress, which it would be important to spot. The manual has a list of them, things that you have to watch out for. If the animal exhibits any of these manifestations they should be euthanized straightaway. It is the humane thing to do, or whatever the mouse equivalent of that word is. A while back I made a copy of the list and Sellotaped it to the wall behind their enclosure. You would be surprised how many possible manifestations there are. Who knew that rodents could be so demonstrative?

The Manifestations are grouped by body system as follows:

APPEARANCE: Piloerection and dull, unkempt coat. Occasional hair loss. Poor skin tension, signs of atrophied muscles on the back, dehydration and weight loss. Eyelids half or fully closed, eyes appear sunken, ocular discharge occurs frequently and can eventually lead to red rings around the eyes.

FAECES: Defecation and urination may occur as a direct response to fear, less evident in the event of pain and long-term stress. Constipation or diarrhoea sometimes occur and indicate angst.

BEHAVIOUR: Animals are initially more alert and aggressive, but later may become passive and unresponsive. Increasing sleep disturbance. They may stop eating and drinking and exhibit less inquisitive behaviour. May become increasingly aggressive and may bite as the pain or stress increase. Fighting back, biting, trying to bite the cause of the pain or the affected area and increased activity are all concerning signs. As the condition deteriorates, the animal becomes subdued or apathetic and isolates itself from the group. Eventually stops responding to surroundings. Stops normal eating and drinking, stops sleeping, stops grooming and scratches a lot. Winces with abdominal pain. Will sometimes damage affected body parts.

POSTURE: Gradually becomes more hunched, often rolled up with the head pressed against the abdomen. Hard, tense abdomen if in abdominal pain. Or extensive swelling secondary to fluid collection. Skews head with earache, for example.

LOCOMOTION: Walking on extended legs is a sign of abdominal pain.

VOCALIZATION: Initially squeaks or squeals, especially when being handled, gradual reduction in noises if the pain or distress continues, unless a sudden painful stimulus is given.

PHYSIOLOGY: Increased breathing rate. Hypothermia is an indication of serious deterioration. A pale appearance can indicate anaemia or blood loss.

None of these are appreciable in Henrietta, with the possible exception of the slightly hunched posture. But that was also present to a certain extent at baseline. The main thing is that her weight is still within the margin for error. In actual fact that is the most sensitive indicator of her well-being. In addition she is still eating and drinking reasonably well. Yesterday she ate at least ten grams, which was how much I specifically measured out for her. She may have taken even more than that from the communal trough when I put her for a short while in with the others. I thought the company might do her good. And I saw her take some drinking water on several occasions. Her bowel motions are also not different from the other animals. Whilst it is true that she is not social-izing much with them, neither is she hiding from them or fighting them, tearing into them with her teeth and her nails. Anyway she was never particularly sociable, tending to keep herself to herself. I think she is probably a little shy by nature. Maybe that is also part of her genetic phenotype. There is certainly no vocalizing, which I would have easily noticed, and her coat is in a decent condition, apart from where the cancer was injected into her flank and where it is growing. Her red tears have not returned.

I rang the vet again, who still hasn't shown up. This time Switch weren't able to connect me. Apparently he's not around on Sundays. I went on the intranet and put in an email request for a review. It was a complicated process which involved filling out an elaborate online form requiring a lot of information – age, species and genetic strain, original litter size, weight, prior vaccinations, infestations or infections – only some of which I knew, and also some of the details relating to the experimental therapy she has received: drug name, mechanism of action if known, date of last treatment, expected toxicities, drug half-life, method of excretion or metabolism. In the dialogue box I put down the following: Awaiting review. Deterioration evident, but no specific mani-festations of distress.

*

When I heard the loud rapping on the door of my apartment I put down my trumpet and went over to answer it. I thought it might be one of the neighbours asking me to keep quiet, which happens from time to time, less often than it should. But when I opened the door Marya was standing there.

'I saw you practising,' she said, 'from over on the ward.'

Her hair had been restored to her head and it was as thick and blonde as ever, although beneath it her face and body seemed thinner. Then again perhaps I was just noticing it for the first time. I invited her inside.

'So this is where you live like monk?' she said, looking around her as she went over and sat on my small couch. I moved around the room tidying it a little, although it wasn't too bad. I generally keep the place tidy and I am a neat person overall. I went into the small kitchenette and put on the kettle but when she heard this she shouted out to me from the couch.

'Do you have anything to drink? Alcohol?'

I turned off the kettle and looked in the small cupboard above the cooker. There was a bottle of Scotch which was about a quarter full. It had been left behind by the previous resident. I've never touched it but I presumed it was fine to drink.

'Is whisky OK?' I shouted in to her.

'Yes,' she said, 'but only if you have some ice. I can't drink otherwise.'

I poured out two glasses and added some ice before going

back out and giving one of the glasses to her. I sat across from her in the armchair and we both sipped our Scotches.

'I can't stay too long, postdoc,' she said. 'Curfew, you know?'

'Like Cinderella,' I said.

'Yes,' she said, and gave a little laugh.

She placed her feet up on the edge of my small coffee table. Her toenails were exposed, painted bright blue.

'So, anyway, postdoc,' she said. 'I'm sorry that I didn't tell you the whole entire truth, you know. About everything. But what do you expect, right?'

'That's OK,' I said, 'I sort of guessed it anyway.'

'Yeah, right, sure you did! Ha! That's a good one! You didn't have a clue.'

'OK,' I said, 'maybe not. So you're not a translator then?'

'Yes. Sometimes. Like I told you already, there are a lot of Russians here and they don't speak English a lot of them. Perhaps even the majority. So I help out. Now and again anyway. Unofficial. I'm here so much, you see.'

'Why didn't you tell me?'

'I don't know, postdoc. Two reasons, perhaps. But mainly it just happened that way. In fact it was nice, you know, to pretend that everything was normal, especially as things look up . . . For a little bit. And it was nice to not answer question. All the time question, question, that you get here. How are you today, Marya, how are you? Oh my God, if someone ask me that one more time I scream! Especially the Americans, you know? How are you? And then they look at you with long horse face and full-on eye contact. They're so extreme, you know? Uccch! Leave me alone, I want to say!'

Both of us laughed.

'Anyway,' she continued, 'it runs in the family. My mother she die of same thing, eight years ago. Back in Russia. She have mutation also.'

'BRCA?'

'Yes. Bracka. I get it from her, actually. Not her fault, though. You know, they say the Jews are cursed. It is not true, only some of us are. The ones who have this thing stamped on our DNA.'

She leaned forward then and looked about the room. She was about to say something but stopped and yawned, making a loud noise. Then she stood up and walked over to the window where the blinds were up. I remained in the armchair and my eyes followed her, evaluating her from behind, as if they belonged to the gaze of a third person in the room with a separate agenda of his own. Is there any situation where that gets switched off?

'So this is your view,' she said, her arms stretched out on the ledge, 'where you stand?'

'Yes,' I said and I stood up and walked over to the window and stood beside her. The entire flank of the hospital was lit up as ever like an enormous ship. At night it is easy to imagine the whole building adrift out on some Arctic sea, moored in black ice and separated from the rest of the world.

We stood for a while in silence. It was the usual night-time scene over there. Nothing much was happening. The odd partial figure was discernible in a window here and there.

'Who are they?' Marya asked.

I looked to where she was indicating, in the other direction. A group of doctors in scrubs were walking along the east corridor. They were pushing the crash trolley, but judging by their relaxed demeanour they were most likely returning from an arrest rather than on their way to one.

'Looks like the crash team,' I replied.

'What is it?'

'They run to the scene of an arrest, when someone collapses or becomes unconscious, to try and revive them and save them.'

'But just in the hospital, right? Not out in general world?'

'Yes, just in the hospital. Or directly outside it,' I said, and I had a momentary glimpse of Mrs X's bright red shoes protruding from the base of a scrum of paramedics, all the crowd standing around watching, which is always the way in an arrest. One or two people doing all the work and the rest just onlookers really.

We both turned away from the window and sat back down, her on the couch and me in the armchair. At her back was my enormous bed. I must buy a screen for it, I thought.

'So are you on treatment?' I asked Marya.

'Yes, clinical trial.'

'Which one?'

'It's one that they have specifically for bracka. On the plus side they have figured it out how to treat it better. So maybe you scientists aren't so stupid after all. But it's like a game show, postdoc. They take three of us, me and two more. Then they give us drug, and if OK you can go up to next level. Increase dose. If not OK then you stop. It's like snake and ladder! You have snake and ladder in Ireland? Maybe just Russia, I don't know.'

'Yes, we have it,' I said.

'Anyway, I've had three cycles already. No snake yet, thank God. Just ladder. It's a response. I've seen the scans. Big response. The doctor, he show them to me on the monitor. The first time he showed them to me, my lungs on the screen, they look like the starry sky at night, you know. I said it to him, hey, it looks just like starry sky at night, kind of pretty actually. But he just stare back. Then he point at the black space and say these are your lungs. And then he point at the stars and say this is the cancer, which was like strange, you know? I mean, you'd think the blackness would be the cancer, right? This I say to him, but he say NO, that is lung. This is cancer. Again pointing. No joke. God of almighty, postdoc, I tell you, he was so serious! Even more worse than you! But anyway, they look nice now, the lungs. No stars. Or if there are any stars they are only small ones.'

'Far away.'

'Yes! Exactly! Far away. Light years away.'

'That's great,' I said.

I did not ask her why it was then that they had needed to drain fluid from her lungs on Friday. Usually there is no need to do that if things are getting better and if somebody's disease is a distant concern, light years off and difficult to see on the monitor. It would certainly have been odd for them to have done that. In addition it is also technically way more difficult, when everything is under control or the tumour or tumours are small and there is less free fluid appreciable. You would be much more likely to cause a complication in that situation or, as it is also called – a little delicately, I think – an adverse event.

'That's great,' I repeated and this time I said it with a little more enthusiasm. I looked at Marya and couldn't help but notice that her breathing was a little heavy.

When you are a doctor and you sit across from somebody who is a patient and they are telling you things – the story of their last few days or weeks, explaining how they felt or what they experienced – you may find your brain flexing and beginning to act a little like a detective, looking for more information. (You say you were breathless, how breathless? How far could you walk before stopping? Was that on the flat or on stairs? Did the breathlessness come on suddenly all at once or did you notice it build up gradually and get worse?) And you can even sometimes find yourself looking for holes in their story, inconsistencies which would suggest that it is not serious (Ah, it comes and goes then, and you've noticed it before, even down the years, therefore it is probably nothing); or alternatively consistencies, which are a lot more damning. (What's that? You say it is there all of the time, and that it is getting steadily worse as each day passes?)

But I didn't want to sit across from the girl like a detective and I didn't want my brain to start looking for inconsistencies or consistencies in her story, and it was nice to simply take it as read that her disease was under control, so that it now looked minuscule on the CT scanner like an expanse of stars, tiny and remote and light years away, against the normal blackness of her lungs.

'That's great, Marya,' I said again, and on this occasion I was aware that I was saying her name for the first time, and I think she noticed it also because she looked at me for a few seconds before she spoke again.

'So you have my cells now, what are you going to do with them?' she asked.

'I haven't done anything with them yet,' I said. 'At the moment they're frozen.'

'Frozen. Like your embryos, postdoc.'

I instantly thought of Yvonne. More and more now I am afraid that she did things the natural way. It would explain why she doesn't want to talk to me. It was foolish of me to jump to those other conclusions where I saw myself as some sort of family man all of a sudden. She has delivered her message and can get on with things now. Her conscience is clear.

'By the way,' Marya added, 'I never told you but mine also are frozen. Not embryo but ovary tissue. I got it done last year just before I started all of this. They preserve your eggs over here. It's routine. I thought they were crazy when they tell me about it. But sure, why not, right? So now, two parts of me are frozen. What are you going to do with your part?'

'Maybe I was going to make a cell line out of them.'

'Like Henrietta.'

'Just like Henrietta.'

'Yes, do,' she said. 'I like it, actually. Immortal Marya. But do me a favour and don't put me into animal, postdoc. I don't want to cause them to be sick.'

Neither of us spoke for a while and she looked around the room, no doubt taking in my efforts at homemaking, which I pride myself on a little, certainly more so than was the case when I was back in Ireland and living with Yvonne. I didn't make much of an effort and neither did she. I wonder if that has changed for her as it has for me, although I think it is harder for people like her who were born into money, because they usually grew up with cleaners or even servants, and with fewer obligations.

'You said there were two reasons, Marya,' I said. 'About why you didn't tell me about your sickness. What was the other one?'

She looked at me and giggled a little, in quite a girlish manner.

'It's a little crazy to say it, to be honest, but basically I thought, y'know, boy girl situation?'

I looked at her without saying anything. She gave a deep sigh before speaking, as if she had little choice but to go ahead and say what she would have preferred not to say.

'I don't know, but I think to myself maybe, you know, he's boy and I'm girl and perhaps small chance that he wants to . . . I don't know . . . but anyway, everything change if he know I'm patient and not normal.'

She said the last part while looking at the floor and now with only one of her feet attached to my little coffee table, as if that sole foot with its painted nails was the only thing stopping her from floating off out the window and back over to the hospital. Neither of us looked at each other. I found myself staring at the painted nails as if they were also the only things stopping me from drifting off, before that foot too became detached from the edges of my coffee table and rested on the floor.

'It's not a question of normal, not normal,' I started to say but she cut me off quickly.

'Yeah, right, talk to the hand, postdoc,' she said, and she held her hand up in the air in front of me before continuing.

'Just so you know,' she added then in all seriousness, 'that I am not here in my official capacity as patient. And also, postdoc, don't forget that I know all about your doctor's speeches. I listen to so many of them, I can probably give myself at this stage.'

I smiled in acknowledgement but was also relieved that she had stopped me in my tracks. The last thing a sick person wants from a well person – especially if that well person is a doctor – is perspective. People can generate plenty of that for themselves, but it must be galling for them to sit and hear it from you, with your countless years ahead of you like an endless patchwork of fields stretching out towards the sun. I once overheard a doctor colleague respond to a patient's question about her prognosis by telling her that she should try to think in a more Eastern way if possible, taking one day at a time and living more in the moment. Fuck you, the patient's polite facial expression said back soundlessly to him. Perspective should be the preserve of the old or the sick or bereaved, in my opinion. The rest of us should just get on with it. Frankly, if in the fullness of your health you need to be reminded to seize the day – or, as is sometimes said, to smell the coffee, or the roses – then you deserve all that comes your way. How can you not know that it might be you tomorrow, sitting in the chair on the other side of the desk that is barricaded by a pile of medical journals which is getting bigger every day? Personally I could do with having a lot less perspective, and smelling the coffee, or the roses, to a much lesser extent. It would be very much better for me if I could learn to take a little more for granted the coffee and the roses and also the Scotch as it melted the ice in my glass, just enough to take the harshness out of it.

Marya said she had better be getting back to the hospital to make her curfew. It had been set by the nurses at ten o'clock. When we stood up we were standing close together and it seemed natural for us to lean towards each other and allow our lips to touch, and it was pleasant because hers were cold. We both opened our eyes as we kissed and I was able to look directly into them for the first time. It was still impossible to describe their colour, except that both eyes were slightly different and their many tints added up to a colour that was rich and beautiful.

She stayed a little longer after that and we did finally move over to the territory of the large bed, which groaned with relief when we eventually made our way onto it. She did not seem breathless at all then and it was easy for us both to forget certain things for a while. She did not spend the entire night but she was late heading back over to the hospital, which nevertheless was still lit up like a docked ship, waiting patiently for her to reboard it. She would not have made her 10 p.m. curfew. She would not even have made Cinderella's midnight one.

25

When the door to the lift opened on my floor, Siobhan Deasy – Cillian's wife – was standing inside it. She looked up and saw me but did not say anything.

'Hello, Siobhan,' I said, but she didn't reply.

I walked into the lift and stood opposite her and the door closed. We stood in a tense silence. Between us in the carpeted floor was a dark patch made no doubt by one of the building's dogs. Siobhan reached over and pressed the button for the lobby, which was already lit.

'Where's Cillian?' I asked, turning towards her.

She didn't reply at first.

'What?' she said then, even though she had clearly heard me.

The elevator stopped a couple of floors down but when the doors opened nobody got in.

'He was supposed to present at the Concept meeting last Wednesday,' I said. 'But he wasn't there.'

The elevator doors closed over again and we descended.

'He's in Ireland,' Siobhan said, but in a very strained manner, 'at a job interview.'

I got the impression that she was holding something back

and keeping what little she did say under tight control. But she wasn't able to maintain that control for very long because she then added: 'Why don't you get that bitch of yours to stay away from him?'

At that moment we arrived in the lobby and the doors of the lift opened. A crowd of people wearing suits were standing waiting. Siobhan barged out through them. I paused for a moment before following her, fighting my way through the crowd which extended all the way to the security desk. I caught up with her at the corner of the lobby.

'What did you say?' I said to her and we went out through the sliding doors together into the cold, sunlit morning. Spikes of glare refracted off the glass and metal of the passing cars on York Avenue like a thousand machetes slicing the air around me. A large truck went by engulfing us in its sound. Siobhan just stared straight ahead with her jaw clenched as if she was biting down hard on something. She took a few more steps forward. I was about to reach out and grab her arm to get her to stop when she stopped of her own accord and turned to me.

'What are you saying?' I asked, barely able to believe or even grasp what I was hearing.

'Do you mean Yvonne?' I asked when she didn't reply. 'My Yvonne? Back in Ireland?' And of course it seemed ridiculous to say 'My Yvonne'.

'Like you didn't fucking know?' Siobhan spat back.

I said nothing.

'The whole of fucking Ireland knows, sure. Getting her

fucking tentacles in. She's been stalking him from day one when he was her intern. And she's still at it. He showed me her email the other day; she was looking to try to meet him when he was home.'

She stood up straight and folded her arms. I noticed for the first time how tall she was. We were almost the same height.

I looked at her without comprehension, and she must have finally noticed this because her face changed a little and she gave a short, joyless laugh.

'You have no fucking clue, do you?' she said.

I stood looking at her.

'You actually have no fucking clue,' she said again, genuinely surprised.

I found it hard to focus on what she was saying. She stood in front of me and I watched her frozen face make its movements as a different story started to reveal itself to me, as solid and self-evident as a building that had been there all along but hidden. I felt the collapse in on itself of a set of circumstances I realized now I'd been counting on. There were vast distances at my back. In front a diminished scope. Siobhan's grotesque smile reminded me of the shame of foolishness. It's an old story, when the past is altered and the future laughs in your face.

Neither of us said anything for a few seconds. Siobhan looked at me with contempt, then she turned and walked off. I stood watching after her. In that direction the heatless sun was blinding.

*

I remember once in medical school they got actors in from the Players theatrical group in Trinity so that we could practise giving bad news. We were each given a little card describing a specific scenario, which we had to then explain – acting as the doctor – to the actor who was improvising and pretending to be the patient. My actor was totally over the top. When I told her what the card said – that her chest X-ray had shown a suspicious, cancerous-looking mass on the lung – she completely lost it in a way that I have not seen a real patient ever do. At first she acted stunned for a minute, then she threw herself on the floor, screaming to the heavens. The entire class was watching me on the sidelines. I was supposed to console her or reassure her in some way. But the whole thing was so absurd – she started crawling around on the ground, trying to grab the leg of my chair – that I simply could not take it seriously and started laughing, and I expected everyone else to as well. But nobody did laugh and the professor running the group castigated me from a height, and then failed me on that part of the continuous assessment.

As I stood and watched Siobhan as she walked off I felt a little like one of those actors, and that I had been given a card with a particular scenario written on it. The problem was that I had no idea how to approach the part and what to think of it. I didn't know whether I was supposed to throw myself onto the ground like that actor did and start banging my fists and screaming to the heavens, or to simply remain standing, like

I had at the time, and in a way have been doing ever since, looking down at what was taking place in front of me, baffled and at a complete loss.

26

There was no cancer cure today. In truth I made very little effort at it. I spent most of the morning out on the bench, staring at the never-ending traffic which broke in angry waves against the 67th Street lights. The drivers leaned on their horns for the slightest reason, their vehicles rearing back and howling like furious elephants, nostrils flared, eager to plant their tusks into each other at the slightest provocation. Then the lights would change and all was fine.

At one point the same builder as before came and sat beside me, the one who was present when I first saw Marya. He sat on the bench and smoked his three cigarettes, one after the other, lighting them off each other. Then he wearily got up and trudged back in the direction of the Tower of Babel. I looked after him as he went. He and his colleagues are nearly done with the tower. Somehow they have managed to get a tiny crane up to the apex and are using it to haul the last girders into position. The apex stretches so far into the sky it is barely visible, almost disappearing into the substance of the clouds. I craned my neck back and looked up at it. I could make out the small orange specks of the workers on the exterior, crawling like ants over the structure's pocked surface. The more I looked the more workers I saw. It was as if they were nibbling at the structure rather than building it. Turning it back into dust, digesting it in order to produce the enormous black hole of its foundations again. I saw on the intranet that it is to be officially opened in a couple of weeks. There will be a ceremony. The mayor is coming.

When I got back up to the lab I saw that Marya had called in again. There was another Post-it stuck to my computer, two of them, actually, her message written across both of them:

Postdoc! You're never here. Do you do any work?!
Anyway I would like for you to take me to Central
    Park. Tomorrow OK? If you have the time and are
    not too busy that is :)
Send me SMS OK.

On the second Post-it which was stuck underneath the first one she added:

By the way, I don't like it how Henrietta looks :(

Next door in the laboratory Deep was sitting fast asleep at the bench, his head resting on his folded arms. He sat up when I came out of the office.

'Did you see the vet?' I asked him, but he shook his head. The vet had emailed me earlier to say that today would be a good time for him to drop by.

'That g-g-g-g-g-girl came by . . .' Deep said.

'I know,' I said, and I walked over to the animal enclosure.

Marya was right about Henrietta. Her lethargy is more pronounced. When I picked her up she made barely any reaction or acknowledgement. In addition, her weight appeared to be down. I could immediately tell that even without the electronic scales. She felt appreciably lighter in the hand. I smoothed out her fur with my hand and stroked the top of her head, which ordinarily she likes, but now she didn't even open her eyes. Her tumours, which are breaking through her skin, are not necessarily bigger but they are a different consistency and are easier to palpate and measure.

I took some of the meal from the dispenser and placed it on the inside of a lid which I had taken from a discarded bottle. I found another tiny container and filled it with some water and placed both objects in front of Henrietta. She was shivering a little so I tore off some kitchen paper and folded over a few pieces and left them over her like a cloak to keep her warm.

I sent Marya a text: 'Sure, I'm free tomorrow. I will meet you at the crosstown bus stop on 66th Street.'

It took the vet forever to arrive. I waited for him by the lifts, having told him to get off at the main elevators on the twenty-third floor. I stood by the large windows and stared down into a silent model New York, surprised as always to find any miniature life movement in it – the crawl of dinky cars on the FDR, the tramway floating through the air to Roosevelt Island – giving an automated look to everything; as if everything was part of some general intelligent design and not just certain things. I followed with my eyes the East River's glinting back studded with the odd vessel. Name-checked the bridges. Queensboro. Manhattan. Williamsburg. Brooklyn. In the hazy distance then the Verrazano – a sleek, alien-appearing thing. The Statue of Liberty that I always look for but can never find. I think it's on the other side. The heat off the thick glass was fierce. It makes you remember how strong the sun is, why the old cults made the most sense.

When the vet finally emerged from the elevator he was breathless, as if the altitude's thinned air had really affected him. He practically burst out of the lift and then bent over with his hands on his knees, gasping for air. He was a big, fat man with thick black hair and was wearing dark blue over-alls. He looked more like a maintenance man than a vet. He raised his head a little and saw me.

'Fucking hate those things,' he said, gesturing back towards the lift.

He straightened up then and walked over to where I was standing by the large window. He stood beside me for a few silent seconds looking out of it.

'Spectacular view,' he said. We turned away then and walked down the corridor towards the lab.

'So who does your inspections up here, generally speaking?' he asked.

'The Research Animal Resource Center,' I said, 'They come by regularly.' As I spoke I took out my swipe card but he stopped me.

'Here, let me make sure my card works, in case I have to come back and you're not here.'

I stood back and he swiped his card.

He walked in first.

'Whoo! It's warm in here,' he said.

'Deep here needs it like that,' I said, nodding towards Deep, who was standing by the enclosure. 'It's for his drosophila.'

Deep stared back at us. He did not say hello.

We walked over to the animal enclosures. I removed the lids from them and both of us stood peering down, the vet with his elbows on the ledges. The mice sensed our presence and moved about at an increased pace, apart from Henrietta, who was sleeping. No doubt they were confused by the sudden appearance of now two Godheads in the sky, one of whom had a crucifix dangling down from his hairy chest. It caught some sunlight and burned in the air. The vet reached out and grabbed it and replaced it back inside his overalls.

'I'm worried about this one,' I said after a while, pointing at Henrietta.

The vet lowered his arm and rested the back of his hand against her back.

'Her eye's much better now,' I said, 'that I rang you about originally. But her weight is down.'

'What is it?'

'One hundred grams.'

'That is on the low side. She eating for you?'

'Yes – about ten grams a day. I've been measuring her stuff out separately.'

'What about her sleep patterns?'

'Now and again she's a bit sleepy but otherwise her pattern seems to be the same.'

'Any aggressive behaviour?'

'No. The opposite. She's very lethargic. Lacks interest in her surroundings. But she was always a bit like that, even to begin with. Disinterested.'

The vet looked at me for a long moment and then looked down on Henrietta. He picked her up carefully and she didn't resist his handling. For a big man he had a gentle touch. He held her in close and then held her out from him.

'It's a male, by the way,' he said, then he put her back.

He picked up a few of the other animals in a similar fashion, before replacing them. Then he stood as before with his elbows on the rim of the cage. After a while he turned and looked at me. I started to tell him about the research drug I am testing in the experiment, a multikinase inhibitor, out-lining to him the treatment schedule – the two-week induction course, long since past, the boost and the observa-tion period. 'We're at Day Forty now,' I said. Then I went on to explain the expected toxicities based on previous data. The whole time the vet just looked back at me, seemingly not very interested in what I was telling him.

'Do you want me to take him for you?' he said then.

'Who?' I said and he looked at me without responding.

'Take her where?' I said.

'Where do you think?'

'For treatment?' I asked.

'No,' he replied.

'No,' I said. 'She's not in any distress. I just wanted to see if there was anything extra that I needed to be doing. A change in antibiotics or whatever.'

The vet gave a small shrug and then turned and walked towards the drosophila enclosure. He completely ignored Deep, who remained rooted to the spot and stared back at him. The vet stopped a few feet from the enclosure and stood there for a few silent moments. It seemed like the insects' buzzing got more intense.

'Fascinating creatures,' he said.

I walked him out to the lift and pressed the button to call it. He was a little friendlier now and handed me his card, which had his mobile phone number on it. But when the doors opened he tensed up. He went into the lift and stood against the back wall of it, his arms spread out a bit, his hand palm-down against the metal. He became breathless again and his face was red and moist with sweat.

'Fucking hate these things,' he muttered.

'Claustrophobic,' he added by way of explanation. 'I can always imagine the fucking breakers failing or something and this thing shooting straight fucking down the tube, y'know. Like a fucking dart.'

'Yeah,' I said, 'I can imagine that all right.'

The door closed over.

27

Marya didn't show up. I waited for her on 66th Street by the crosstown bus stop just outside the hospital. It was very cold, though, so I didn't wait long. The sun was strong but heatless. It was one of those days that you get in New York all the time, where the edges of the buildings are delineated extremely sharply and you can't imagine the atmosphere being capable of supporting anything that tried to fly in it, even particulate matter. Directly above me the side of the hospital was a cliff-face of windows stretching up forever. The glass panes of it caught the sun and were pure white sheets, hard on the eyes, as if there was a forcefield around the hospital, emanating from it. It would scarcely surprise me if there was. Last year two window cleaners went to their deaths off its surface. The internet said a rope came loose and their crate plummeted as they were flung to their concrete deaths.

I left after fifteen, twenty minutes. In any case my apartment is just across the street from the bus stop and I figured that I could still keep an eye out for her from there if she showed up late.

And then I did see her from my apartment window,

although she was not down at the bus stop, which was starting to fill with people going home. Instead I saw her across the way in the hospital. She was part of a small group moving along the Bridge of Sighs corridor in the direction of the wards. I recognized her yellow cardigan. She was sitting in a wheelchair and was being wheeled by a man wearing a suit. He was not a porter. Marya's blonde hair was big and even from where I stood I suspected it wasn't fitted on properly.

The man was staring straight ahead. They moved slowly and ahead of them was a nurse with some clothes over her arm and an attendant carrying what looked like luggage. I followed them with my eyes as they went down the long corridor until they finally disappeared from view. A minute or so later the nurse appeared in the window of the small room down to the left in the corner. I saw with dismay that it was the same room the Chinese billionaire had been in a few weeks ago. The nurse opened the wardrobe and hung the clothes in it. I went down to the leftmost window of my apartment to get a better view. The nurse turned around and moved close to the bed although I couldn't see what she was doing. There was also the movement of the attendant and the man in the suit as they assisted Marya getting into bed. Finally the nurse pulled over the television which hung down on a mechanical arm over the bed and she turned it on so that it flickered and glared on Marya's face. The light went on in the room and the man in the suit came to the window and pulled down the blinds. I couldn't see anything any more.

*

I stood in front of the door and was about to knock on it when the young man in the suit spoke to me. He was standing off to the side speaking into a mobile phone. I only saw him at the last moment. He was the same person I'd seen the other week arguing with Marya on First Avenue.

'Are you Berger?' he said to me, his voice raised. 'I want to talk to you.'

'No,' I said, 'I'm not Berger.'

He held the mobile phone away from his ear as he spoke to me. Then he slowly brought the phone back up to the side of his head. He spoke into it in Russian and then hung up. He did not take his eyes off me the entire time. Despite his expensive suit and crisp white shirt there was a wildness to him, the way he stared at me, without inhibition.

'Who are you?' he asked me.

'I'm a friend.'

'Friend? With white coat? What friend?'

I told him my name and held out my hand, which he looked down at first before shaking.

'Where is Berger?' he asked, 'I want to talk with him now.'

'I don't know,' I said.

His phone went off but he ignored it and stared at me.

'I was going to go in,' I said to him.

He took the phone out of his pocket and, answering it in English, he walked off.

I knocked on the door and pushed it open.

'Postdoc!' Marya said. 'I was wondering when you would come.'

She was in bed, wearing her dressing gown. Her yellow cardigan was over her lap and she was using it as a blanket. She did not have her hair on and just like before I had to allow my eyes to adjust a little to recognize her. She did not look well. There were nasal cannulae in place, delivering oxygen through her nose. I went up to her and kissed her on the cheek. It was both warm and cold at the same time.

'Is my brother out there?' she asked. 'You met him, right? Uri?'

'Yes. He's guarding your room, I think.'

'Ucch, he's being ridiculous! He wants to find Berger.'

'Why?'

'Clinical trial didn't work, postdoc. I come across big snake after all just after I left you note. And so last night they stick this big tube into me.' It was only then that I noticed the chest tube emerging from her side. It was draining into a glass box on the floor beside the bed.

'So we ask what next, you know,' she continued, 'and the answer is nothing. For my brother there is no such thing as nothing. He's too much of an American now. He wants Berger to, I don't know, do some crazy surgery or something.'

'Surgery?' I said.

'I know, postdoc, it's nuts, you don't have to tell me that. But he needs to feel like he has something to do.'

'Who? Berger?'

'Ha! More like my brother, but perhaps him also. Anyway,' she continued, 'I'm sorry that I stand you up. I get fever and all this happened. Tube and scan and blood. You have no idea. It's shit, actually. They say disease has progressed. Doesn't feel much like progress.'

'You must have been short of breath.'

'Yes. And all of a sudden too. Did you go to park?'

'No,' I said.

'Why not?' she asked.

'We can go together, when they remove all this stuff,' I said.

'Yeah, right,' Marya said, 'won't be today or tomorrow.'

The door opened and Uri came into the room. He started speaking to Marya in Russian. He sounded agitated, his voice raised.

'English!' Marya said back at him. Uri looked at me and then shook his head very slightly.

'I'm going to call up to his office,' Uri said. 'This is ridiculous. Why don't these people have cellular phone to call? Why?'

'Don't go up there,' said Marya.

'Why not? They fuck everything up, now they fix, that's all. It's simple.'

'No!' said Marya and then she shouted, 'I don't want!'

'I'll be back in less than one hour,' Uri said, and he walked out of the room, closing the door behind him.

Marya slapped the bed in frustration then she bent her head into her right hand. I went over to the window and looked out. You could see my apartment on the other side of the street.

'So,' Marya said after a minute, 'now you meet my brother.'

'Is it just the two of you?'

'Ucch, he's so annoying. He interfere always in everything.'

'Is it just the two of you?' I asked again.

'Yes, yes,' she said, 'ever since our mother died. Our father die years ago, but I don't even remember him. Uri of course must act like big man of house.'

A nurse came in pushing a blood pressure cuff on a stand. She paused when she saw me before continuing up to the bed. She wrapped the cuff of the blood pressure monitor around Marya's arm and pressed the button on the machine. Then she took out a thermometer and put it in Marya's right ear and held it there until it beeped. The blood pressure cuff also beeped and she wrote down the values on the back of her hand with a biro before removing it. She lifted up the chest drain and shook it a little before setting it back down again. She bent and looked at the glass and then wrote down another number also on the back of her hand.

'Hey, postdoc,' Marya asked, 'will you do me favour? I'm sorry to ask but go after Uri, will you? I'm worried about him, that he'll make some scene. I don't know, start fight or something. If possible talk to him, or try, only if possible. I'm too tired to do it.'

Both her and the nurse looked at me.

'Of course,' I said, and I turned to leave the room.

I didn't have to look very far for Uri. He was outside talking to Solter, who was wearing a white coat. Solter caught my eye when I came out of the room and motioned me to come over to where they were standing near the nurses' station.

'I'll tell you what,' Solter was saying to Uri as I approached, 'why don't we sit down over there,' and he motioned towards the patient lounge area which was behind the nurses' station. Uri looked around as if he was being led to a trap. Solter and I walked towards it and he followed cautiously. The area was empty but noisy from one of those vacuous afternoon TV shows. The presenters on the large flatscreen television were prattling away loudly to the empty room. The three of us walked over to the large couch but no one sat down, and Uri seemed reluctant to. I went over to the television and turned the volume down but not off entirely.

'You're not Berger,' Uri said to Solter, 'where is Berger?'

'Dr Berger called me,' Solter replied. 'He asked me to come around to talk with both you and your sister. And you've met my colleague here, he works with me also.'

'Are you surgeon?' asked Uri.

'No,' said Solter.

'I want to get surgical option for Marya,' Uri said. 'It's the only way. We have tried the drugs, the chemotherapy, the . . . the experiment. Now let us try surgical option.'

He stood in front of us with his hands on his hips. Solter looked at him for a long moment without saying anything. He made direct eye contact with Uri and his face looked blank and expressionless. In actual fact his manner reminded me a little of Dr Harding's. I had never seen Solter interact with a patient before. I had only ever seen him in the laboratory or in his office where he is generally an arsehole. We were all still standing beside the couch.

'Let's sit down,' Solter said and he touched Uri on the elbow. 'Please, Uri,' he added.

Both Solter and I sat down, Solter on the couch while I sat on the armchair off the side a little.

Uri looked around and then reluctantly sat down on the couch.

'I've had a look at Marya's X-rays and the scans,' said Solter, 'and I'm afraid there is no surgical option, Uri. For Marya. I wish there was, believe me, I really do. But I'm afraid it would do only harm to her now. It would only hurt her.'

'But that is only chance for cure!' said Uri, leaning forward. 'I've looked on internet and spoke also to friends. Surgery is best chance. Best chance.'

I looked at Solter. He was entirely different from normal. He didn't fidget or shake his head and each word he spoke appeared to have been carefully selected. He also spoke them slowly with plenty of space behind each word, and with no obvious glance to see his own appearance reflected in them as is usually the case. He leaned forward and put both elbows on his knees, making himself very small so that Uri appeared to tower over him. He looked up into Uri's face and after another very long pause he spoke to him.

'I'm sorry, Uri,' Solter said, 'I know she's your sister and you want what's best for her. I'm very, very sorry.'

At first Uri said nothing. He was sitting forward on the

edge of the couch and a little hunched over. I got a glimpse of him as a boy; which is relatively easy with men anyway, to see us as boys, certainly much easier then it is to picture women as girls. Probably because we act more and pump ourselves up a lot more than women do. But the glimpse only lasted for a moment because Uri recollected himself and, looking around the floor, he muttered something about putting in some calls to San Francisco. One of his assistants had a contact in one of the hospitals there and they would let him know what was available. He nodded and said thank you under his breath and then got up and walked away, taking out his mobile phone as he went.

Solter then came in to see Marya with me but she was asleep so he said he would call back again. As he pulled open the door to leave I touched him on the elbow to make him turn.

'You handled that very well, David,' I said to him. A bit of colour came to his face, and he couldn't suppress a little smile. It was particularly easy to see the little boy in Solter, he was almost always visible, jumping up and down and looking for attention and praise.

'Thank you,' he said without looking at me.

After he left I stood for a while longer and looked at Marya. She woke up and asked me what time it was and I told her.

'I'm tired, postdoc,' she said, and she rested her head back against the pillow. I stood for a few minutes more and then I left the room, closing the door quietly after me.

28

The man in overalls had an upright trolley in front of him. There was a cardboard box on the trolley that appeared to be very heavy, judging by the effort the man had to make in order to manoeuvre it into the lift when it had stopped on the fifteenth floor. We looked at each other briefly and nodded but did not speak. He wrote something on a clipboard using a pen that was attached to it by a piece of string. One floor down another man, with straw-like hair, got on. He was wearing a Hawaiian shirt and shorts, despite the cold outside. He stood facing both me and the man in overalls, looking down at the cardboard box and once or twice at me. You could tell he was anxious for conversation. He had one of those extroverted faces, which are so common over here.

'What, is there like a heart in there?' he said then to the other man.

'Possibly,' the man in overalls said, looking up from his clipboard, and the two of them laughed, the man with straw-coloured hair especially so.

'They don't tell you what's in the box?' he asked.

'Yep, they ship everything now,' said the man in overalls.

The lift stopped on the seventh floor and he got off, taking a minute to manoeuvre the heavy trolley. I imagined an enormous heart inside the box, packed in ice, a whale's heart, perhaps, blood seeping out of it and turning the ice a deep red, weighing a ton. The man with straw-coloured hair got off on the ground floor just as I did. I allowed him out first. We walked down the long corridor. The man went towards the main exit and I turned off towards the 69th Street exit which leads to the Nathan Institute.

29

Henrietta's tears have turned red again and the cancer has broken through her skin. I picked her up and brought her over to the window. She was listless and appeared to be more sleepy than anything else. I held her as gently as I could, enveloping her in both hands. It was warm in the glare of the sun through the window and it was almost pleasant, standing there holding her and swaying soundlessly as if there was music playing. We stood like that together for a while. It was almost as if we were dancing.

I brought her over to the euthanasia station in the corner of the laboratory. I lifted the lid and placed her on the white tray, then firmly reattached the lid. She opened her eyes briefly but other than that she did not show any interest in her new surroundings. I turned the knob on the gauge until the delivery pressure was at five. I looked at the clock on my mobile phone to mark time. I had brought the phone with me especially. The three minutes went by slowly. Henrietta leaned forward, motionless, her chin pressed to the floor. I turned off the knob. The manual said to leave her there for thirty minutes. I stood and watched her slumped body, looking for any signs of life. I looked closely. There weren't any.

After thirty minutes I took her out of the chamber. I lifted her using a piece of tissue paper. You are supposed to perform an additional, further method to ensure death. You have four choices. Decapitation. Cervical dislocation. Bilateral thoracotomy with scissors. Barbiturate overdose via intracardiac injection. But I didn't want to do any of those and instead I took her back to the cage area and placed her on the bench next to it and simply observed her. After some time her body was cool and stiff.

I brought her over to the dissection area and performed the necropsy. It was not a surprise to find that her tumour was very extensive. It was really a wonder that she had survived for so long. The peritoneal cavity was studded and there was free fluid which was a little chylous, probably from a blocked thoracic duct. The omentum was thick and matted. The surface of the liver was studded. I removed her arms and legs and – using a syringe and needle – separated the bone marrow by injecting the bones with some saline solution. I separated out the lungs and the liver. There were many metastases appreciable in the lung parenchyma and there was free fluid there also. I took out the heart and weighed it. It was enlarged but I didn't dissect it. For some reason the cancer never goes there, no doubt because of the rapid blood flow through it. The cells can't lodge. I replaced the heart back within her body cavity. Then I removed the spleen and crushed it with a pestle and mortar before mixing it with some FACS buffer for staining later.

When I was finished I took her to the biological disposal

unit which was a yellow plastic bin saying HAZARD: BIOLOGICAL WASTE MATERIAL. I slid her off the dissection board and through the narrow slit of the unit. Then I went back to the bench and took out the ledger from the drawer and marked in the appropriate column the date of death. It was Day 45 of the protocol. She made it to the halfway point, which I suppose was not so bad. I made a few more notes in the lab book and closed it. I will enter the data into the computer tomorrow.

30

Cillian's back. He was at Grand Rounds this morning. I saw him as soon as I entered the hall. I stood just inside the door for a minute letting my eyes adjust to the reduced light. I looked over and there he was. He saw me also but he quickly averted his eyes and aimed his gaze off in the other direction. Unusually for him he was sitting towards the back of the hall, on the other side of the room, as opposed to where he normally sits up front near where Solter invariably is. The lecture hall was packed and people were standing at the back and along the sides. There was a seat free on the same row as Cillian but on the near side of the room. I went over and sat in it. The row was curved so I could still see him. He didn't look once in my direction. My gaze would have felt like heat on the side of his face. When the lights dimmed completely and the speaker stood at the podium and tapped the micro-phone it must have come as an enormous relief to him to retreat into the darkness.

The speaker was Dr Berger, presenting on behalf of the hepatobiliary group. I thought it strange that there were so many people there to hear him. Perhaps he had swapped with somebody else at the last minute. And sure enough when

Berger appeared on stage a lot of people did make for the exit. His talk was on some new technique that they are using to perform liver resections. The surgeons are always coming up with new ways to simply cut out or remove something. There can't be many more refinements to make before they announce on the news that the field of surgery has now fully evolved, having reached the limits of its potential.

I kept an intermittent eye on Cillian throughout. He barely moved a muscle, nor did he laugh along with everyone else at Berger's stupid jokes. I thought he looked tired, as if he had just stepped off the plane. His eyes were black circles. The whole time his gaze remained fixed on the floor or off to his right, certainly well away from my side of the room.

Berger's talk wasn't bad, diverting enough despite the fact that my thoughts veered frequently to Cillian and what I was planning to say to him. The lecture was entitled 'Multi-Stage Approach To Hepatic Resections'. It had an italicized subtitle, *'moulding the remnant'*, the remnant being the good part of the liver that is left behind after a surgeon has removed a tumour from it. What is left behind needs to be a certain size in order to support life, otherwise the operation would have been in vain. The patient would wake up from the operation, their cancer gone, but die in the following weeks of liver failure from the inadequate remnant left behind. Or in extreme cases, not wake up at all.

Berger presented the case of a forty-year-old woman with bowel cancer which had metastasized to the liver. The original colon tumour had already been removed and now all the disease that was left was confined to the liver. They could cut the tumour out, of course, but if they did that the liver remnant would not have been big enough to support life. So they performed the operation in three stages, each two months apart, removing part of the tumour each time, and relying on the liver's ability to regenerate in between. That is the unusual thing about the liver, where it differs from all of your other organs: it regenerates, growing back to pretty much its normal size, and it does this quickly. This seems to have been known about for a long time, possibly as far back as the ancient Greeks, judging by the myth of Prometheus, who was strapped to a rock, as punishment for stealing the gift of fire from the gods, while a giant eagle turned up each morning to eat at his liver, which would then regenerate overnight in time for the eagle to return the next day and for the whole ordeal to begin again.

When the patient's CT scan was projected on to the monitor behind him, in cross section, Dr Berger stepped out from behind the podium and walked towards the front and centre of the stage like a performer. He was rigged up with a hands-free set, the small mike suspended in front of his mouth. He looked ridiculous.

'I am going to explain to you how to look at this CT scan,' he said to the audience, a little breathlessly. 'Some of you know already, but anyway. Just imagine that the patient is lying flat on her back,' and he turned and pointed at the enormous cross-sectional image on the screen behind him.

'OK?' he continued. 'And that you all are sitting at where her feet are. OK? Got it?'

There was silence in the auditorium.

'Now,' he continued, 'imagine that the patient's head is on the other side of the wall,' and he turned his body and pointed towards the wall on which the patient's CT scan was massively emblazoned in cross section and where, on the other side of which, in the next-door room, he wanted us to visualize her head and shoulders. And of course – because the images on the big screen were enlarged to many times their normal size – we all visualized the woman as being a giant, lying on her back, her giant legs and feet coming out from the wall towards us, her head and shoulders and chest on the other side of the wall beyond, strapped into the CT scan like an enormous creature against her will, or like that poor bastard Prometheus strapped to his rock.

'Now,' Berger continued, 'imagine that we have cut across her in sections with a saw,' and when he said that he stood to the side and made a funny sawing motion with his own hand across his own belly which he protruded out even further than it does naturally. There was laughter.

'Of course,' he said pointing at his belly, 'it would take a chainsaw to get through this,' and there was more laughter, mostly from the nurses, who he was obviously playing to. I looked over at Cillian, who didn't laugh.

'Now that you are orientated,' he said, 'these are the cross-sectional images.' And then, using his laser pointer to indicate the basic anatomical reference points: 'These are your kidneys, this is the colon, this is your aorta and your vena cava, and of course this big thing here is the liver itself. And this,' he said, pointing the laser at a darker area in the centre of the liver, 'this ugly thing is the tumour. The metastasis. OK?'

He then showed each of the scans sequentially, from immediately following the first operation right through to after the third and final operation. The initial post-operative scan did indeed show both the liver, with a big chunk missing out of it, leaving barely enough of a remnant, and the tumour, which was now much smaller. But on the second scan you could appreciate that although the tumour had remained small there had now been a lot of regeneration in the normal liver, such that it had grown back almost to its normal size, as it had for Prometheus. In his case, though, the liver had regenerated more quickly, which was bad luck for him, because it was just in time for the eagle to descend from the sky to tear at it each morning, its talons fixing him in position as the glistening beak rooted around under his ribcage, his agonizing screams heard all over the mountain and down the valley.

It was the same thing with the third operation, after which the post-operative scan showed again a large chunk missing, but this time the tumour had been removed completely, the eagle having taken his last mouthful. The final scan – two months after all the surgeries had been completed – showed still no sign of the tumour, and the liver had completely regrown, although the shape was a little odd and knobbly. You could easily see that chunks had been removed from it, but that it had been pushed out in places by the regrowth. There were no more scans, the eagle having flown off, hopefully never to return.

At the end of the lecture, when the lights went on and we all stood up, I waited for Cillian to walk out past where I was sitting, which would have been the obvious route of exit for him. But instead he went out the opposite side door near to him, which nobody ever uses. I had to wait for the row of people to empty past me before I could go out after him, pressing down the heavy bar of the fire door with both hands. On the other side was a long corridor that led to the radiation suite at one end. There was no sign of Cillian so I took a guess and went in the opposite direction. When I turned the corner he was standing waiting for the service elevator. He looked up, seeming not at all surprised to see me. He nodded and then we stood for a few seconds ten feet apart. Neither of us spoke.

I am not good at conflict and in general try to avoid it. I don't have that on-the-spot cleverness which you need, and which my wife for example has in abundance; that short connection between your mouth and your brain which allows you to say exactly what you are thinking. But more than that, I think I am too reasonable a person for conflict, my brain too fertile a ground for circumspection. If someone makes any sort of cogent attempt to dissuade me or defend themselves I immediately start to see things from their end. Ah yes, I find myself thinking, I can see why you might have thought like that, or done that, or acted in that way. No hard feelings then.

Except that there were hard feelings. I had realized that the moment I saw Cillian upon entering the lecture hall. He had been with my wife, that seemed clear. He had been with my wife possibly even in my bed, my old bed, in the house I still own or half-own; although I didn't want to think about those details and my brain – not for the first time – shut down that particular line of thought before it got up and running.

'I see you were back home,' I said to him, and he looked up at me, but he didn't reply and just gave a sigh.

At that moment a bell rang and the elevator opened. Inside it a man in overalls was revealed. He was standing behind a trolley with a stack of boxes on it. Cillian went into the lift first and I followed him, both of us standing on either side of the man. Neither of us said anything and the lift doors closed and descended. The usual sterile music made the silence a little less awkward.

The man with the boxes looked at both of us. Each box on his trolley was marked 'Live Animals' on the side. He first looked at Cillian and then at me. You could tell he was another extrovert.

'You want B2 also?' he said.

Neither of us responded.

'Right you are,' the man continued, and he bent over and pressed the button to close the doors. Then he put his head close to the boxes.

'Hey, you guys got the white coats. Can you tell me what's in here?'

264

He addressed Cillian but I answered him.

'Most likely they're mice,' I said.

'Yeah, that's what I figure too,' he said laughing, 'coz whatever they are they sure is quiet in there. 'N mice are real quiet. Ha! Even a small child knows that!'

'That's true,' I said. 'But you'd never know in this place. They could also be dogs or even small monkeys.'

The man laughed uncertainly.

'Well, I don't think they're monkeys,' he said. 'Monkeys cause a racket. I know that much.'

On B2 the lift doors opened and the man manoeuvred the trolley out. Cillian and I remained in the lift and the doors closed over. The lift shuddered and then started to ascend, even though neither of us had pressed a button.

'Did you meet Yvonne when you were back?' I asked Cillian, staring at him and making my voice clipped and hard. 'My Yvonne,' I added, and again it seemed ridiculous to say that.

Still he wasn't returning my gaze and this made me feel like I had the upper hand. He appeared resigned, almost a little depressed. He gave another deep sigh and leaned back against the wall. I looked down at his shoes, which were long pointy ones, the sort you would wear to a wedding. For sure they were no match for my boots if it came to it.

'I went for an interview,' he said.

'But you saw Yvonne while you were there,' I said, quickly cutting him off and making it a statement rather than a question.

'Who told you?' he replied quickly, raising his eyes off the floor. He looked wrecked. The black circles around his eyes looked like they had been applied with thick make-up. 'Look, mate,' he said, turning to face me. 'I never wanted to say anything to you. I mean, she's your wife and everything. But, I don't know, she sort of lost it there, man. No harm to her, but. Like we were friends and all, and we hung out and all that, but then . . . I don't know, she sort of lost it. She starts fucking texting my wife and ringing me and . . . She even called round to the house one night a couple of months before we left for here, and fucking parked outside it!'

What he said made me suddenly think of that night Yvonne had told me she was not coming to America with me. I saw her now in her make-up, damp from tears, dressed up in that leopard-print blouse she was wearing, taking her car keys off the sideboard and going for the front door.

'Was it a Saturday?' I asked. 'What was she wearing?'

'What? I don't know!' Cillian said. 'I mean, Jesus!'

He lay back against the wall of the elevator. Neither of us spoke and the earlier tension dissipated completely.

'Like I'm not saying I was perfect in all this,' he said then. 'I admit that at the start there was a bit of flirtation and all. And OK, maybe once we did . . . eh . . . eh . . . but that was after you guys had split up . . . I thought we were just hanging out like . . .'

'What? Like buddies?' I said sharply to him. He just looked at me and shook his head.

The lift stopped and the doors opened. Four scientists

walked in, a tall one and three small ones, all bearded. The tall one had his hands joined behind his back and walked with long, slow strides while the small ones scampered around him like Jack Russells, all talking excitedly and at the same time. They didn't appear to notice either Cillian or me.

'That is what you'd have to do if you really wanted to prove it!' one of the Jack Russells said.

'Correct, correct.'

'But, even then.'

'You'd have to normalize.'

'NO! You could simply expand the N and buff up the other.'

'I completely disagree.'

'But what about . . .'

'Where are we?' the tall one said then, and the Jack Russells went quiet, looking around themselves, as lost as children. Nobody spoke. The lift wasn't moving.

'Perhaps we should press one of the buttons?' the tall scientist said in a droll manner.

His three short colleagues laughed and two of them went to press the button for the ground floor.

'No, no. Let's go to seven,' the tall scientist said and the same two Jack Russells reached for number seven.

Now it was my turn to lean back against the wall. The six of us stood perfectly still listening to the bland music. I thought once more of that night, Yvonne leaving the house in tears in that leopard-print blouse which I probably most associate with her. It had some extra material at the shoulders which almost looked like shoulder pads. I used to make fun of her by calling her Sue Ellen. They made her look like a little girl pretending to be a grown-up. The image made me smile out of tenderness for her. I didn't want to hear anything more from Cillian.

After the scientists got off on the seventh floor Cillian and I were once more on our own. He was now staring at me.

The elevator landed on the ground floor and the door opened. His hand came towards me.

'Congratulations, by the way,' he said.

I looked down at his hand.

'On the baby,' he added.

I nodded and shook his hand. We walked out of the lift and went our separate ways.

When I got back to my apartment there were several missed calls showing on my mobile phone, which I had left on the kitchen table. I scrolled through them, relieved that the Irish number which showed up on it wasn't my parents' landline or my mother's or Donal's mobile phone. I didn't recognize the number and there had been no message left. I was still holding the phone in my hand when its face lit up and the same number was again displayed on it.

'Hello,' I said.

'You finally decided to answer,' the voice on the other end said.

'Yvonne,' I said to my wife.

Neither of us spoke.

'What number is this?' I asked after a delay.

'My new mobile,' she said. 'Don't tell me you don't have it. I specifically remember giving it to you.'

'I've been trying the old one,' I said.

Yvonne sighed. I could feel her breath on my face.

'I figured,' she said then without anger.

'How are you feeling?' I asked her.

'Fine,' she said. 'It's like, fine.'

'How many weeks are you?'

'Eleven.'

'I didn't know you tried again,' I said. 'In London.'

'Yeah well, you wouldn't, would you,' she said quickly.

'Is it the boy or one of the girls?' I asked her. Of the frozen embryos all but one were female.

'It's the boy,' she said after a delay.

I sat down at the kitchen table.

'He's fine as well, by the way,' she added. 'Genetically.'

'What?' I said, but I already understood that she was referring to Down's syndrome, because of Donal.

'I had him karyotyped,' she added.

I didn't say anything and for a few moments there was silence apart from my own breathing into the phone.

'Listen,' she said then. 'We need to sort this out.'

'What?' I said.

'THIS!' she replied.

There was more silence before she continued.

'My father's solicitor is sending you some papers to sign. I thought I'd let you know to expect them.'

I didn't say anything and I allowed her words to hang in the air a little. Her breath was more pronounced against my face.

'You'll sign them?' she said.

'Will I see much of him?' I asked.

'That's up to you,' she said. 'But I think you know I'll be good about all that.'

'Yes,' I said.

In fact I did not know that and I could see straightaway that it could just as easily be the opposite. Either way there was no doubt who would be in the position of control.

'I know about you and Cillian,' I said to her.

'Christ, not fucking you as well!' she shouted into the phone, exasperated. 'His fucking psycho wife has been sending me vicious emails. She always hated my guts.'

I said nothing and allowed the silence to gather.

'Anyway,' Yvonne said, her tone briefly changed, 'there's nothing . . . Not that it's any of your business!'

But then she said, more to herself than to me, 'I'm over it anyway, whatever it was. It was all a bit stupid, the whole thing. I just want to forget about that period of my life, to be honest. And besides,' she added, her voice gathering speed, 'I mean, I wasn't exactly getting what I needed with you, was I?'

Again neither of us spoke for a while. We both knew the other was still there on account of our breathing.

'I want to be involved,' I said then.

Yvonne started to say something but then stopped herself.

'I want to be involved,' I repeated, and this time I tried to make it sound like less of a request.

Yvonne said nothing and I could sense her weighing up what I had said.

'What I mean is . . .' I added.

'I know what you mean,' she said quickly.

'I just wanted to clarify,' I said.

'It's clear enough,' she said, again quickly, and I knew that it wasn't the point whether she did really know what I meant or whether it truly was clear. It was a technique she had for winning or at least not losing any argument and I knew from experience that we could go on all night like that. So I didn't say anything else.

'So you'll sign them?' she said. 'The papers.'

'I'll take a look at them,' I said.

'Do more than that,' she said.

There was a short delay where it seemed possible for anything to be said and then she was gone.

31

Uri was standing in the Bridge of Sighs. He was at the far end of it and I walked the length of the light-filled corridor towards him. Only a few days had passed since I had seen him wheel Marya along it but that seemed so long ago. Her ward was situated through the double doors at the end of the corridor. The inner wall was glass and I looked down into the central atrium eight floors below. The tables far below were half filled with afternoon coffee drinkers, a lot of them wearing white coats. There was nobody else in the corridor and Uri was sitting back against the windowsill. He was staring at the floor in front of his feet.

'She sleeps,' he said without looking up, when I was still twenty or so yards away. I continued walking until I was standing in front of him.

He looked up at my face then and added, 'Post. Doc.'

His eyes were red and dry as if he'd been rubbing them. One or two days of hair growth on his face. But he wasn't as tense as he had been when I met him with Solter. He was wearing the same clothes but his appearance was more unkempt, ruffled. You did not now get the sense of somebody coiled tightly down in himself and ready to spring up suddenly. He stood up straight and stretched his arms over his head, giving a loud yawn. His naked belly showed briefly beneath his untucked white shirt. Then he turned around and faced out of the window, bending over and resting his elbows on the ledge. I went to the window and stood beside him.

'I might go in and check on her,' I said, 'if that's OK.'

Uri didn't say anything and we remained standing beside each other in silence. My apartment was directly across the way. I searched it out, half expecting to see myself in the window of it looking back.

A girl in a floral-patterned dress walked by down on the street. The wind caught her dress and pressed the light material tightly against her. Uri's attention descended on her like a small bird of prey coming out of the sky. For a few seconds he stared at her, thinking of nothing else. It really is ridiculous that for us men that never ceases, no matter what the circumstances. You could be running for your life and still your head would turn. The girl went around the corner and out of sight and Uri was present again. I stood up from the window.

'I'm going to go in,' I said. 'Don't worry. If she's asleep I won't wake her.'

Uri half turned his head to look at me then turned back to the window. Something else caught his attention.

'Look at this,' he said.

I went back to the window and looked at where he was indicating. A homeless man was making a commotion down on the street about fifty yards away on First Avenue. He was pushing a supermarket trolley filled with cans, inching his way across the wide avenue in front of angry cars. But now he had stopped and was screaming at the traffic, waving his arms in the air, before pushing on. Uri laughed. The cars screamed back at the man as they stopped suddenly in front of him. Eventually he made it to the near side and then began the struggle of lifting the trolley onto the sidewalk. When he eventually did this Uri stood back clapping his hands and laughing, but too much, like an idiot telling a tale full of sound and fury, signifying nothing. For a second I thought he was drunk or had taken something. But when I looked at his face I did not see any laughter. I noticed again that his eyes were red and sore.

Marya was drowsy but awake. When I partially opened the door she stirred and recognized me. I opened the door fully and went inside.

'Where's Uri?' she asked, propping herself up on her elbow. Her voice was thick and I got the impression she had just woken up.

'Outside in the corridor,' I said.

'Is he behaving himself?' she said, giving a cough and now sitting fully upright in the bed, using the tips of her fingers to stretch open her eyes and shaking her head a little.

'Yes,' I said.

I walked around to the other side of the bed. There was a chair next to the bed but there was a lot of stuff on it, so instead I stood against the windowsill. Marya was leaning fully forward in the bed now, hunched over, stretching her back, her arms fully extended, the fingers interlocked. At the head of the bed there was an IV stand. Otherwise she wasn't connected to anything.

'They've removed the chest drain,' I said.

'Yes,' said Marya, before breaking into a bout of coughing.

'I told them to,' she said when the coughing eased. 'Too uncomfortable . . . If they want they can stick needle in again. I prefer it actually . . . That way at least I get visit from gorgeous Georges.'

'Jorge Seabat?' I said.

'Yes, of course,' Marya said. Another small bout of coughing.

'All women in hospital have hots for him,' she said, her voice now weak.

'Really?' I said, genuinely surprised. Jorge is on the short side, I would have also thought him ugly if I had put any thought into it, which of course I never did.

'It's his eyes, postdoc,' Marya said. 'And the way he talks to woman . . .' She looked at me. 'It's OK,' she said, laughing. 'Don't be jealous.'

I laughed also, although something physical now stopped short Marya's laughter and she put the palm of her hand on her sternum and sat very still for a moment.

'What's he doing anyway? Uri?' she asked. 'On telephone as usual?'

'No,' I said. 'He's just looking out the window.'

Marya fixed the pillow under her, then lay back against it, turning on her side to face me, seemingly not bothered now by whatever discomfort she'd just felt a minute ago.

'It's hard for him,' she said. 'Because of our mother . . . Bring it all back.'

We looked at each other.

'I can stay in touch with him,' I said, but it came out with more gravity than I intended, and I felt foolish, even though the offer was genuine enough.

Marya looked at me for an instant and then gave a little laugh, as if she was already picturing Uri and me as fast friends, calling each other up and going out for a beer.

'Only if you want to, postdoc,' she said. 'But Uri will be fine, actually. Maybe not so good with picking girlfriend . . . but . . . he's smart. He'll be rich and successful. No doubt about it. If it wasn't for me he would have moved to San Francisco already . . . So maybe you should stay in touch. For your sake, you know. Good to know rich people.'

She started coughing again and this made her sit up in the bed. I went over and filled the glass on her bedside table with water, even though it was already half-full. When the coughing stopped Marya lay back against the pillow, exhausted.

'Anyway, postdoc,' she continued, her voice weak again, her throat not fully cleared. 'You need to go to Ireland.'

I looked at her and then retreated back to the windowsill. I told her about the baby, that I had finally spoken to Yvonne.

'There you are, then, postdoc, it's settled! What are you

going to do?' she said. 'Hang out with mice in laboratory for the rest of your life?'

'There are worse things,' I said.

'Tell me about it,' Marya said.

I went to say something but stopped myself and neither of us spoke for a few minutes. There was more coughing, and afterwards Marya leaned over and took a drink of the water. She sat back heavily against the pillow. I looked around the room. Every object had its own shadow. The window blinds were fully open and the declining light was perfectly, brightly grey. Things were either lit by it or not, there was no in-between.

'Which reminds me,' Marya said then, her voice again thin. 'Your strange lab creature friend.'

'Deep?'

'Yes. I spoke with him for a little while the last time I call up to your lab. I forgot to tell you before. Anyway I like him now, actually. He tell me all about his wedding. Show me picture, even.'

'He did?'

'Yes,' she said, giving a little giggle. 'His wife is really beautiful. I mean, no offence to him, but . . .'

We both laughed.

'He gets these ideas into his head,' I said. 'At the moment he is obsessed with cleaning the lab from top to bottom.'

Marya laughed.

'No,' she said, 'I can't imagine it. I can't!' and she laughed some more, finding what I had said really hilarious for some reason, whatever image she had concocted. 'I'm picturing the two of you with washing-up gloves,' she said, 'cleaning floor and windows.' She started laughing again, and this time there was no coughing.

Neither of us spoke much then. Marya seemed happy to lie back on her pillow and I was happy to just sit there, trying to make each moment as long as possible. We had never sat together in so much silence but it was pleasant. Outside, the thick windows insulated all the sound of the world which was darkening by the minute. The objects and architecture of the hospital room retreated into the murk, as if it was trying to disguise itself as simply any other type of room. The only exception was the lanky drip stand, whose small battery face had neon figures on it. But even its sounds were subtle, a tiny whirr every few minutes as it delivered more of its fluid into Marya's veins. The blind was fully open and again when I turned around I registered the wall of windows across the way in my apartment building. Some of them were lit now.

'I'm so tired, postdoc,' Marya said then. 'All I want to do is sleep, to be honest.'

'That's allowed,' I said.

'Maybe it is,' Marya said, turning to look at me, 'but I feel like I should be having big significant conversation with everyone . . . you know?'

I nodded.

'But to be honest I don't want . . .' she said, and suddenly she seemed upset.

I moved over closer to the bed and sat down on the chair,

having to move the things off it. It was only coats, a blanket and a bag, so I thought it was OK to put them on the floor. Marya made a noise of frustration and lay directly back on her pillow and stared up at the ceiling with her eyes tightly closed. I reached over with the intention of just patting her on the arm but she surprised me by quickly grabbing my hand and holding it tightly in hers. The rapidity of her movement immediately made me think of Yvonne, the way she used to hold on to me at night, clinging to me with her fingers. I pulled my chair closer to the bed. Marya's hand was very warm and I could practically feel the blood pulsing through it. She gripped me tightly.

I don't know how long I stayed. There was nothing to mark time except for the fact that it was soon night. After a while I could tell Marya was going in and out of sleep. Occasionally she woke, only to check if I was still there, or so it seemed. Then her breathing grew deeper and her grip relaxed. I stayed for another long while after that in case she woke and looked for me. Then I left the room, closing the door quietly behind me.

She died later in the night. At three o'clock in the morning. I found out when I came in to check on her at seven thirty. Her room was empty and I went urgently to the nurses' station. The nurse I spoke to didn't know much, only what she had heard at report, but what she told me was enough to make me stare back at her, not getting what she was saying. The nurses' station was full of people all talking at the same time.

I wanted to shout out, telling them all to keep quiet. The nurse was looking at me, her mouth moving. She pointed towards a young Hispanic man who was coming out of the staff room with his jacket on. 'Ask him, she said. 'He was the attendant last night. Annette has gone home. Or at least I think she has. Ask him. I don't know what his name is, he just started last week. José or something.'

I walked away without a word. I went up to the man and my voice said something to him, and he looked at me. I asked him what happened and still he just looked at me. 'To Marya,' I said, 'what happened?' José's face changed and he started talking. He seemed happy to be able to talk about it. I recall that. As if he wanted to share an experience. He said that the patient's brother came out to the corridor looking for help, calling out. It was maybe two thirty. Before three anyway. Because that was the time of death. When he and nurse Annette went in Marya was sitting up in the bed breathing fast and shallow. 'Distressed?' I said, and he said, 'Yes, doctor.' He went on. 'Nurse Annette held her very tightly and told her over and over that it was all right, everything would be all right. Marya seemed frightened, her eyes wide open. But Nurse Annette held her tight. She kept telling her everything would be all right. After a while Marya relaxed and Nurse Annette laid her back in the bed and then that was it, it was over.'

He looked at me and neither of us said anything.

'What about her brother?' I asked him then. He shook his head.

'He was crying, doctor. He stayed in the corner and cried.

Shouting out her name. Man, it was sad. Ms Annette stayed with him, talking to him. For maybe one hour. She had to get the on-call resident to give him something. A pill. Then they came and took away the body.'

I said thank you and he smiled and said no problem and walked away.

I went down the corridor to Marya's room and stood by the door. It was more than empty. Even the bed sheets had been removed and the mattress was bare, like an open wound in the centre of the room. I stared at it, trying to make myself remember that only a few hours ago she had lain on it. I tried to make my mind absorb this simple fact. As if Marya's absence was just a failure of concentration. I went into the room and around to the other side of the bed. It was much quieter now. Less noise coming in from outside on the ward. The shift change, the morning hustle up and down on the corridor, preparing for the new day. No matter how recent it was and how much I tried to force it, there was no sense of Marya in the room. It could have been any room at any time. I turned around to face the window. The blinds were fully open and I stood looking out at the nondescript view, the blank face of my apartment building across the way, the drab winter morning, the people down at street level making their way along the sidewalk in the rain.

32

It came as a surprise that I should see Uri again. Especially as he had me paged overhead by the operator. That is something they generally only do in an emergency, blaring your name out through all the speakers in the building. When I called the operator she told me to go and meet 'a Mr Uri' in the atrium. I said OK and made my way over to the main hospital.

It's been three days since Marya died. Each intervening day has been indistinguishable. I have kept busy doing not much, cleaning the lab mostly, working on the new protocol. I assumed I wouldn't see Uri again. But now here he was waiting for me at a table, looking once more like a sharp young executive on the move, his hair gelled, a pristine white shirt unbuttoned at the neck. He got right to the point, barely greeting me and not even waiting for me to sit down.

'Marya wanted me to give you this,' he said.

On the table was a paper bag. He nodded at it and I took my seat. I stared at the bag. Uri was watching me intently.

'What is it?' I asked.

'Gift,' Uri said.

I took the bag up and opened it. A child's toy, a little blue horse. It looked old, handed down through the generations. I looked at Uri. He had a strange smile on his mouth, one of pure curiosity, as if he was conducting his own little experiment.

'Traditional Russian toy,' he said. 'From our childhood, actually, mine and Marya's. She told me to give it to you. She say you are going to need it . . . So you have child?'

'Not yet,' I said.

Uri shrugged.

'Well anyway, she tell me to give it to you . . . She was very specific about it. It was number one on big list of things for me to do . . . Tick,' and he made a movement in the air with his hand. Then he took up his coffee and drank from it. His manner was a little flat. It wasn't hard to see that he hadn't yet emerged from the devastation, that his grief was coexisting with his efforts at revival, the polished appearance, the immaculate shirt and nice dark suit he was wearing.

I held the toy in my hand. It made me smile, the thought of Marya still trying to prompt me a little, even now. I looked at Uri and said thank you, my face beaming foolishly. He gave a little nod and said 'postdoc'. Then he smiled and took a final drink of his coffee. We both stood up and shook hands and he handed me his business card. I watched him as he walked quickly away towards the nearest exit, taking out his phone as he went.

When I arrived back at the lab Solter was there. He was sitting on a stool in front of the CO_2 incubator, holding an enormous coffee.

'There he is!' he called out as soon as I came in the door.

I stood for a moment, surprised to see him. It's been a long time since he called up to see us.

'Where's Deep?' I asked and Solter nodded towards the cell incubator, which had been pushed forward a few feet. Deep was down on his knees behind the machine cleaning the back of it.

'The place is looking good,' Solter said, looking around him.

'Thanks to Deep,' I said, which was the truth. About a week ago Deep came up to me and proposed a general lab clean. He said it with a great solemnity, as if it was the most serious thing in the world. I thought it was a good idea, although I didn't appreciate what a big undertaking it was going to be. The timing was right given that we had both recently come to the end of the experiments we were doing. Deep drew up the list of tasks on the whiteboard and we divided them between us. He was surprisingly pernickety about it then. Yesterday, for example, after I had spent a good hour cleaning the sterile hood, I left the lab only to come back to find Deep redoing it. He was kneeling up on the high chair and leaning all the way into it scrubbing its back panel. His sleeves were rolled up and he was wearing yellow dishwashing gloves that went up over his elbows. I told him that I had already done that. He stopped working for a moment but then went back to it.

'Anyway,' Solter said. 'I just thought I'd check in on you guys . . .'

He stood up straight and looked at me, drinking again from his coffee.

'. . . See what you were up to,' he said.

I knew the other reason Solter was here was to check on whether I had made a decision on the new position he offered me the other week. He's been pushing me for an answer. Dropping not so subtle hints at every opportunity. The other day he sent me a draft of my job spec, the one that would go on the web to look for my replacement in the event that I turn him down. 'Look over this, will you,' was the terse instruction. When I opened the attachment I saw that he had only written two brief lines. It was very generic and didn't remotely capture the job, either the good or the bad parts of it. I found it wholly inadequate. Not that I think we aren't all replaceable. If anything I find that reassuring, the fact that we are. That there's always someone coming along behind you to pick up the slack. They may even do it better. Regardless I didn't rise to the bait. I corrected his grammar and sent it back to him.

'I've finished the new protocol,' I said. 'Do you want to see it?'

'Sure,' he said.

Solter followed me into the office. He stood behind me as I sat and opened up a file on my computer, showing him the schema of the experiment I had drawn up. He looked at it in silence for a while, leaning over and using the mouse to move forward through the document, then finally going back to the schema.

'What cells you gonna use?' he asked then, standing upright and sipping from his coffee. I opened up the section in the background which explained this. I had chosen a fairly broad panel.

'What about using some of the first generation cells, from the fluid you've been collecting?' he said. 'It would be cool to use those . . . depending on how they're growing.'

'True,' I replied, which I hadn't thought of, actually.

'Anyway, see what you think,' he said, and he took another big swig from his coffee. He seemed fairly relaxed, at least by his standards. Perhaps the coffee was only a decaf.

'Could be interesting,' he said, getting up from the chair, but more to himself than to me. We walked out of the office and back into the main part of the lab. Solter looked around the lab again as he went.

'Keep up the scrubbing, Deepak!' he shouted out, before heading out the door.

In the afternoon I went for a run over to Central Park, around the Jackie Onassis reservoir. I love it up there. When you stand at the north end of the reservoir and look back across the water Manhattan seems to rise like a cliff. It is easy to imagine that the entire universe is concentrated there. For those moments standing there, nothing exists other than what you are seeing in front of your eyes. It's no wonder Jackie O decided to live nearby. I'm sure she could have had her pick of places.

It was good running weather. The sun wasn't out and it

was a homogenous sky, texture-less, grey. Many hefty breezes came roaring out of it, stampeding about the place like young wild horses all of the same herd. I could tell them apart from each other by their colour as they tore at the trees, playfully scattering the year's last cull of leaves which they set down wet against the concrete.

The papers have arrived from Yvonne's solicitor. They came the day I found out about Marya so I hardly glanced at them. But this morning I took them out of their FedEx package. I kept my word and signed them, but I haven't sent them back to her yet and I'm not sure that I will. Perhaps I will deliver them to her in person. I intend to go back to Ireland in a few weeks and scope things out a bit. Yesterday she sent me an email. It was just a brief message with a link to a new oncology job that is being advertised by one of the Dublin hospitals. 'Knowing you,' Yvonne wrote, 'you probably didn't even know about this.' I clicked on the link and then looked up a few things about the position online. It would be purely clinical, of course, no lab work, but perhaps that wouldn't be so bad. No doubt Cillian has also seen the ad. He is probably already rehearsing his patter in front of the mirror. It would be almost worth it just to see the look on his face when I turn up in the waiting area outside the interview room. I'll give him a big wink and wish him all the best.

On my way back across town from Central Park, every inch of 66th Street all along both sidewalks was crammed with parked cars, no daylight in between them. It was as if they formed part of an enormous machine that had conked out years ago, stretching off up side streets in an inert and endless chain.

At the 66th Street junction I waited for the traffic to stop to cross First Avenue. The smoking bench across the way was unoccupied. The only person smoking at the back entrance of the hospital was the elderly protester, his foot on his upturned sign. The lights changed and I continued on. It started raining a little. As I went past the protester I nodded at him and he smiled back at me. Perhaps he has finally heard back from St Michael, telling him that he is on his way. Down to my right a crowd of people had gathered by the entrance of the Tower of Babel. I had forgotten that today is the official opening. There were police about. Although it is not one hundred per cent finished you can tell the tower is going to be spectacular.

33

This morning a new Henrietta arrived, six of them, actually. When I got into the lab first thing the delivery man was waiting for me. He seemed pissed off that I hadn't been there to meet him. 'You need to fill this out,' he said, handing me a clipboard with a form attached to it. Then he lifted up the transport cage which was at his feet and placed it up on the bench counter. He was about to raise the cover from around it when I told him to wait. I went over and lowered the blinds on the window.

'So as not to give them too much of a fright,' I explained, as I walked back over to where he was standing. 'The sudden light can be disorientating for them.'

The delivery man shrugged his shoulders. A spurt of static came from the walkie-talkie on his belt.

I brought the transport cage over to the area next to the main cage, which was now entirely empty. I removed the cover slowly and the animals, who seemed a little dazed, started moving around the place, slowly at first, then quicker. They are Black 6 mice, three females and three males. The males have a genetic mutation on chromosome 6 and the females have one on chromosome 7. After they mate their offspring will have both. That will be the second phase of the experiment.

'I'll fill this out in a minute,' I said, putting the clipboard down. 'Let me transfer the animals first.'

The delivery man said nothing, but his body language was impatient. I opened the side hatch of the transport cage and picked the mice up one by one and placed them on either side of the central divider in the main cage, separating the males and females. I had already given the cage a good clean after the passing of its previous inhabitants, using bleach to sterilize the area. It is good basic practice to do that but it also formed part of Deep's general lab clean-up, which thankfully is complete now. In any case I have literally nothing to do at the moment. It is always like this when you are in between experiments and waiting for the conditions to be right to begin the next one. All you can do is wait. It takes longer than you would think to get to baseline. The protocol is totally silent during this period, like an extinct god, not yet making any of her inflexible demands. The freedom is a little unnerving actually, but you have to make the most of it.

As I filled out the form for the delivery man, his walkie-talkie kept producing its spurts of static. It was distracting. The form was very detailed, requiring me to look up on the computer various pieces of information – the institutional review board animal protocol number, the drug dosing I will be using, the radiation dose in centigray, if applicable (which it is not), and various other items. Once I had finished I handed him the clipboard and he took his transport cage with him and went towards the door.

'Good luck,' he said over his shoulder, possibly in the direction of the animals.

Tomorrow I will inject them. As per the protocol I will assess them daily until we can get to Day 1 and begin their treatment. How long that takes will depend on their biology. I went over to the CO_2 incubator to check the various cell cultures that are ongoing and which have all been initiated from the fluid samples that I have been collecting on the wards in recent months. There were a number of culture flasks in the incubator, stacked on top of each other, and they were all warm to the touch, the temperature setting being at 37.2 degrees – human body temperature – which is optimal for the cells to thrive. I removed each of them in turn, holding the flasks up to the light and tilting them to and fro to move the fluid about, seeing with the naked eye the cell populations as they adhered like grit to the bottom of the flasks. Not all of them had grown, however, and even with those that had you could already discern biological differences between them in terms of their behaviour. The woman I met in the lift, for example, the Velazquez subject, her cells have been very slow to divide. I had them in a single culture flask for a week before I needed to change the medium at all. And even now the fluid was only slightly discoloured, reflecting a fairly minimal metabolism, as if the cells were completely burnt out. When I looked at them under the microscope there were hardly any mitotic figures visible. There was hardly any life in them really.

I removed the last of the flasks from the incubator and held it up to the light. They were Marya's cells. I could tell from the altered colour of the medium that they had already started to proliferate and that the medium needed to be changed. I closed the incubator door and brought the flask over to the microscope, looking at the cells under low power. Even though I had only split the cells the previous day there was hardly any free surface area left. Contact inhibition had been easily overcome and the cells covered the entire bottom of the flask in a monolayer like a thick blanket. They were an off-white, flesh coloured, appearing to emerge out of the blood water tinted medium. You could easily make out the mitotic figures where the cells had started to divide into their daughter cells. I switched to high power and their tiny nuclei looked out at me like a million eyes, shimmering in the fluid, appearing to pulse almost from within their bed of rich cytoplasm dotted by the organelles, the mitochondria especially heaving away at their immortal task. But the centres of the nuclei were densely black and you had to imagine the coiled DNA compacted in their centromeres, emitting their signals and commands, controlling the eternal programme of continuance.

I must have been standing at the microscope for way too long because Deep got curious about it. He came over and asked me what I was looking at. I stood aside and gestured to him to come and look for himself. I told him I had only started the culture the previous day. He had to alter the focus of the microscope on account of his eyesight. After a while he raised his head and looked at me.

'Astonishing,' he said.

I turned off the microscope and replaced the flask back in the incubator. After closing the door I adjusted the settings on it a little to ensure their optimal growth. Then I turned away and went back into the main part of the lab. I walked over to the animals' cage and stood looking down on them as they continued in their rapid motions around their new home. They showed no awareness of my presence. Later I will email the Animal Resource Center to let them know about the delivery. Someone will come over in the afternoon to register them on to the system and do a baseline check to make sure they are OK. After that we will start again in earnest.

Acknowledgements

I would like to sincerely thank the following people: my parents Vincent and Pauline Duffy; Faith O'Grady; Bella Lacey; Sarah Bance; Sydney Peck and – from the Writers' Studio in Manhattan – Lisa Bellamy, Peter Krass and Cynthia Weiner; and my first reader, Naomi Taitz Duffy.

Keep in touch with
Granta Books:

Visit grantabooks.com to discover more.

GRANTA